ELLE GRAY
BLAKE WILDER
FBI MYSTERY THRILLER

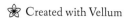 Created with Vellum

PROLOGUE

Industrial District; Briar Glen, WA

A THICK MARINE layer had rolled in off the ocean, blotting out the moon, which made the night darker than normal. Tyler hated nights like that. He always thought they were inherently spooky. He sometimes felt like the bogeyman was going to reach right out of the shadows blanketing the entire town and snatch him up.

Tyler shivered and pulled his tattered jacked more tightly around him, then fished the dirty, threadbare floral scarf out of his pocket. He wound it around his neck, then pulled it up over his mouth. It didn't help all that much, but it was better than nothing. Turning to the wallet in his hands, he discarded some papers and an old condom, then pulled out the cash and quickly counted it out.

"Twenty-three bucks. That's it?" he grumbled.

But he pocketed the money, knowing it would buy him a couple of meals and a few other necessities. If nothing else, it would keep him from having to dig through the trash cans for something to eat for a couple of days, which he was glad for. Tyler hated eating out of trash cans and avoided it whenever he could. The stench alone was off-putting enough, but the food usually tasted like crap to boot.

He was pragmatic enough to know that when you live on the streets, you usually don't have much in the way of options. So, given the choice between eating what he found in the can and starving, he always chose to scrape off the moldy, dirty bits, and pretend he was eating a five-star meal. It beat going hungry.

Sitting on the stoop of a building that had been long abandoned, Tyler rifled through the rest of the wallet and held up the driver's license he found tucked into one of the side flaps. The photo was of a young kid, twenty-three years old by the date of birth. He had blond hair, blue eyes, was listed at five-foot-nine, one hundred and sixty-five pounds, and he wore corrective lenses.

"Sorry 'bout this, Jake Fontenot. But hey, ya do what ya got to do to survive, and I reckon I need this more than you right now. Maybe you'll be in the same spot as me later on and learn that valuable lesson," he mumbled to himself.

He didn't really believe that. Tyler thought Jake Fontenot had the look of spoiled entitlement about him. And the Lexus he'd broken into where he found the wallet to begin with certainly didn't do anything to contradict that belief.

"What kind of idiot leaves their wallet in the car anyway?" he grunted. "A kid with more money than common sense, that's who."

Tyler doubted Jake Fontenot had ever gone without anything in what he assumed was the kid's privileged, pampered life. He certainly didn't look like a kid who'd ever suffered hardships or had ever wanted for a damn thing.

"Not like I have. This kid don't know tough times or what a hard life really is," he muttered to nobody in particular.

He picked out the credit cards but left the debit card behind. Without the PIN number, it was useless anyway. But Tyler reasoned that he might be able to use the plastic to buy some things when the stores opened in the morning. Best to try to use them before Jake Fontenot got wise and canceled them.

"A jacket. I'm definitely gonna get me a new jacket. And some warm damn socks. Yeah, definitely warm socks."

Not finding anything else of interest or value, Tyler tossed the wallet into a pile of trash on the stoop beside him and started to mentally compile a list of things he'd want to buy in the morning. He figured he'd go find a place to sleep near the local Wal-Mart, so he was nearby when they opened, and he could grab what he needed. Tyler had found the cashiers were less apt to hassle him first thing in the morning, before they'd had their coffee, than they were if he came in during peak hours.

Tyler clocked a guy walking down the street, heading in his direction. The guy was tall and slim. Not very threatening looking. But Tyler noted he had a pretty expensive looking coat, nice shoes, and he glimpsed what looked like a Rolex on his wrist. One thing living on the streets had taught Tyler, it was to size somebody up and calculate the value of their clothing and accessories in a heartbeat.

He liked to call his ability to almost instantly take somebody's measure his predator's instinct. It made him feel like a lion out on the savanna, stalking a gazelle. And as he watched the guy walking down the sidewalk, Tyler thought fate was suddenly smiling down on him for a change. Given the money he saw they guy wearing, he figured he had a fat wallet on him too. Roll the guy, take his cash, and who knew? Maybe he could get himself a room somewhere for a night or two.

With thoughts of a warm shower and a warmer bed filling his head, he got to his feet and descended the steps. The mark was walking toward him, hands stuffed in his pockets, his head down. He didn't even seem to notice Tyler coming his way. That put a grin on his face.

"Easy peasy, lemon squeezy," he muttered to himself.

He flexed his hands, clenching and unclenching his fists a few times and shrugged his shoulders, getting himself ready.

"Hey man," Tyler said. "Can you spare a little cash for a guy down on his luck?"

As if startled, the guy jerked to a stop and raised his eyes. But then a slow, ominous looking smile crawled across his face. It was enough to stop Tyler in his tracks and send a wave of uncertainty rippling through him.

"Hey, you're Tyler Salters, right?" the guy asked.

It wasn't his predator's instinct, but the sound of a shoe scuffing the sidewalk behind him, that alerted Tyler to somebody's presence behind him. A hand snaked around from behind him, grabbing his hair and yanking his head to the side. Tyler felt the pinch of the needle sliding into his neck and grimaced.

His vision wavered and he started to feel lightheaded. Tyler felt weightless and had the sensation of the ground rushing up to meet him. He hit the pavement with a hard thud and a groan as his head bounced off the concrete. Tyler could hear them talking and the sound of a car pulling alongside them on the curb.

And then his world went black.

TYLER GASPED AND SPLUTTERED. THE WATER WAS SO COLD, it nearly stole his breath as it rained down on him. He shook his head, trying to clear his vision as the wet cloth of the hood stuck uncomfortably to his skin. Tyler was unable to lift his arms or move his legs for that matter. It was then that he realized he was naked and seated in a cold metal chair.

His hands had been bound behind him and his ankles secured to the legs of the chair by plastic cuffs. They were strapped so tight, he felt the edges cutting into his skin, cutting off his circulation. Tyler struggled against his bonds, but they only scratched him roughly as he tried to move.

"Hey, what in the hell?"

His shout echoed around the large, obviously empty space. Tyler shivered as the cold from the water seeped into his bones. The sound a footstep splashing in the water that had pooled around him announced somebody's presence a moment before the hood was yanked from his head. Tyler gasped.

Standing around him in a half circle were seven figures in deep purple robes that looked made of velvet. They all had hoods pulled up over their heads, and on their faces, they wore masks. One looked like the mask of a medieval plague doctor. Another looked like a harlequin mask from the theater. Every mask Tyler saw was different, but they covered the faces of the people behind them completely, sending terror-fueled chills running down his spine.

Behind the seven, he saw more figures, though he couldn't say how many. As he turned his head, he saw the figures had ringed him completely. They too were robed and masked, and some of them held torches, casting the circle around him in a flickering orange light.

"What the hell is this?" he shouted.

The robed figures remained silent. The only sound was his own breath echoing in the vast dark space. The eerie, surreal feeling of it all pressed down on him so hard, he felt like he might crumble beneath it. Tyler saw that he was in some sort of abandoned plant or something. The ceiling was high overhead and cloaked in shadow, and all around him, he saw large pipes, the skeletons of old machinery, and tall stacks of wooden crates.

"What's going on here?" he screamed at the silent figures. "Who in the hell are you? What in the hell do you want?"

Finally, the man in the center of the semi-circle immediately in front of him stepped forward. He wore a mask that was half black and half white, the features twisted and contorted into something that looked more animal than human and was altogether terrifying. Tyler shrank back and whimpered, his face burning with shame as he wet himself.

"Tyler Salter," the figure intoned. "You stand accused of a number of serious crimes, for which you have escaped justice. We are here tonight to correct those wrongs."

"Who are you people? I didn't do nothin'!"

Tyler struggled against his bonds, but they held him fast. He let out a growl of impotent rage.

"Let me go. I didn't do nothin'!"

"We adjudge you guilty of three counts of rape. Multiple cases of theft. Breaking and entering. Assault—"

"I didn't do any of that! I've never been convicted of nothin'!"

"We have weighed the evidence and have deemed you guilty," the man in the mask said, his voice calm and steely.

"Screw you! I didn't do that stuff!"

The man in the mask closed the distance in the blink of an eye and delivered a vicious backhand that snapped Tyler's head to the side, cutting off his words. The coppery taste of blood filled his mouth as his cheek throbbed with heat and pain. Turning to glare at the man in the mask, Tyler spit a glob of phlegm and blood on the concrete floor.

Tyler looked around at the other shadowy figures who ringed him. The flickering shadows cast by torches danced around him, sending a finger of ice sliding up Tyler's spine. He swallowed hard as the gravity of his situation began sinking into him.

"Who are you people?" Tyler gasped, his voice quavering.

The man turned the vacant eyes of his expressionless mask upon Tyler, sending a shudder through him.

"We are *Manu Dei*. God's Hand," he said.

"Please. Let me go. I swear I didn't do anything. You've got the wrong guy. I swear it. Please!"

"You are guilty in the eyes of God, and we, acting as agents of our Lord, shall carry out your punishment," the man said. "And for your crimes, your punishment will be death. It is decreed as our Lord wills it."

"As our Lord wills it," the rest of the group repeats in unison.

Tyler trembled hard, and not just because of the cold. The gaze of all those eyes on him was heavy. Oppressive.

"Please," Tyler said, his voice barely louder than a whisper. "Please don't do this. I'll change. I won't do that bad stuff anymore."

A smaller figure, one Tyler thought looked feminine, emerged from the crowd and stood beside the man who'd slapped him. She carried a long lacquered wooden box in her arms. She opened it gently.

The firelight from the torches gleamed off the long, curved dagger that lay inside the box, nestled on a bed of crimson velvet. Its blade looked sharp enough to cut through human flesh like butter. Tears spilled from the corners of Tyler's eyes and he shook his head in disbelief at what was happening.

"Please don't," he sobbed.

The man reached into the box and lifted the dagger out almost reverently. Cradling it in both hands, he raised it above his head, all faces in the crowd turning upward. The flames of the torches glinted off the cold steel he held.

"Our Lord demands true justice be done," the man intoned, his deep voice echoing around the large open space.

"And our Lord will not be denied."

The man approached him, the torchlight gleaming off the cold, cruel blade in his hand.

Tyler opened his mouth and let out a blood curdling scream that echoed away into the darkness.

ONE

"I'VE JUST RECEIVED an email from the Director of the FBI," Astra announces breathlessly as she bursts into our office.

I look up at her, a grin already playing across my lips as Astra closes the door and drops down into the chair behind her desk.

"From Director Wilkins himself, huh?" I raise an eyebrow.

She nods soberly. "Yes. And it concerns you."

"Oh, this sounds serious."

"It is serious. Very serious. It's a directive from the Director himself."

I drop my pen and lean forward, clasping my hands together, giving her the best expression of faux concern I can muster.

"Do tell. What is this directive?" I ask.

"The Director has ordered you to loosen up and remove the stick you have up your backside. He is also ordering you to go out and have a few drinks and some fun with me tonight," she announces.

I laugh. "Is that so?"

"Hey, it's an order from the Director. I'm just the messenger here."

My officemate Astra has been a good friend of mine since we both went through the Academy together, and we were both elated to have been assigned to the Seattle Field Office together coming out of Quantico. I was doubly thrilled since I grew up in the Pacific Northwest. It was a homecoming for me and a bonus since I get to work in an area I'm intimately familiar with.

Astra is a fantastic field agent. She's intuitive and intelligent. And she's also one of those people who take that old t-shirt slogan, "work hard, play harder," as their personal life challenge. I think she's the only person I know who can be up drinking and dancing all night, then kicking in doors and running down bad guys the next morning. It's impressive, if a bit reckless for my taste. But hey, she gets the job done.

She's also stunningly beautiful. I like to call her a supermodel with a badge and a gun. At five-foot-six, she's three inches shorter than me, has hair blacker than midnight, and eyes a shade of blue so light, they're practically silver. She's got tawny colored skin, has legs for days, and curves that I'm jealous of. She's also fit and strong. The guys in the workout room used to challenge Astra to spar as a juvenile way of flirting with her. But after she whooped the ass of almost every guy in the field office, they stopped asking.

It's one reason I don't enjoy going out for drinks with her after work. I don't think I'm an unattractive woman, but standing next to her, I sure feel like it. And it gets a little old to watch the men in the bar flocking to her like they're a bunch of moths and she's the only source of light in the room while I sit there talking to my damn swizzle stick. Not that she goes home with every single guy who looks her way. She'll hook up with a guy every now and then, but more than anything, Astra likes the attention and the fact that she never has to buy a drink.

Yeah, I guess you could say I'm a bit envious of her. Not that I'm actively looking for a guy or anything. A relationship is about the last thing I want or need right now. I'm focused on my career and taking bad guys off the street. And I'm really good at it. I have plans and goals that I'm going to accomplish and getting involved with anybody at this point will likely only complicate things.

But that doesn't make feeling like an outcast or the Ugly Duckling when I'm around Astra at the bar and guys are flocking to her, all but pushing me to the side, any easier to swallow. Yeah, I guess I can be shallow and vain sometimes. Sue me.

"Well, tell the Director that's an order I cannot follow, since I'm trying to do my job," I tell her.

"But that's all you ever do. Like twenty-four hours a day," she complains. "All work and no play makes Blakey a dull girl."

"Not all of us are like you, Astra. We don't just fall out of bed brilliant. Some of us have to actually work at it," I reply.

"You exaggerate."

I scoff at her. "You're like this girl I knew back in high school who never studied — like ever — and yet still rolled into class and got A's on every test."

Astra looks at me, a mischievous grin curling her lips upward. "You're talking about yourself there, aren't you?"

"No," I say immediately. "I'm definitely not talking about myself."

I did study, but the truth of the matter is that school came easy to me. Not that I'll tell Astra, that since it would blunt the point I'm trying to make. But judging by the way she's looking at me, she's not buying what I'm selling.

"You act I don't know just how smart you are. Or that most people think you're the best agent in this field office," she says.

"That's not even true," I reply.

"Stop being so damn humble. You've done some amazing things in the time we've been here. Your star is on the rise, Blake. I wouldn't be surprised if you made Director one day," Astra tells me, her voice thick with sincerity.

I laugh and wave her off. "I think we're getting a bit ahead of ourselves here. Personally, I think you would make a far better Director than I ever would. You're good with people and can navigate those political waters better than me."

She arches an eyebrow at me. "The way you say I'm a people pleasing ass-kisser sounds so nice."

I laugh and throw a piece of balled-up paper across the office at her. She laughs along with me and swats it away harmlessly.

"That's not what I'm saying, and you know it," I tell her.

"I know. It's just fun watching you get all uptight about it."

"You're an ass."

"Thanks for noticing," she chirps.

I've had some success here; I won't deny that. My investigations have taken a few major criminals off the board. But it's certainly nothing to get complacent or big headed about. There will always be new bad guys to chase, and in this modern day and age, with more information about how we conduct our investi-gations out there in the public sphere, catching them is getting more and more difficult.

The only way I can stay on top of things and keep that edge is to keep working. To keep grinding. And to never rest on my laurels. If there's one thing I've learned, it's that things can turn on a dime, and the moment you let yourself get smug about scoring a win is the moment you will lose. And in this game, you could lose everything. Including your life.

"Seriously. Come have a drink tonight," she presses.

I groan dramatically. "I've got something cooking here though."

"Is an arrest imminent?"

"No," I admit.

"Are you even looking at a particular suspect right now?"

"I'm gathering the data and crunching all the numbers — "

"So, that's a no," she cuts me off.

I roll my eyes. "That's a no."

"Good. Then since it's Friday night, and you're nowhere near making a bust yet, you can gather the data, crunch the numbers, and work whatever voodoo you do, on Monday, and go have a drink with me tonight," she argues.

I blow out a long breath, knowing she's right. At the moment, I'm working on a theory, and that's all. But as I look deeper into it, I really feel like there's something here. It may just be a theory, but it's starting to solidify. I really think there's something there. Something that needs to be investigated. And having that taste of something happening makes me hate stalling my momentum, such as it is.

But if I'm being honest, I've had to slog through the last couple of hours, and I feel like I'm looking at so much information on my computer screen that I'm going blind. And perhaps a bit loopy as well. Maybe Astra's right. Unplugging for a bit, then coming back and hitting it hard with fresh eyes will be beneficial to me and to the case I'm starting to build. Perhaps it'll help me get my momentum back.

I look up at her. "Okay. I'll stay for one drink, or until you find somebody to go home with, whichever comes first."

She laughs. "Deal."

TWO

Barnaby's Social House; Downtown Seattle

Whoever coined the phrase, "meat market" to describe a bar obviously had Barnaby's in mind. It's an 80's-themed bar that plays nothing but music from that era. It's full of neon, 80's movie posters, drinks named after stars and films of the decade, as well as all kinds of memorabilia and kitsch. Clearly, the owner is stuck in the days of his youth or something. Most people think it's got a fun, quirky vibe. But I find it kind of tacky and seedy that it preys on people's sense of nostalgia. It's kind of sad watching the aging patrons try to recapture their youth to songs that came out before I was born, but at least the drink specials aren't so bad.

It's also a well-known cop bar. Barnaby's is the place local law enforcement and those of us from the field office all tend to congregate for whatever reason. There are also the hordes of badge groupies who descend on this place every night, of course. It's a phenomenon I don't personally understand, but if you've got a badge, be you a man or a woman, the chances are good that you can find somebody to take you home at the end of the night, if that's what you're looking for.

Which is why Astra likes this place. Barnaby's is not our usual haunt, so I know when she talks me into coming here, it's for a purpose. Aside from the attention and free drinks, Astra is guaranteed to find somebody to go home with for the night. Not that she couldn't snag a guy basically anywhere we go, but for whatever reason, Barnaby's has always been her go-to place to scratch that carnal itch.

"You know what your problem is?" Astra asks.

"Not sure I can narrow it down to just one."

She chuckles and shakes her head. "For the purposes of this discussion, we'll only delve into your biggest issue."

"Oh, well this should be fun then."

"You don't know how to lighten up and have a good time," Astra says. "You're so focused on work and being FBI Super-Chick that somewhere along the way, you seem to have forgotten how to smile and have fun."

"That's not true. I smile. I have fun."

"Yeah? When was the last time you cut loose and had a good time?"

I quickly take a drink to give myself a moment to think. Unfortunately for me, I don't really have an answer to her question. It's not that I don't know how to have fun. It's just that I've been so focused on work that I haven't really had time to go out and have any. Which is her point, of course.

"That's what I thought," she says, a triumphant smile crossing her face.

I harumph at her but laugh, taking the L on that argument. Taking a sip of my drink, I look out across the mob jammed into the bar and hope that if I ignore her, the lecture will just go away.

"Blake, you're young. You're gorgeous," Astra presses. "You should be enjoying yourself. Your life. We only get one crack at this, y'know? You should be sucking the marrow out of life."

No such luck, apparently.

"You did not just quote Thoreau at me," I say dryly.

She shrugs. "Who?"

"Henry David Thor — forget it," I say with a laugh. "I enjoy my life. I get a lot of satisfaction out of my job."

"Spoken like a woman who hasn't gotten laid in a really, really long time," she says. "You get satisfaction out of your job? I mean, who says that?"

"There's nothing wrong with getting satisfaction out of doing a good job," I protest, cringing at how defensive I sound.

"Nothing at all. And the job satisfies me too. But you really should be getting satisfied by more than just your job," she says with a laugh. "I mean, you know you could have any man in this bar, don't you?"

I shrug. "I'm not the one-night-stand kind of girl. You know that about me."

"Yeah, I do. But I hate to see you alone, Blake."

"I'm fine. I promise. Believe it or not, there's more to life than men and sex."

Astra takes a drink of her martini and nods. "Absolutely. There absolutely is," she admits. "But men and sex make life a little more fun, interesting, and can provide us with a distraction when we need it most."

I take a drink and look off again, letting her words rattle around in my mind as I savor the flavor of it. I'll say this for Barnaby's... they can make one hell of a White Russian. It's about the only reason I ever agree to coming here.

"Girl, we are surrounded by death and blood all day, every day. We deal with some of the worst in humanity," she continues. "Every now and then, we have to find a release. We have to find something to connect us to this world and get us out of our minds for a while. Away from the evil we see on a daily basis. And so far as I can tell, you don't have that pressure release valve. You keep going on the way you do, grinding twenty-four/seven, you're going to burn out, Blake. And I don't want to see that happen to you."

I'm loath to admit it, but somewhere deep down, I know she's right. Burnout is pretty common among law enforcement, but it takes a variety of different forms. For some, it leads to a sense of ambivalence and sloppy work. Some just go through the motions. Others choose to simply walk away. And still others, when they hit critical mass and can't deal with it any longer, choose to eat a bullet.

I don't plan on doing any of the three of those things. I'm dedicated to the job, I do it well, and I'll keep doing it because I feel like I'm making a real difference out here. How many lives have I saved because I got a monster off the streets? How many families have been kept together, didn't lose a mom or dad, son or daughter, because I'm good at my job?

That's what keeps me going. It's what keeps me getting out of bed every single day. It's knowing that I'm keeping people safe and putting monsters in cages where they belong that staves off the feeling of burnout. On the contrary, the thrill of hunting these evil people down never fails to send an electric charge through me.

"I know you're not a hook-up girl. I get that," she says. "But having somebody in your life can help take the edge off. It can turn a bad day into something better."

"Or it could turn a bad day into something worse."

"I never knew you to be such a fatalist, Blake."

I shrug. "I'm not a fatalist. Just a realist. Relationships are complicated. Messy. They can really muck up the gears — "

"Or they could provide you with solace and relief from the unrelenting darkness we are immersed in all day, every day."

A small grin touches my lips. "I never knew you to be such a poet."

"There's a lot you still don't know about me."

"That might be true, but there are some things I do know that I'd rather not. Things I can't scrub from my memory no matter how hard I try," I say with a laugh.

"What about that local cop you told me about? Arrington, right?"

"Paxton?" I ask.

She nods. "Paxton Arrington. Yeah, that's the one. What about him? He's filthy rich, drop dead gorgeous —"

"And my friend. He and I get each other," I cut her off. "He also lost his wife less than a year ago. Even if I was interested in him in that way — which I'm not — it's not even remotely appropriate right now."

She raises her hand in mock surrender. "Fine, fine. I didn't know that. My bad," she says. "But my point still stands. You need somebody in your life, Blake."

"I'll get a cat," I tell her.

Astra sighs and shakes her head. "I can see you shutting down, so I'll get off my soapbox for now."

"Thank you."

A slow smile creeps across her face. "Don't think I'm not going to keep pestering you about this. You need some balance in your life."

"Thank you, Dr. Russo."

"Speaking of a little balance in my life..."

I don't even reply as a large, good looking guy comes over to the table, his eyes fixed on Astra. Because of course they are. He introduces himself as Detective Sergeant Renfrow... as if his rank is supposed to impress her. But she gives me a wink, letting me know she's impressed with something.

"Well, I'll take that as my cue," I say and down the last of my drink. "I'll see you later, Astra."

"Yeah. Call me," she replies.

THREE

Wilder Residence; The Emerald Pines Luxury Apartments, Downtown Seattle

I STAND on the small balcony off the living room of my third story apartment, glass of wine in hand, trying to get Astra's words out of my head. Soft jazz music is playing inside the apartment, but outside, my ears are filled with the sounds of the city. To me, it's the most beautiful music in the world.

I know most people think the sounds of a city — car horns blaring, people shouting, laughing, and talking, trucks rumbling, and everything that goes with it — is noise pollution. They say it's loud and obnoxious. And yeah, I suppose there are days it annoys me too. But there's always been something about it I've loved. Astra says it's because I wasn't born here, and I guess maybe there's something to that.

I was born in Cockeysville and spent the first twelve years of my life out there. It's out in the sticks in the middle of Maryland, boasting a population of about twenty-thousand people. It's an affluent little community that isn't without its charms, I suppose. But there isn't a whole lot going on out there and it's usually so quiet, even your thoughts echo. It's a pretty place, but it lacks the sort of energy and vitality of a city like Seattle. I'm not quite the social butterfly Astra is, but I do like a place with a bit of life to it. I like having options, just in case I ever do feel like hitting the town. But believe me, Barnaby's is not the place I'd choose.

Both of my parents worked for the NSA, which is situated at Fort Meade. They opted for the half-hour commute, rather than sticking us on base housing. They said they didn't want us to grow up surrounded by soldiers, but with relatively normal, everyday people. They wanted us to go to normal civilian public schools and have that normal family experience.

And for a while, everything was great. For a while, I'd say I had the ideal childhood. Until it wasn't. Until I came home from school one day to find that my entire world had come crashing down around me.

Draining the last of my wine, I wander back inside and refill my glass. It's Friday after all, so why not? I pluck the framed photo off the shelf and carry it with me as I drop down onto the couch. As John Coltrane softly issues from the speakers, I look at the picture of my family. A family that was taken from me.

Kit and I both got our mom's strawberry blonde hair and green eyes. My sister also got her long, lithe frame, and delicate features. I more took after my dad body-wise. I've always been lean, but I'm also toned and athletic. Probably because of his influence, I've always enjoyed sports and even followed in my father's footsteps, becoming proficient in a couple of different martial arts.

Knowing how much I took after our father in temperament and interests, it often makes me wonder what Kit would have done. Would she have started to share our father's interests as she grew? After all, I was eight or nine before I became interested in sports and the like. My best guess is that she would have turned out more like our mother, a bit of an introverted bookworm with a natural knack for computers. It wouldn't have surprised me to see Kit follow our folks into the NSA.

"I still miss you guys. Every single day," I whisper.

It was more than a decade ago, but the pain is every bit as fresh today as it was back then. Coming home to find what I did has stayed with me. I've done counseling. In fact, I still see my shrink, for all the good it's done. But having that outlet isn't a bad thing. Dr. Reinhart has given me some tools that have helped me cope when times get really dark. She's helped me through some of my rougher moments.

But what she hasn't been able to do is take away the lingering pain completely. She says it's a process, and that it's going to take time for those wounds to heal. I personally don't think they'll ever heal completely, but I at least want to get to a point where I can look at photos, or think of them, and not have it be accompanied by a searing, blinding pain. But it's been fourteen years now, and I'm not sure that day is ever really going to come.

What makes it doubly hard to get over is the fact that I may never know what happened to my kid sister. Unlike my folks, what happened to Kit — my sister, Katherine — is a complete mystery to me. She was just gone. At least I got to bury my folks. Dr. Reinhart says that helped me find some semblance of closure with them — whatever that means.

Personally, I don't believe in closure. I think it's a myth. Simply something we tell ourselves to help us feel better about things. I don't know if you can ever truly get over a loss of the magnitude of the one I endured. To have the people I loved and everything I've ever known just ripped away from me like that? Yeah, I think that's a wound that's never going to fully heal.

But hey, I got to say goodbye to my parents, at least. Katherine disappeared from the face of the Earth like she'd never even existed. She was just... gone. Kit did exist, though. She was kind and beautiful, she had a vibrant personality that lit up every room she walked into, and I loved her fiercely. I still love her.

But I'm realistic enough to know she's probably dead. As much as I'd like to say otherwise, I have little hope she's still alive after all this time. I'd still like to know what happened to her all the same. If for no other reason than to lay her to rest and give her some peace. She deserves that.

I take a long swallow of wine as I look at the pictures, trying to focus on the fonder memories and reflect on happier days. It's not easy when all I can seem to recall with vivid clarity is coming home and finding the lifeless bodies of my parents sprawled out on the living room floor. Their hands had been tied behind their backs and they each had two bullets in the back of their heads.

That's what I remember first and most clearly when I think of my family. That and all the blood. There was so much blood that sometimes I feel like I can still smell it. Silly as it seems, one thing it's done is turn me off to the color red. After that day, I took everything red out of my wardrobe, and my life. I refuse to wear it or have it in my home. I know it's irrational, but it is what it is.

If not for what happened, my life might look very different right now. Instead of hunting monsters, who knows what I'd be doing. It's a question I've pondered a lot over the years but have never been able to come up with a definitive answer for. It's impossible to guess which path I would have taken. As a four-teen-year-old with interests ranging from music to cooking, and parents who supported and encouraged my every whim, I could have been anything from a singer to a chef.

But because of what happened, here I am. A professional monster hunter.

After what happened, I came to Seattle to live with my Aunt Annie, my mom's sister. Annie has a daughter a few years older than me, so we basically grew up together. I still consider Maisey one of my closest friends, and in so many ways Annie is just like a mother to me. We're as close as sisters, and I might not have gotten through the dark days in the immediate aftermath if not for Maisey and Annie. I am forever grateful to them.

I went to school at the University of Washington, where I double majored in Criminology and Psychology — with an emphasis on Abnormal Psychology. I knew before I ever enrolled for classes that my goal was to join the FBI. My first preference all along has been to join the Behavioral Analysis Unit. I want to be a profiler tasked with hunting down the most notorious and prolific killers. Before I can join the BAU though, I've been told I need seasoning. Experience.

So I'm here at the Seattle Field Office cutting my teeth. I'm getting results and have been praised for my work. I've been here for a couple of years now, and I like to think I'm developing a solid reputation. I've taken a few high-profile killers off the board before they could wreak any more chaos and destruction. It's something I'm proud of, and it's gotten me a bit of recognition from the brass.

What I appreciate most about the successes and recognition it brings is that my bosses have started giving me some leeway in my investigations. They're allowing me to work independently and find cases on my own, rather than wait for one to be assigned to me. Personally, I'd rather be proactive in hunting a killer and preventing another life from being lost, instead of waiting for a body to drop, and only then reacting to it.

I wasn't lying to Astra earlier when I told her that I love my job and derive a tremendous amount of satisfaction from it. It's all true. I just hate that I had to get to this point, doing what I'm doing, because of a horrible tragedy. I hate that my career came at the cost of my family. I hate that no matter how much good I do, how many bad guys I get off the streets, or lives that I save, I will forever bear the scars of my youth.

No matter what I accomplish in this career, I'm always going to know that it comes on the backs of two dead parents, and one missing sister, who is presumably also dead. Any success I have in my life will have been paid for with their blood. I'd like to think otherwise, but that's how it is. Being able to forge something productive and good out of such a senseless tragedy is the only silver lining I can take away from it. It's all I have, so I'm going to hold tight to it and hope that one day, it doesn't taste so bittersweet in my mouth.

I get to my feet abruptly and feel myself swaying unsteadily for a moment before I right myself. I've obviously had a bit too much wine tonight. The fact that I was feeling so morose and nostalgic enough that I picked up the family photos should have been tip-off enough. But I didn't think about it too much until I almost went toppling to the floor.

"Time for bed," I mutter.

Depositing the wine glass in the sink, I stagger to the back bedroom and start to get ready to shut myself down for the night and go to sleep. Or maybe more accurately, to try and shut my brain down for the night.

FOUR

"ARE YOU EVEN LISTENING TO ME?"

I look up from the computer. "Of course I am."

Astra gives me a long look and then resumes her story. The truth is, I tuned out shortly after she started telling me about how she and the Detective Sergeant from Barnaby's got back to her place for a weekend of adult fun and games. And I get to hear all about it. Lucky me.

Astra is the sort of friend who wants to share everything. In excruciating detail. And I just don't have the heart to tell her I really don't need to hear about every last groan and grunt of her weekend sexcapades. While I'm glad she feels I'm the kind of friend she can tell anything and everything to, Astra really needs to learn that having some boundaries isn't a bad thing.

It's strange, because I'm normally confident and assertive, and have no problem putting people in their places. With Astra, though, I can't seem to force myself to tell her there are some things I don't want or need to hear. Sharing her life with me is just part of how she shows love. And I can't help but think if I tell her I don't want to hear that level of detail, she'll take it as a sharp rebuke.

She and I have been open with each other about most everything since the Academy, and I cherish that relationship with her. The last thing I want to do is hurt her. There are precious few people I let into my inner orbit, and I'd rather not damage my relationship with Astra by shutting her down just because I'm uncomfortable.

Or maybe I'm just jealous of her for having these wild carnal adventures when I'm sitting at my computer staring at crime trends and murder statistics night after night. That's a disturbing thought that I quickly push away.

"So are you going to see him again?" I ask when she finally finishes her tale.

"Maybe. I don't know. I haven't decided yet," she replies. "Life is a buffet and I plan on tasting a little bit of everything before I shackle myself to just one man."

I laugh and shake my head at her. "You are truly one of a kind, Astra."

"I shouldn't be. I'm simply a woman who is in control of my own sexuality and there is nothing wrong with that."

"No, there's nothing wrong with that at all," I reply.

"You know, I think if you — "

"Oh, would you look at the time? I've got a meet with Rosie in ten minutes," I cut her off.

She gives me a knowing smile as I gather up all of the papers I've been putting together and stuff them into a file. After that, I grab my tablet and return her smile as I head for the door.

"This isn't over, Wilder," Astra calls after me.

"It never is," I shoot back as I close the door.

I stop in the kitchen to grab a cup of coffee before heading for my meeting with Assistant Special Agent in Charge, Rosalinda Espinoza, aka Rosie, my direct superior. Rosie is a tough, no-nonsense kind of woman who's had a long and illustrious career. After she very nearly single-handedly took down a notorious drug cartel, Rosie's ticket was punched. Astra thinks I'm going to be the first female Director, but even though her career arc seems to have stalled a bit here in Seattle, my money is still on Rosie getting to that chair long before me.

Not that I have any grand designs on it anyway. I'm not much for politics and would much rather remain where I am, doing the work I'm doing. Taking bad people off the streets is what I do, and I'm good at it. Far better than I am at the politicking necessary to sit in the Director's chair. It could be why Rosie is still stuck at ASAC after all this time. She's not the type to kiss people's butts. She'll tell them the hard truths, rather than give them empty platitudes. It's something about her I've always respected and admired.

I get to her office and go inside. On my left in the anteroom is Rosie's receptionist, a bookish looking guy named Stephen — not Steve or Steph, always Stephen, or he's likely to cut you. To my right are two plush wingbacks and a small table set between them that make up the waiting area.

"Good afternoon, Agent Wilder," he nods, his tone as clipped as always.

"Good afternoon, Stephen. How are you today?"

Rather than actually using his words to answer me, Stephen merely gives me a smile that's about as warm as an ice cube and picks up the phone. He quietly murmurs into it as if he's passing along state secrets. It's hard for me to not roll my eyes. I used to wonder what it was I did to make him hate me so much, but then I realized he's like this with everybody and stopped taking it personally.

"You may go in now," he says curtly.

"Thank you, Stevie."

A devilish grin on my face, I quickly open the door and step into Rosie's office, practically feeling the laser beams that are undoubtedly shooting from Stephen's eyes and into my back. Closing the door behind me, I find Rosie sitting back in her seat, an eyebrow raised, a small smile on her lips.

"Stephen seems exceptionally pleasant today," I note.

"Why do you antagonize my assistant?" she asks.

"He makes it so easy. Besides, maybe if he didn't act like such a jerk, I wouldn't take such satisfaction out of tweaking him a bit now and then."

"Ever think that's why I keep him around? It's kind of nice having somebody who everybody thinks is a bigger jerk than I am acting as my human shield," she says with a small smile. "Have a seat."

I drop down into one of the large, comfortable chairs situated in front of her desk, my file and tablet sitting on my lap.

"You're not a jerk, Rosie. You're just blunt, and most people can't handle it when somebody's that direct," I tell her.

She whistles low. "That's as close as you've ever come to kissing my butt, Wilder. You must have a big ask."

"Oh, I don't think asking to do my job is a big ask."

"No, but asking me to sign off on one of your wild theories is."

I lean back in the chair and arch an eyebrow at her. "And haven't my wild theories always panned out? How many times have I been wrong?"

"Touché," she replies, pursing her lips as she considers me.

Rosie knows better than anybody that I don't go solely off gut feelings, or wild hunches. My cases are all data driven. But I also know that what I do isn't exactly standard FBI protocol, so Rosie, and by extension, SAC Potts, are going out on a bit of a limb for me. But they do it because I get results, and when I have success, it shines on them as well.

Not that Rosie is truly all that interested in taking credit in much of anything. She's all about the job. It's probably why she hasn't made a big stink about being stuck as the ASAC when she had more seniority, and an arguably better track record when Potts was named the SAC over her. The difference is that Rosie doesn't play politics anywhere near as well as Potts. For her, it's about doing the job, completing cases, and serving her country. She's a genuine believer in the mission, and I respect the hell out of that.

Potts has gone from solid field agent to bureaucratic administrator in record time. For him, it's less about what's going on out on the streets, and more about what's going on inside the ivory halls and towers of the Bureau, back in DC. He's a climber and wants to be in a position of power and authority, whereas Rosie couldn't care less about that. Personally speaking, I think it's made Potts less aware of what's actually happening out there in the actual world.

That's not to say that Potts isn't a capable and solid SAC, or that I don't respect him. I do. It's just different. He can be a bit predictable, and a little too rigidly by the book sometimes. But the one thing I can always count on with Potts is that he's got my back. He always looks after the agents under his command, which is why he's earned the loyalty of so many within the field office, as well as with some of the command staff back in DC.

"So lay it out for me, Wilder."

I nod and open up the file in my hand and start to pass some of the articles I've printed across the desk to her. Rosie picks them up and glances at them.

"And what am I looking at?" she asks.

"Briar Glen. It's a town a few hours southwest of here, along the coast, and sits near the Oregon border," I start my pitch. "Current population is two hundred thirty-five thousand people, and yet they've got a murder rate of just about eighteen per hundred thousand."

Rosie leans back in her seat, steepling her fingers in front of her. Her eyes flick to the papers on the desk in front of her and a small frown pulls the corners of her mouth down. Cities have spikes of violence now and then, but it isn't always indicative of a larger pattern. But those numbers are out of whack.

I pull up the file on my tablet and push it across the desk to her. "Going back fifteen years, you can see the escalation and see that Briar Glen has been well above the state's average murder rate. And within the last four years, things have escalated even further. If this rate holds for another four years, they'll be looking at nearly twenty-three per hundred thousand. That's almost to the level of Chicago."

Rosie picks up the tablet and starts to scroll through some of the data I've pulled up, which to me seems pretty black and white: Briar Glen has a murder problem.

"So, you think a serial's been operating in this city for the last fifteen years? Is that what I'm hearing?"

"Not necessarily. Details are a little thin at this point, but I think the fact that their murder rate is so out of whack with the state and national average that it warrants a closer look."

Rosie rubs her chin, her frown deepening. I can tell she's bothered by the murder rate but turning me loose on Briar Glen — or perhaps more specifically on Briar Glen's Sheriff — seems to be troubling her a bit more. It's true that historically, relations between the Bureau and local LEOs have been strained, and we're reluctant to intervene when we've not been invited.

But I tend to operate below the radar and try to show the locals that I'm there to help. That I'm raising issues they may not be aware of and working with them to resolve the problems.

It's always dicey, given how territorial locals can be, especially when it comes to the Feds, but we usually find a way to make it work. It helps that I'm usually solo and don't have a battalion of Bureau suits at my back.

"There are plenty of small cities around that rate well above the national average," Rosie points out. "Off the top of my head, Pittsburgh and Indianapolis — "

"The difference is, Briar Glen has a fraction of their population and yet, their murder rate has exceeded the state and national average for a decade and a half," I counter. "This isn't a big major metro area, nor is it central to a lot of interstate commerce. This is a sleepy little beach town hours away from everything else."

She pauses, seeming to be thinking it over, the silence lingering for a long moment. She finally gives me a nod.

"Talk to Potts," she tells me. "You're good from my end. Just... tread lightly down there. We don't want a repeat of Pine Valley."

"In my defense, Sheriff Bagins was a sexist pig who doesn't know his ass from a hole in the ground."

"Be that as it may, it wasn't a good look for us, so let's just go easy on the locals. We're trying to keep things smooth and easy, yeah?"

A small grin curls a corner of my mouth up. "I got this, ma'am. I mean, that's what I do best."

As I get to my feet and head for the door, I hear her groan and mutter under her breath behind me. I laugh to myself as I close the door, earning a dirty glare from Stephen.

FIVE

Federal Bureau of Investigations, Seattle Field Office

THE FOLLOWING MORNING, I stop by my office, sifting through my messages and emails. Astra's not at her desk and I wonder where she is briefly before recalling that she's part of a big drug raid today. After saying a silent word for her safety, I lean back in my seat and enjoy the quiet in the office for a minute before my meeting with SAC Potts.

I run through all of the data in my head again and think about what I'm going to say. Though he's willing to back me up, he demands a little more convincing than Rosie does. He's got more on the line than she does, so he's a lot more cautious than Rosie, and wants to be absolutely sure there's something there before he turns me loose. I get it, but it doesn't make the bureaucratic red tape any less annoying.

I'm normally a pretty patient person, but when I've got the scent of something bigger, I hate the waiting. And although I don't know what it is I'm looking at exactly, and can't quite see the shape of it yet, I'm positive there's something there that's worth looking at. In my experience, brief though it might be, smaller cities don't have a murder rate as high as I'm seeing in Briar Glen without something darker and more nefarious going on.

It's time to go, so I get up and check myself over, then grab my things and head out the door. As I head down the hall, I've got my head down, lost in thought. If I'd been paying attention to my surroundings, I would've heard him coming up from behind long before he was walking next to me; he's got a very distinctive walk and an annoyingly loud way of breathing.

"Golden Girl looks like she's on a mission," he cracks.

Determined to say nothing, I grit my teeth and walk on. If I were a superhero, Grant Bryant would be my arch nemesis. He would be the villain I'd find myself locked into mortal combat with for eternity. But I'm definitely not a superhero, so here in the land of mortals, Grant is just another irritating jerk I have to deal with. I'm not entirely sure why he seems to take such bitter resentment to me, but it's escalated well beyond workplace rivalry and into actual enmity.

It wasn't always like this. When I was first assigned to the SFO, Grant was warm and welcoming. He was gracious and kind. But then we butted heads on the first case we worked together and that facade crumbled pretty quick. The problem was he'd zeroed in on a murder suspect in a case we were involved in, and I disagreed with him about it. And he didn't take me disagreeing with him well at all.

The guy Grant had homed in on didn't strike me as a serial killer. In fact, he didn't even match the profile he'd put together on the killer we were tracking — a profile I personally found incomplete and lacking. But Grant targeted the guy because of a couple of inconsequential coincidences. Things I found easily explained away. But the harder I pushed back, the harder

Grant went after the guy. He made it his mission to take the guy down.

In the meantime, I worked up my own profile with the information we had in hand and it pointed to somebody very different. I shared it with Grant, but he rejected it out of hand. With nothing else to do and not wanting to see an innocent man get railroaded just because Grant wanted to prove his superiority to me, I went to Rosie with my concerns... and my profile.

Suffice it to say, it wasn't a popular move with Grant, or his buddies. But my profile led us to the real killer, and he was forced to admit that he was wrong. For a guy with an ego like his, it must have been about as easy as flaying himself. Ever since then, he's been on a crusade to destroy me. Or barring that, to make my life so miserable that I'll transfer out of Seattle just to get away from him. Hence his ridiculous little nickname for me. He thinks he's clever.

That just proves he can't profile worth a damn. If he could, he'd know there's no chance in hell he's going to chase me out of Seattle. It's my home. If he were able to profile at all, he'd know that when somebody comes at me the way he does, I tend to dig my feet in and fight back. I'm not easily intimidated. Especially not by arrogant jerks like him.

"So what are you going to dazzle them with today, Golden Girl?" he snarks.

"Aren't there some boots you need to be licking somewhere?" I finally fire back.

"There's that searing wit again."

"I'm surprised you recognize it for what it is."

Grant fancies himself a climber, and since he's clearly lacking in the smarts department, he's relying on his superior power of ass-kissing. That's the one thing he can do ten times better than I can. A hundred times.

"Are you ever going to get tired of trying to show me up, Wilder?"

"I'm not trying to do anything. Your incompetence just makes it look that way."

"You're just a little ray of sunshine today," he replies.

I roll my eyes and grunt in frustration. "What do you want, Grant?"

"Nothing. Just wanted to remind you that stars may rise quickly, but it's just as easy to get knocked off that high horse."

I stop and turn to him. "Are you threatening me?"

He shrugs. "No. Just trying to keep you humble. You have yourself a good day now, Agent Wilder."

He walks off, leaving me glaring at his back and feeling slightly unsettled. There's no question in my mind that it was some sort of veiled threat. It makes me wonder what he and his boys are planning. What I don't know is if it's real or if he was just trying to knock me off my game, obviously knowing I'm going to meet with SAC Potts. If it's the latter, he's a bigger idiot than I thought. If it's the former, all I can say is, "bring it on." I don't get that rattled very easily.

"Jerk," I mutter as I turn and walk away.

A couple of minutes later, I'm sitting in front of SAC Potts, watching him look over the data on my tablet, his expression skeptical. He's a tall man with broad shoulders, icy blue eyes, and hair that's slowly ceding its dark color to the ravages of time as it slowly turns gray. It's mostly around the temples, which gives him something of a distinguished appearance and a gravitas he tries to cultivate.

Potts is fit, trim, and very obviously takes care of himself. His presence just screams baseball, Mom, and apple pie, and he's got this chest thumping, flag waving aura about him. If you ask me, you can't see him and not think Fed. He looks like the stereotypical FBI agent you see in the movies — minus the dark aviator shades and darker trench coat. At least indoors.

After a few moments, he looks up at me and frowns.

"ASAC Espinoza gave me a quick briefing, but I wanted to look at your information and speak with you about it myself," he starts.

"Thank you for taking the time this morning, sir," I reply. "As you can see, Briar Glen is a city about a third of the size of Seattle, and yet it has a murder rate that's six times as high."

"I can see that. And do you have a theory? Are we looking at a serial?"

I shift in my seat and clear my throat, trying to summon the might of my powers of persuasion. Such as they are. Ordinarily when I come to Rosie and Potts, I've got a specific theory and data to support it. But right now, I've got little more than some numbers and a feeling. A feeling I know is right, but a feeling nonetheless. And I'm not sure how that's going to play with the SAC. Rosie is usually willing to give me a bit more leeway in most things.

"At the moment, whether there is a serial operating in Briar Glen is unclear. I would need to be on the ground there, with access to their case files to make a final determination on that, sir."

"Then why am I even looking at this?"

"Because I'm of the opinion that there is something happening in that city, sir," I urge. "Their murder rate is — "

"Higher than normal. Yes, I gathered that."

"Not just higher than normal, sir. Alarmingly high," I argue. "I've gone back thirty years in Briar Glen's history, and this violent trend started roughly fifteen years ago, and took an even higher uptick four years ago. Prior to that, the city was well below the state and national averages. It was, by all accounts, an idyllic place to live."

"From what I'm seeing here, there's no pattern. We've got shootings. Strangulations. Stabbings. There's no signature."

"That we know of, sir. Again, I won't have specifics until I review some of their case files. I'm willing to admit the spike could be... natural. For lack of a better word, anyway."

"But you obviously don't believe that."

I shake my head. "Not at all, sir. I think there's something going on in Briar Glen. Something bad."

Potts sighs and leans back in his seat, his eyes on the tablet in front of him. He's working through the cost benefit analysis in his head — the cost of turning me loose in a city, and the benefit he will reap from it if I'm right. We go through this every time I bring something to his attention that I want to investigate. He's also, of course, weighing out how much of a hit he'll take if I'm wrong and/or cause a scene. It doesn't happen often, but I've been known to butt heads with the locals now and then, and I'm sure he's factoring that into his equation.

"Sir, it's my belief that if we do nothing, people in Briar Glen will continue to die," I press him. "Their murder rate is so out of whack with state and national averages, there is no other conclusion to draw than somebody, or perhaps multiple people, are out there killing people, and have been doing so for over a decade."

"I've got to be honest here. This is really thin, Agent Wilder," he sighs. "A lot thinner than what you usually come to me with."

"I understand, sir. This one is somewhat unusual, I admit. But my gut is telling me there's something there. Something we need to be looking into."

He's wavering, caught somewhere between trusting me and doing the right thing, and making sure his own backside is covered. Although I love my job and doing what I do, this is the one thing I really despise about it — letting your need to give yourself some political and professional cover get in the way of doing the right thing. I want to scream at him, tell him this isn't some political calculus to consider. These are people's lives at stake.

"Look, if I'm wrong, I'm wrong. I'll come back to the field office, no harm, no foul," I push. "But if I'm right, just think of how good it will look for the field office. And for you, sir."

He arches an eyebrow at me. "You really shouldn't try politicking, Agent Wilder. You're lousy at it."

My smile is rueful. "Had to try, sir."

"You feel this strongly about it, do you?"

"Yes, sir. I do."

His eyes flick to the tablet again before he looks up at me. "You're to tread lightly, Agent Wilder. You are not to antagonize the locals. I don't want another phone call from an angry sheriff," he says. "Are we clear?"

"Crystal, sir."

"And if there is nothing there, you get your butt back here ASAP. I won't have you trying to force the facts to fit your narrative."

"I hope you know me better than that, sir."

His face relaxes and he nods. "I do. I don't question your integrity," he replies. "I'm just looking out for you and this office."

He knows I would never try to trump up a case when the facts aren't there, nor would I try to force them to conform to my view of things. I know he doesn't question my integrity. I've never given him cause to. When I've been wrong, I've always been the first to admit it.

But I'm not naïve. What he's actually looking out for is himself. He's simply trying to hide behind the facade of protecting me and the office, when his biggest concern is how big of a chunk of his hide will be torn out if I make him look bad in all of this. That's outweighed, only slightly, by his concern over how big of a chunk will be torn out if he does nothing and more people are murdered in Briar Glen. Deaths we could possibly prevent.

"Understood, sir. I'll tread very lightly. They won't even know I'm there," I say.

"Stop being smart with me." He can't quite stifle his smirk entirely though. "Dismissed, Agent Wilder. And good luck."

SIX

Marco's Corner Diner; Downtown Seattle

"So where are you off to this time?"

A smile crosses my face as I take a drink of my iced tea, then set the glass down. My cousin Maisey is sitting across from me, a small grin curling the corners of her lips upward, a knowing gleam in her eyes.

"What makes you think I'm going somewhere?" I ask.

"Whenever you get ready to leave town, you invite me out for dinner," she replies simply.

"What? That's not true."

She nods. "It totally is."

"We just had dinner a couple of weeks ago and I didn't go anywhere," I protest.

"That's because I asked you," Maisey says.

I screw up my face and think about it for a second. "Really?"

"Yup. Sure did. I can show you the text messages."

"No arguing with physical evidence."

"You should know that better than most," she says.

A soft, rueful laugh escapes me. As I think about it more, I come to the conclusion that she's right, I do usually only call her to meet for dinner right before I blow out of town. Maybe on some level I think it could be the last time I see her or something, which is incredibly morbid. But I can't deny that's the way my mind works sometimes. A sunshine and rainbows girl I am not.

I'm sure Dr. Reinhart would tell me it stems from the loss I suffered as a child. That I have dinner with Maisey before I head out on a case to make sure I can at least say goodbye on my own terms, in case everything goes wrong — a goodbye I never got to say to my parents. Having seen a therapist for most of my life, as well as having one of my two degrees in Psychology, I've got a pretty good idea of how my brain works. But sometimes, things still pop up and surprise me.

"Wow. Maybe you should be profiling for the Bureau," I comment.

"Yeah, I'm not really a fan of being put in a position where I have to shoot, or be shot," she says wryly. "I kind of like the quiet solitude of the library."

That's a very Maisey thing to say. She's very risk averse and has avoided things that might be considered dangerous all her life. I can't even get her to go on a roller coaster with me when the fair comes to town.

I give her a soft smile. "I'm sorry. I just never realized..."

"It's fine. You're a busy woman with an important job," Maisey says. "I'm just glad we get together as often as we do."

"Even if it's you facilitating it."

She shrugs. "Doesn't matter to me how it happens. Just that it happens."

I never realized before that she's usually the one who puts in the effort to make it happen. Knowing that makes me feel a little ashamed. Maisey is an incredibly important person in my life, and I now see that I'm not doing a good job of showing that. The fact that I apparently only try to connect with her before I leave town — and that she's noticed it — sends a wave of guilt washing over me.

It's true that I'm busy most of the time, but I like to check in on her as often as I'm able, just to be sure she's doing all right. I send her texts fairly regularly and give her a call when I have a chance to sit and talk. Granted, it's not often I have the time to sit back and chat for an hour, but I do my best.

"I'm sorry, Maisey," I tell her. "I promise to do better."

She gives me a smile as the waitress drops off our meals — a steak, skewer of shrimp, and baked potato with all the trimmings for me, a pistachio crusted salmon filet for Maisey — and we tuck into them. Marco's is a quaint little place that has a log cabin, hunting lodge motif, complete with faux animal heads mounted on the walls, and a massive fireplace set into one wall. There are pictures of Seattle from a bygone era on the walls, and other kitschy decorations all over the place.

It's Maisey's favorite place to eat when we go out, and while the food here is outstanding, I'm relatively sure her fondness for the place has more to do with Marco, the owner, than it does with anything else. Marco is a tall, lean, guy with tawny skin, dark hair, and darker eyes, and looks to be of maybe Mexican descent. He's a good-looking man and I can see why my cousin has a crush on him.

Not that she'd ever admit that to anybody. Not even to me. She's always been incredibly shy around men. Maisey has only had a handful of relationships in her life at most, and none of them ever lasted more than a couple of months. With dark hair, green eyes, and a curvy little body, Maisey is a knockout. Her biggest problem, and the reason she can't seem to connect with most guys, is her confidence. Or rather, her lack of it. If she'd only believe in herself, I have no doubt Maisey would find a man who would love her the way she deserves to be loved.

"How is Mom?" I ask. Even though she's my aunt, it's important to me sometimes to think of her as another mother. Annie never once tried to replace my real mom, but she made sure I always knew I could call her Mom, and I could be her mother too, whenever I needed a mother. I didn't quite understand it at the time, but I appreciate it now.

"She's good. Keeping herself busy as always," she replies. "She'd like you to come for dinner soon. She misses you."

"I'll do that. It's been a little while since we got together and I miss her too," I tell her.

I'm not as close with my aunt as I am with Maisey, but we get along well enough. Annie is even more reclusive than Maisey. She really tried her best raising us, but the years have been tough on her, and when my mom died she took it hard. She almost makes my cousin look like a towering monument to confidence. Annie had a bad marriage and left just after Maisey was born before things got worse.

Probably because of that, Annie's lived a quiet life alone, distrustful of men and avoiding personal connections of any kind. Her experience has turned her cold. Bitter. And unfortunately, that's rubbed off on Maisey a bit. While my cousin isn't nearly as bitter as Annie, she's definitely distrustful of men. That, combined with a sense of self-esteem that's in the gutter, explains why Maisey can't find or keep a man.

I've tried working with her on it. Tried to get her to be a bit more open. I've encouraged her to be bolder, more adventurous, but I can never seem to pull her out of that pit where her confidence resides. I'll never quit trying, though. I want her to live a life filled with love and happiness. And I'll do whatever it takes to keep her from being the surly spinster my aunt has become.

"So where are you headed this time?" she asks.

"Briar Glen," I say around an incredibly tender mouthful of steak. "On the coast down near the Oregon border."

"What's happening down there?"

I take a sip of my tea and shake my head. "Not sure yet. Just going to down there to check some things out."

"People being murdered down there?"

I nod. "Yeah, but I'm not sure what's going on yet. I'm basically just going down to see if there's something bigger going on, or if it's just coincidental."

Although she isn't big on blood and guts, Maisey has a peculiar fascination with true crime. She's always watching documentaries about serial killers and TV programs about notorious murders. She's probably read every last book on the subject in the library she works in. Maisey always has a million questions and loves to talk to me about cases I've worked — minus the gory details, of course.

"What does your gut tell you?" she asks.

"There's something bigger happening."

"Then I'm sure there is," she replies. "You're never wrong about these things."

I give her a smile. "I appreciate your faith in me."

"It's well-founded, given your history. I'm surprised the Bureau hasn't given you a blue spandex suit and a cape yet."

A small laugh escapes me. "Yeah, let's not get carried away."

Maisey's eyes flick over to Marco, who is standing near a table, chatting with the patrons. Her gaze lingers on him, an expression of desire etched into her features. Marco looks over at her, and when their eyes meet, I see her cheeks flare with color and she quickly averts her gaze. Maisey turns back to her plate, her attention fixed firmly on the remnants of her meal.

"Why don't you go talk to him?" I ask.

Never looking up, she shakes her head. "I can't do that."

"Sure you can. It's easy," I urge her. "It's just like talking to me."

"Hardly. I'm not like you. I can't — "

"You only can't because you tell yourself that," I press her. "The only thing holding you back is you, Maisey. I mean, even from here, I can tell that Marco's interested in you. And I know for a fact that you're interested in him."

She screws up her face and gives me an awkward smile. "I don't think he's interested in me."

"Maisey. Trust me, he is."

"Can we not talk about this?" she asks.

The color in her face deepens and she's rendered speechless for a moment. I open my mouth to speak but pause as the realization that I'm doing the same exact thing I give Astra grief about. I try to justify it in my own mind, telling myself that I'm only doing it for Maisey's own good — and then realize Astra's said the very same thing to me before. I silently chastise myself.

But still, I think it's a little bit different. This isn't me telling Maisey she needs to start taking people home every weekend. This is me trying to help her overcome this crippling lack of confidence in herself. This is to help her see how much she has to offer somebody, and that she deserves to be happy and loved. My pushing Maisey is different than the way Astra pushes me.

At least, that's how I'll justify it to myself. If nothing else, I am a master at rationalization. But for now, I'll back off. I don't want to be quite as pushy and domineering as Astra can be. Maisey is a bit more delicate than I am and pushing her too hard might result in the exact opposite effect of what I'm trying to accomplish. Which is for Maisey to get over her fears and develop a little confidence.

I smoothly steer us away from talking about Maisey's love life and onto safer, more neutral subjects instead. We spend a couple of hours laughing and talking, enjoying our time together like we always do, and it makes me regret the fact that we don't do it more often. That I don't make more of an effort to get together with her.

And as we're leaving the diner, I silently vow to myself that from now on, I'm going to make sure I try to do better. She turns to me, a gentle smile on her face.

"Be careful down there. I want you home in one piece," she says.

"I will," I respond. "If for no other reason than because I will get you and Marco together at some point."

She laughs, but the twinkle in her eye tells me she's not opposed to the idea at all.

SEVEN

Pacific Crest Motor Court; Briar Glen, WA

"How... RUSTIC," I mutter.

I throw my bags on the bed and frown as I look around at what's going to be my home away from home for a little while. My room is a small, one-room bungalow set at the far end of the grounds. It's got a king-sized bed against the wall with cheap pressboard nightstands that are pitted and cracked on either side of the headboard.

There's a highboy dresser against the wall across from the bed that doesn't quite match the color of the nightstands, or the battered table that sits beneath the window on the wall next to the door. A flatscreen, off-brand TV sits on top of the highboy so I can enjoy the free HBO the desk manager was so excited to tell me about. Assuming the TV works anyway. At least I've got a nice view of the Pacific through that window. That's a plus.

The carpet is a low pile brown color that feels more like a layer of Astroturf stretched over the concrete foundation of the bungalow. The comforter on the bed, printed with pictures of trees and deer, is done in shades of red and brown, giving it an autumn-like feel, as well as providing plenty of camouflage for the myriad of stains I'm sure cover the fabric. I'd really hate to see this thing under a UV light.

That it's otherwise clean is probably about the best thing that can be said for it. But hey, I guess I should count my blessings that it is. I've had to stay in a few places that had me questioning whether or not I should sleep in the rental car instead.

"My life is so glamorous," I say to the empty room.

With nothing else for it, I get to work. After quickly stripping the bed of the sheets and comforter, I toss them into a pile in the corner, then remake it with the bedding I'd brought along. I learned not to trust motel bedding on a case long ago, when I found a bed covered in faded spots of blood. Now, whenever I'm out in the field, I bring my own.

Others think me eccentric, a germaphobe, or perhaps a touch bougie for it, but the last thing I want to have to worry about is catching some freakish skin-eating disease while I'm out on assignment. They can call me whatever they want. I couldn't care less. All I know is I sleep better at night on my own sheets.

After getting myself squared away, I lock up and head into town, which is about ten minutes from the motel. Briar Glen looks like it's frozen in time but is desperately trying to break from the past and move forward. Up and down the main drag of town — Pacific Avenue — there's a mish-mash of old timey Mom-and-Pop shops and modern chain stores. It's cute. A little mismatched, but quaint.

I should go by the police station and check in with the sheriff. I know I need to announce my presence and I'm pretty sure Potts would be chewing me out if he knew that wasn't my very first stop. But I like to get a feel for a town. I like to see how it is without any agenda-driven, perhaps biased eyes looking over my shoulder. I don't want my initial impressions of a place tainted by outside influence.

But I know that I have to play nice with the locals. It's not like we Feds have a terrific history with local LEOs. Back in the day, the Bureau would descend upon a town and steamroll anybody who got in the way of an investigation. Including local cops. But in the interest of preventing the hostility and resistance from local law enforcement by bringing the full weight of our power to bear, the Bureau has pivoted over the years.

It's a brave new world. We rely on cooperation, so today, we make every effort to work hand in hand with local LEOs as partners, rather than subordinate agencies. More or less. The Bureau, in its infinite wisdom, has found it more beneficial to not antagonize the locals and work with them in a collaborative fashion, rather than pit them as adversaries from the jump.

That's not to say there aren't still the usual territorial pissing matches. Some guys — and yes, in my experience, it's always men — just need to prove their manhood and assert their dominance. It usually makes for sticky and tense situations where the focus of the investigation sometimes gets lost in the shuffle. It sometimes makes for sloppy police work. Things get missed. And there's nothing I hate more than things getting missed.

I find a parking space and pull in, then get out and start walking along the street, peering into the storefronts as I go. About halfway down the block, I find a coffee house, so I step inside, place my order, and carry it to a table out on the patio. Taking a seat near the railing, I sip my coffee and watch the flow of traffic passing me by as I sit back and take it all in.

There's a rhythm and a flow to a city. A natural vibe. Whenever I start an investigation, I like to tap into that. I like to try to get a feel for the city. Just a little taste of the local flavor. In this stage of the investigation, I always kind of feel like Jane

Goodall, just sitting and observing the native wildlife. Which is what I spend the next few hours doing. Just observing.

See, I have this idea that you can pick up on the energy in a place. It's not as woo-woo new agey as it sounds. I just think you can get a sense of it simply by watching how the people interact with one another. It's obviously far from scientific and leans more toward the soft sciences like anthropology or sociology. Potts would undoubtedly call it pseudo-science, but I think watching a person's behavior is critical to doing our job thoroughly. Granted, it's not admissible as evidence in a court proceeding. But it can help you narrow your focus.

To me, being able to work up an accurate profile, one that will lead you to the suspect you're looking for, you have to include things like environment. You have to know the people around you to be able to accurately pick the one out of the group who's actually guilty. To my mind, if you're not factoring everything into your profile, including the vibe of the city you're in, you're handicapping yourself. I see value in the soft sciences others reject out of hand.

If you go into a city like say, Chicago, specifically the South Side, you're likely going to pick up on a lot of anger. A lot of tension. You'll be able to see it playing out in how the people interact with one another. When there's a lack of basic resources like decent housing or meaningful employment, people don't trust each other, and they especially don't trust law enforcement. Suddenly what should be a community becomes a desperate grasp for survival, and that survival instinct overwhelms people. Small arguments blow up into full scale melees in the blink of an eye. People get shot and killed at the drop of a hat for petty, inconsequential things every day. And I think, after a while, that sort of thing leaves an imprint on a city. On the energy and soul of a city.

Now, contrast that with a place like Centennial, Colorado,

or Sterling Heights, Michigan, which are among the safest cities in the United States and have some of the lowest violent crime rates in the nation. There are so little violent crime in those cities, you don't see the same sort of instant escalation of hostility. You don't see the same sort of violent reaction to those same inconsequential things that would get you shot on the South Side of Chicago. Of course, it doesn't hurt that those cities have robust economies and opportunities for people to succeed. When people don't have to scrape by just to survive, they can thrive.

This is all purely anecdotal. Some would say idle conjecture. It's not scientific in the least, nor is it admissible in a court of law. I'm aware of all of that. But I believe observation is an important tool. A key arrow in my quiver I can use to sight in on a target.

The one thing I've learned from my observations as I wandered about the town today is that there doesn't seem to be any sort of underlying anger or hostility. People don't seem to interact with each other very much in Briar Glen, and from what I've seen, when they do, it's nothing more than the usual pleasantries. Interactions are short and polite. But I don't think this place is a hotbed of violence. From my research, the economy seems decent enough here, and I couldn't find any notable gangs or organized crime. It just seems like a... well, a normal small city. Not a paradise, but not the kind of place where you have to worry about rampant gun violence.

What I do pick up on is a sense of wariness that runs below the surface of the city. There is a current of tension among the people I've been watching today. It's very slight, but it's there. It's hard to describe, and impossible to quantify, but they have the sort of tension prey animals have when there is a predator about. I can see it in the way they look at other people on the street. There's a familiar hunch in their shoulders, a tightness in their bodies, and sideways glances.

To me, it feels as if the violence and death that's occurred in Briar Glen over the past fifteen years or so has left an imprint. Maybe one so subtle that its own citizens don't quite realize it. It's perhaps not the same sort of indelible mark that you'd find in a city that's more known for its violence, but it's there all the same. I can feel it.

Satisfied with my conclusions and first impressions of the town, I pack it in and head back to the hotel. I want to bone up on Sheriff Morris before I go and have a sit down with him. The more I know about him, the easier it might be to manage him if needs be. I know how these small-town law enforcement types can be and I'd rather not ruffle this guy's feathers like the last one.

The last thing I want is to give Potts more ammunition to use against me.

EIGHT

Industrial District, Briar Glen, WA

I STAND at the second-floor window of the old factory, looking out at the other derelict buildings, and the forest beyond that. Scattered clouds roll by overhead, hiding and then uncovering the moon, bathing the land in a light that flits from shadow to silvery luminescence, creating a slow strobe effect.

This part of town has been abandoned for years, but still stands as a crumbling artifact of a time long gone by. Briar Glen was founded as a fishing town more than a hundred years ago. The town flourished and grew quickly. Briar Glen was prosperous and was quickly becoming the jewel of the state.

But then, with increasing political pressure and men with deep pockets, the industry shifted north. Seattle became the prime hub of the fishing industry, and Briar Glen was left behind to languish and decay like the building I'm standing in right now. This was once the biggest fish processing plant and cannery in town. It's been in my family for generations but hasn't been used for anything in... I don't even know how long anymore.

Oh, we've tried to convert it for another use several times. We tried to revitalize this area by manufacturing different items over the years. None of them panned out though, and the factory was finally shut down and boarded up. Briar Glen itself has enjoyed a resurgence over the last thirty years or so, drawing new jobs and people to settle here, thinking it an idyllic place to raise a family. But this section of the city, what used to be the center of the fishing industry, has been cast out and left to rot.

It suits me just fine though. This factory, or rather the shell of what used to be a factory, is still owned by my family. And with the surrounding area deserted, it is the perfect place for our group to meet without being observed. We are free to gather and mete out God's justice.

Briar Glen has grown. In many ways, it has become that suburban utopia many believe it to be. But there is a dark underbelly here as well. There is a criminal element that preys on the weak and the vulnerable. That victimizes people. What makes it worse is that most of these animals get away with it. Our police department is so inept, and has been since the dawn of time, that these people — and I hate to call them that — literally get away with murder. The incompetence of our police department is costing good people their lives.

I know this better than most. My people know this better than most. It's a situation that's untenable, which is why we gather to do what needs to be done. To do what our police department has neither the intelligence nor backbone to do. We gather to make Briar Glen, our home and a town we love, safer and more secure. We gather to do God's justice.

"Everybody is here. It's time," he announces, his voice slightly muffled by his mask.

The voice behind me echoes around the cavernous, empty room. The light from his torch casts flickering, writhing shadows upon the walls as I turn and give him a nod. I raise the mask in my hand and put it on, situating it so that it's comfortable, then pull the hood of my cloak up.

"I'll be down shortly," I reply.

He gives me a nod and turns away. I listen to the echo of his footsteps ebb as he goes back downstairs, plunging the room around me back into a silent darkness. It is a very special night for us. I can practically feel the excitement below radiating up to me. The dedication of my people fills me with a sense of joy and renews my sense of purpose. It confirms for me once more the righteousness of our work.

I take a deep breath and let it out slowly as I stride from the room, head down the corridor, and then descend the staircase. As I walk across the open floor and step up onto the small dais, the group falls silent. All eyes turn to me. The light from the flickering torches glimmers off the masks of my people, all of them assembled and waiting for me, and I feel a rush of pride flow through me.

"Fourteen years ago, there were seven of us. We were bonded by a shared grief that quickly became a sense of purpose. A mission," I begin. "Over the years, we have grown. Others who share the same bond of grief, now share that same sense of purpose. They have come to join us. They share our vision and we have become one."

Applause and cheering erupts from the crowd. I can feel the pride and conviction they all have for what we're doing. I can feel how much they, too, believe in the righteousness of our cause. My heart swells from their adulation.

"We original seven, back when we first started our work, decided that every seven years, we would renew our bonds. That we would purify ourselves and consecrate our work," I continue. "The time to do that has come again. Tonight, we begin the ritual of renewing our faith. Tonight, we begin the ritual that will renew our bonds to our work, and to each other. Nos servo fidem."

"Nos servo fidem," the group replies as one.

"We are the ones who deliver true justice in Briar Glen. God's justice. We are the ones who hold the line here, because we are the only ones willing to do what must be done to protect our homes. Our families," I intone. "We alone have the will and the conviction to do the work that others will not. Some might call us monsters, but they do so while living beneath the safety and protection we provide. Never forget that. Our work is critical to the health and welfare of this town and everybody in it. It is vital to the safety of our loved ones. Nos servo fidem."

"Nos servo fidem," they call out in unison.

"We are the Sword of Michael," I reply, my voice rising. "We are Manus Domini Dei."

"We are the Sword of Michael. We are Manus Domini Dei," they call back to me as one.

I stand still for a moment, looking over the eighteen people before me. My people. My army. Warriors all. I slide an eight-by-ten photograph out of my robes and lay it on the table at the front of the dais, glancing at the dark haired, dark eyed beauty. I can feel their excitement rising, along with my own. The renewing of our bonds and faith is an event we all look forward to. Perhaps me most of all.

"Let us begin," I call.

NINE

"I'D LIKE to see Sheriff Morris, please," I say.

The man behind the inch-thick plexiglass at the front counter has sergeant stripes on his uniform sleeves, dark hair that's obviously been colored recently, dark eyes, and a bushy mustache that would probably would have fit right in on an adult film set in the 1970s. He takes off his glasses and looks me up and down, appraising me, and clearly finding me wanting.

"Got an appointment?" he asks.

I shake my head. "I don't — "

"Sheriff's busy. Make an appointment and come back then," he snaps.

He puts his glasses back on and returns his attention to the phone in his hand. It's painful watching his brow furrow as he struggles to hunt and peck his way to keying in a text message. Clearly, this guy isn't incredibly tech savvy, and would probably feel more comfortable with a rotary dial phone. He notices I haven't moved and looks up at me, his expression darkening.

"There somethin' else?" he grumbles.

"Yes. In fact, there is," I say and slap my credentials down on the counter. "Special Agent Blake Wilder. I'd like to speak with Sheriff Robert Morris."

I hate badging people and asserting my position like that. It definitely starts things off on the wrong foot. But when you run into an obstinate buffoon, you do what you have to do.

If the man's expression was any sourer, it would curdle milk. But he picks up the phone and turns away from me so I can't hear him, or read his lips apparently, as he mutters low into the receiver. He drops the phone back into the cradle a little harder than necessary and turns to me, his face etched with his displeasure.

"Go straight back, take the first hallway on your right, and the Sheriff's office is at the end of the hall," he says.

A moment later, a loud buzzer sounds, so I walk to the door to the right of the window and pull it open. I step through and wind my way through the desks that fill the administrative area of the station, heading for the corridor at the back the Sergeant so helpfully directed me to.

I know I should have called ahead to schedule a meet with Sheriff Robert Morris. It would have been the proper way to go about introducing myself and all that. But I'm not a big fan of bureaucratic protocols. They're cumbersome, and in many cases, entirely unnecessary. I've found that people so often get hung up on the protocols and following the proper channels that things get lost in the translation. Especially when it's we Feds dealing with local LEOs.

I much prefer showing up unannounced. I've found that walking in on these guys in their natural habitat without giving them the benefit of time to sanitize things or put on a happy face is more beneficial. At least, it is to me. I know that some of them get their panties in a bunch about it and it puts them on the defensive, but I'd rather have them unscripted and blunt, than listen to them pour honey and garbage in my ear. Ten out of ten times, I'll take the truth. Even if it irritates me.

As much as the Bureau has tried to soften our stance — or at least, tried to make a public show of softening our stance — when it comes to dealing with crimes in local municipalities, old feelings and rivalries die hard. Not all of the locals trust us, and although I can't say I necessarily blame them, it would be nice if they would at least make a good faith effort to work with us. Meeting us halfway would go a long way toward bridging that divide.

That's not to say all local PDs are that way. Many aren't. But there is a large number of small-town sheriffs who resent us and would just as soon shoot us as work with us. They're protective of their towns and don't like outside interference. While I get that, most of these guys are simply too proud to ask for help and view our presence as something that will make them look bad. It's pure egotistical macho idiocy. Plain and simple.

I find my way to Sheriff Morris' office and knock on the door.

"Come," he calls, his voice muffled.

I open the door and step in to find him sitting behind his desk, a cup of coffee in one hand, a breakfast burrito in the other. Morris is a large man, wide through the shoulders and chest. His hair is iron gray, he's got dark, piercing eyes that I don't think miss much, and a strong jawline. He's a fit man who looks like he takes good care of himself. He's clean cut, looks freshly shaved, and has that Old West, small town, gunslinging Sheriff look about him.

Morris sets his mug of coffee down, but doesn't get up when I come in. He simply looks at me from the other side of his desk, his feet propped up on the top and crossed at the ankles, munching away on his burrito.

"Special Agent Wilder," he says around a mouthful of what smells like egg and chorizo. "To what do I owe the distinct dishonor of a visit from the Federal Bureau of Intimidation?"

I chuckle softly to myself. This is starting off well. Everything I'd read about him last night had said he was a straight shooter, no nonsense, tough as nails guy. He's known around here as a solid lawman who takes the job of protecting his town very seriously. As a sacred duty. I didn't read anything about him having any particular axe to grind with the Bureau. So, this is a fun surprise.

Without waiting for an invitation, I shut the door behind me, walk across his office, and drop down into a chair across from him. He arches an eyebrow at me, an amused smirk on his face, but says nothing. Morris takes a big bite of his burrito and stares at me while he chews. It's clearly a tactic he's using to try and assert his dominance. By remaining silent and making me wait, he's trying to intimidate me, and at the same time, show me that he's the boss and he's in control.

It's a common enough tactic and pretty easy to spot. I'm frankly surprised that Morris would try it with me, since he's got a reputation as a fair and open-minded guy who's willing to do whatever is necessary to do the job. Apparently, that willingness might end when it comes to dealing with the Feds.

I lean back and stare right back at him, showing him that I not only know what he's doing, but that it doesn't intimidate me in the least. I'm used to dealing with cocky, arrogant, chauvinistic men. The Bureau's full of them, so I'm well versed in dealing with their types. I lost any sense of fear or intimidation of them a long while ago. If I hadn't, I never would have made it through the Academy in the first place.

"What are you doing here, Agent Wilder?" he finally asks,

his slow drawl only adding to the Old West Sheriff image I have in my head.

"Nothing as sinister as it seems like you're imagining right now."

"I guess time will tell."

I let out an irritated breath. There's a rather large piece of me that would like to put this man in check. There's a part of me that would like to shut him down and put him in his place. But the calmer and more rational side of my personality takes control and throttles back my irritation. It reminds me the best way to catch flies is with honey, rather than vinegar. Or whatever that old saying actually is.

"Look Sheriff, there doesn't need to be any animosity between us. I'm not here to get into your hair, or — "

"Then why are you here?" he interrupts me.

I bite back the pointed and sarcastic remark that's sitting on the tip of my tongue and force myself to take a breath. When I feel reasonably calm, I start again.

"I'm here because I've noticed that Briar Glen has an unusually high violent crime rate compared to the state and national averages," I say. "We thought it warranted taking a closer look at."

He scoffs and shakes his head. "Ain't you guys got enough to deal with on your own instead of pokin' around here in our business?"

"Forgive my impertinence, Sheriff, but doesn't it concern you that Briar Glen has one of the highest violent crime rates in the entire country, especially for a town this size?"

His expression darkens as he puts his feet down and slams his burrito down on his desk, scattering egg and meats across his blotter. He frowns as he glances at the mess and I can see his jaw clenching tight. Clearly, I've hit a nerve with the man. He grabs a napkin and wipes his hands, then scoops the mess into the trash can and drops his burrito on top of it all. Morris takes a long swallow of his coffee, then leans forward.

"To answer your question, of course it concerns me," he growls.

"I just want to understand how you can have a violent crime rate six times higher than Seattle when you have a third of the population."

"I'm afraid I can't answer that, Agent."

"Can't?"

He sits back in his seat, taking a long swallow of his coffee, and as he does, I see the emotion in his eyes. The number of deaths and violent crimes in Briar Glen does indeed weigh on him. I can see it's taking a toll. It's not much, but it at least gives us some common ground to operate from. If he's willing to work with me, that is.

"Look, Sheriff Morris," I start again, adopting a more conciliatory tone, "me being here isn't an indictment against you. It has nothing to do with your work —"

"Then why are you sitting in my office?"

His constant interruptions are starting to wear on me. As is his defensiveness. He's sitting here acting like I'm accusing him of being incompetent or something, when I've done nothing of the sort. I need to find a way to break through that barrier and make him see that I'm not actually trying to denigrate him or the job he's doing. But he's so busy trying to cover his ass that he's not giving me an opening to do that.

"I'm sitting in your office because what I do at the Bureau is a little bit different. I analyze data and look for patterns."

"So you're a number cruncher?"

I give him a small shrug. "Not exactly. But in some ways, yes. I use the data and look for patterns, like I said. For instance, in Briar Glen, I went back a little more than fifteen years and saw the trend of violent crimes rising steadily... getting it to the point it's at now. Which is fairly alarming."

He runs a hand over his face, then takes a swallow of coffee, his eyes never leaving mine. But the flip side is, he hasn't interrupted me again, and seems to be absorbing what I'm telling him. I find it encouraging, so I plow forward.

"Now, what I've been able to determine is that you have a large number of unsolved homicides. Your open-unsolved rate sits at about sixty-four percent." I tell him, and when he opens his mouth to object, I raise my hand to forestall it. "To be fair, major cities always have high open-unsolved rates. This isn't like television where every case gets neatly wrapped up in an hour. Actual homicide investigations rarely go the way we think, and unfortunately, more times than not, finding the actual killer is more difficult than fiction has led us to believe."

He lets out a grunt and rolls his eyes, but nods for me to continue.

"What troubles me is that smaller municipalities usually don't have an open-unsolved rate as high as yours. To put it in perspective, Cedar Creek is a town in the northeast of the state that has a similar population density to Briar Glen. Their violent crime rate is roughly three percent, well below state and national average. And their solve rate is ninety-six percent. They've got very few open-unsolved cases."

Morris takes another pull from his coffee mug, looking at me over the rim the whole time. Then he sets it down gently and looks at me curiously for a moment. I can see the wheels turning as he puts all the pieces of what I said together in his mind. The numbers I laid out for him paint a stark picture and he knows it. The fact that he hasn't dismissed me and genuinely seems to be thinking about what I've presented him tells me he's a thoughtful man. One who, his earlier defensive outbursts aside, usually doesn't speak without thinking.

"So, are you tellin' me, you think we've had a serial killer or somethin' runnin' around here for the last decade and a half or so?" he asks.

"No, that's not what I'm saying. Not exactly," I reply. "I'm just saying that something is happening in Briar Glen, Sheriff. I don't know what yet, and I'm definitely not saying you're to blame in any way. But I want to find out what's going on here. The violent crime rate is alarming, and if there's some way we can figure it out, maybe we can save some lives."

He blows out a long breath and seems to be thinking about what I said. Finally he sits forward again, his expression stern. I can see him warring with himself. The statistic I cited is bothering him, no doubt about it. He hates that there are so many open-unsolved homicides in his city. I can tell he wants to do something about it. But the other side of that coin is that to do that, he'd have to work with me. The Feds. He'd have to give up some of his control, which I can see is something he is absolutely loath to do.

But then he nods to himself as if he's come to a decision. He raises his gaze to me, his expression no less grim, but I see a steely determination in his eyes.

"What do you need from me, Agent Wilder?"

TEN

Pacific Crest Motor Court; Briar Glen, WA

THE POUNDING on my door jerks me out of a fitful sleep. Not that I can actually call what I got sleep. According to the clocks, it's just after six, so I'm not even sure it qualifies as a nap. On the bed all around me, pages and files are scattered, the result of a long night's work. I've only barely scratched the surface of what Sheriff Morris let me take from the station yesterday. And according to him, there is a lot more being held at an off-site storage facility.

We came to a meeting of the minds yesterday. He's still not thrilled that I'm here, and remains skeptical of everything I laid out, but he's willing to work with me. At least for now. It shows me something about his character — confirms it for me, actually. He's a man willing to set aside his own pride to do what's in the best interest of his town and the people in it. It's something I respect.

As for the files, Morris explained that they're in the process of digitizing their files and are working backward, so they've only gotten to 2015 so far. Anything prior to that is paper. The boxes and files I have spread out all around me are from the years 2013-14. To be as thorough as I normally am, I've got a ton of work and a lot more sleepless nights ahead of me.

The banging on the door resumes, so I roll off the bed and stagger across the room, trying to wipe the sleep from my eyes as I shuffle along like a zombie from *The Walking Dead*. Which is a pretty accurate description of how I feel right now.

"I'm coming, I'm coming," I call, my voice sounding thick and slow in my ears. "Keep your pants on."

I unlock the door and open it, wincing and hissing like a vampire as the sunlight slants in. I hold my hands up to shield my eyes from the intrusion of light, and find Sheriff Morris standing there with a large, steaming cup of coffee in his hand.

"Well, you look like hot garbage," he observes, thrusting the cup into my hand.

"You say the sweetest things," I say, inhaling the rich aroma wafting from the cup. "But I'll forgive you for it this time."

I take a drink of the coffee, wincing at the heat on my tongue, but not really caring in the moment since I desperately need the caffeine boost. I swallow it down and look up at him.

"I assume you didn't stop by just to deliver coffee?" I ask.

"Afraid not," he says, his expression grim. "There was a body found this morning. Figured you'd want to go check it out with me."

I nod and take another drink of coffee. "I appreciate that, Sheriff. Give me a minute to get dressed?"

"Sure thing."

I close the door and take another swallow of coffee before throwing on some clothes, pulling my strawberry blonde hair back into a ponytail, and brush my teeth. I decide to forgo makeup and figure I can grab a shower when I get back from the crime scene. Finished getting ready, I bound out of the room to find Morris leaning against his SUV, drinking a cup of coffee, and looking out at the ocean. His face is clouded over, as if he's lost in thought about something deep, though not something entirely unpleasant.

Standing next to him really highlights the size discrepancy between us. I mean, even with him sitting in his chair back at the office, I could tell he was a big man, but I didn't really realize just how much bigger than me he is. I'm five nine, and though I'm fit and in good shape, I'm lean. Morris is about six inches taller than me and is a bull of a man. He looks like the kind of guy who'd enjoy wrestling bears for fun in his spare time... and could probably win.

"You all right, Sheriff?" I ask.

He nods and instantly, his face clears as he turns to me. That almost wistful look on his face vanishes, quickly replaced by what I imagine is his default stern and gruff expression. But for a moment there, he looked... human.

"Right as rain," he says, turning to me, his expression betraying a sense of surprise. "Didn't expect you to be ready so quick."

I give him a wry smile. "I'm not somebody who needs to get all dolled up before I go out. We're going to a crime scene, not a club. I'm not here to impress anybody with anything other than my investigative skills."

The corner of his mouth quirks upward in a smile, a small expression of approval on his face. I've never been a typical woman like that. Makeup and fashion just aren't my thing. I much prefer function and comfort over form. Like, I can't imagine how much money Astra spends on makeup and clothing. Yeah, she always looks runway ready, and I usually feel like the Ugly Duckling standing next to her, but that kind of thing's never been important to me.

That's not to say I'm not without my own sense of vanity. I

think as humans, we're all vain in our own ways. I think I'm an attractive woman, but I usually put more effort into my work, or into learning something that will be beneficial to my work, than I do into dolling myself up for a night out on the town. Yeah, Astra thinks my work-life balance is out of whack, and maybe she's right, but I'm driven by the mission at hand. There is literally nothing that brings me more pleasure in life than bringing justice to those who deserve it. Both to help the victims and their families gain some sense of closure, and to lock up the monsters who would harm the innocent.

"Well all right then. Let's get out of here," Morris says. "Hop on in."

I slip on a pair of sunglasses and climb into his SUV as he gets behind the wheel, and he roars out of the motor court parking lot. Metallica is playing on the radio, which surprises me. I thought for sure he would have Kenny Chesney or Luke Bryan pumping through the speakers. He gives me a sideways glance and a grin, as if he's reading my mind. But he's good enough not to comment on my stereotyping him.

"So what can you tell me about the vic?" I ask.

"Not much yet, I'm afraid. I only got the call out half an hour ago," he replies. "Woman in her mid-twenties. That's about all I know right now."

"And your deputies have cordoned off the crime scene?"

He gives me a sour look. "We ain't rookies at this, Agent. Nor are we stupid."

"Right. Sorry," I reply, realizing how condescending that sounded. "I didn't mean to offend you, Sheriff. I'm just used to —"

"Being in control of everything, from soup to nuts, huh?"

A rueful laugh escapes me. "Yeah. I suppose so. Sorry. It's my nature."

A wide grin stretches across his face. "I think the same is

true of most of us who go into law enforcement. We've all got some control issues."

It's a surprising sentiment coming from him, given that just yesterday, he was railing on me for trying to bigfoot my way into his town. That he's offering me a concession like that is an olive branch, and one I appreciate.

"I guess we do," I say, offering him a smile.

We ride in silence for a couple of minutes and I take in the town around me as we pass through. There is something charming about it, I have to admit. If I were ever going to raise a family of my own, a place like Briar Glen — at least on the surface — seems like a quaint, ideal place.

"I appreciate you taking me out to the crime scene," I say, breaking the silence between us.

He smirks to himself. "I'll be the first to say I don't know everything," he says, never taking his eyes off the road. "And as long as you're here, I figure I might as well lean on your expertise. Maybe we can start chippin' away at that violent crime rate. Believe it or not, it's somethin' that bothers me every damn day. Some nights I can't sleep because of it. I know you're right. There shouldn't be this many murders in a town this size. We're like a small town with big city problems."

A faint smile touches my lips. "I do believe it bothers you. And I have to admit that I don't know everything either, Sheriff. But maybe between the two of us, we can figure this out."

He finally looks over at me and gives me a nod. I feel like we're finally on the same page here, and while he might still have some reservations about working with the Feds, I'm glad to see he's willing to quash them for the greater good. Now I just need to justify his leap of faith by helping him here.

Morris pulls into a parking lot that sits on a small bluff overlooking the Pacific. The sun is just starting to begin its ascent, and the sky is cast in vivid hues of pink and purple. The ocean below looks blood red in the morning light, which somehow seems both ghastly and appropriate.

He shuts off the engine and looks at me. "Time to dazzle me, Agent Wilder."

Right. No pressure or anything.

ELEVEN

Rhodes Beach; Briar Glen, WA

"Usually, the only people who come out to Rhodes are the surfers," Morris says. "A small group of 'em is who found the body this morning."

I look over to where three young men, no more than nineteen or twenty years old, in wetsuits are standing with a couple of Morris' deputies. They all look annoyed, as if resentful this whole thing is cutting into their time on the water. But underneath the irritation, I can see that they're shaken to the core. I don't blame them. It's not every day you find a dead body. It can rattle you pretty hard.

Rhodes Beach is a small, secluded section of beach separated from the larger coastline of Briar Glen by a natural finger of land that reaches out into the Pacific on one side. The waves here seem to build larger than what I've seen from my bungalow window. It reminds me of a small beach down in Southern California called the Wedge that's famous for its larger than average waves, as well as for its several deaths a year, thanks to the shallower than normal water. But I guess if you're a surfer, it's a risk you're willing to take for the rush of riding a beast of a wave.

"It's isolated out here," I note.

Morris nods. "Yeah. This isn't the first body we've found dumped out here."

"No?"

He shakes his head. "We've put up cameras around here a few times, but they're always busted within a week. I've upped the patrols in this area, but I can't have men sitting here twenty-four/seven."

"Yeah, I get that. Makes it the ideal dumping spot."

"Exactly," he says.

The crime scene is taped off in a large square, and a pair of deputies are stationed just outside the perimeter to keep people back. They both give me a curious look as I approach with the Sheriff but say nothing. I glance at them from behind my shades though and can see them staring at me. Given the sour looks on their faces, I figure they've made me as a Fed and are none too happy with my presence here. I expect that Sheriff Morris is going to have some explaining to do.

We duck under the tape and move to the body of the woman in the sand. She's been wrapped in a thin robe that looks made from something like muslin, her arms crossed over her chest. She was pretty in life. Her raven black hair is splayed out around her like a dark halo, and she has naturally smooth and milky colored skin. She's got eyes that are almost as dark as her hair, and are wide open, staring off into nothingness. I wouldn't put her age at more than twenty-one or twenty-two years old, and that makes me not just sad, but angry for her. She had so much life yet to live.

A bookish-looking woman is kneeling down in the sand next to her, jotting some notes on a clipboard. She looks up and gets to her feet as we approach. Her long sandy brown hair is tied up into a knot on the top of her head, held there with a pair of pens. She's in her mid to late forties, has a long, slender neck, high cheekbones, and is thin. She wears the ME's office coveralls, hiding her frame from view. Like me, she's not out here to impress anybody. She's here to do a job and I instantly like her for that.

"Sheriff," she says, then turns to me and extends her hand. "Dr. Sofia Carville. City medical examiner and crime scene tech."

I take her hand and give her a firm shake. "You wear a lot of hats," I say with a smile. "Blake Wilder. Nice to meet you, Dr. Carville."

"Special Agent Blake Wilder," Morris adds.

Sofia's eyebrows rise as she looks at me. "Please, call me Sofia. FBI, huh? And what have we done to attract the attention of the Feds?"

"Numbers and patterns," Morris explains, casting a mischievous grin at me.

"Huh?"

"I'll explain it later," Morris says. "Tell me what you got."

"Cause of death seems obvious, but I'll run some more tests back at the lab," Sofia starts.

I nod, my eyes falling upon the long, clean slices across the throat. The cause of death is obvious, but there may be more to it than simply a woman having her throat cut. In fact, I kind of guarantee it based on the preliminary evidence I see. Sofia squats down and points to the bruising with the tip of her pen.

"I believe these bruises were inflicted antemortem," she says. "The girl took a beating before she was killed."

I point to her hands. "She put up a hell of a fight."

Sofia turns the girl's hands over and looks at the nails, which are chipped and broken, and her hands are covered in scratches that look like defensive wounds to me. I glance at the other hand, and notice that the middle finger of that hand has a clean, unbroken nail on it. And unlike all the others, which are coated with a dark nail polish, this one is white with a cross painted in red on it.

Fishing a pair of latex gloves out of my coat pocket, I snap them on, my eyes fixed on the girl's hand.

"You carry latex gloves with you wherever you go?" Morris asks, his own eyebrows raised this time.

"Don't you?"

He chuckles, his voice low and rumbling. "You must be a lot of fun at parties."

"Actually... I am," I reply and shoot him a grin.

Kneeling down next to the body, I lift the hand and look at the nail. I can tell right away that it's an acrylic. The only acrylic on either of her hands.

"What do you see?" Morris asks.

"This nail. It's not hers. It was put on her hand, I'm guessing after she'd been killed."

"Why would somebody do that?" Sofia asks.

"It's what we call a signature. In a sense, it's the killer's way of claiming his victim. Think of it like an artist who signs their work," I explain. "And the fact that she's been dressed in this robe and posed this way... it's ritualistic. I can already more or less guarantee that when we find our offender, we're going to find that this wasn't his first kill."

"That's grim," she says.

"How can you be sure that nail's not hers though?" Morris asks.

I point to her hands as I get back to my feet. "Every other nail on both of her hands is broken. Or at least cracked," I tell him. "Yet that one is pristine. It's the only one that's fake, and it's a different color and pattern than the rest. What are the odds of that?"

He frowns. "Not very good, I suppose."

I turn to Sofia. "Can you make sure you bag her hands? There could be trace evidence."

"Absolutely."

"Preliminary time of death?" Morris asks.

"She's starting to come out of rigor, so I'd say she's been dead for at least twelve hours, give or take," Sofia says.

"What do you think?" Morris asks me.

"I think I want to take a closer look at her in the morgue. I'd like a controlled environment," I tell him. "I'd also like a sweep of the area to see if there's any evidence sitting around out here. Like an ID. That'd be nice."

"Nothing's ever that easy," he chuckles. "But I can make sure the area's swept anyway."

I nod. "In that case, we'll need to see if any missing persons reports came in overnight," I say. "She's definitely not a transient, so somebody is going to be missing this girl."

"How do you know she's not a transient? We don't have many here, but we've got a small population. Junkies and the like."

"She's too clean. Too healthy looking," I respond. "Also, despite their condition now, I'm pretty sure she gets regular manicures."

"And how could you possibly know that?"

"Did you see her toes? They weren't destroyed like her fingernails. Her toes were impeccable. How many transients do you know who get mani-pedis on the regular?"

A wry grin curls his lip, and Sofia is looking at me like I've sprouted a third eye. But they both look impressed, which to me, is a sad testament to policing here in Briar Glen. Those are basic observations any newbie recruit at the Academy would have spotted. But I pull that line of thought back. These people weren't trained at the Academy, so they're not going to automatically spot inconsistencies like that. They probably would have gotten there eventually, but it's not second nature to them, like it is to me. I have to remind myself that it's not their fault.

"Do you want to talk to the surfers?" Morris asks.

I shake my head. "Not yet. I'll read the report and see if anything pops. I don't think they're guilty of anything other than stumbling upon her body. But I'll talk to them later if needs be."

"Fair enough."

I duck back under the tape and walk to the shoreline, looking out at the ocean. The sun is climbing higher and the surface of the water is glittering like liquid gold. The waves hit the shore with a sound like thunder, and a gull overhead cries plaintively. It's a lonely sound. A sound of sadness, which fits my current mood.

This girl, whoever she is, should still be alive. She should be planning for her life and her future. Not lying dead in the sand. But as I think about my observations, specifically that white nail with the red cross, it confirms my initial thoughts: there is definitely something bad happening in Briar Glen.

And I'm going to find out what.

TWELVE

City Morgue; Briar Glen, WA

THE MORGUE in the ME's office in Briar Glen is the same as every other morgue I've been in. Done completely in tile — light blue and white here — with everything else done in stainless steel. For a city that boasts a police force of just over a hundred, it actually looks a lot more modern than I'd expected it to.

Part of me thinks it's a sad testament to how often the morgue and the medical examiner are needed in cases. It's actually kind of surprising Briar Glen has their own ME at all. I mean, I guess with a population of almost two hundred and fifty thousand, they're big enough to justify it. But most smaller towns and cities usually farm out their ME work to a larger city with the capacity to handle the influx of bodies.

For a city that doesn't have a detectives bureau or homicide squad, the fact that they've got a sleek, modern morgue is kind of telling. It's also a source of curiosity for me as I stand next to Sheriff Morris at the window, watching Sofia do the autopsy. He looks distinctly uncomfortable.

"How many of these have you watched?" I ask.

"Including today? One."

I laugh softly. "You don't need to be here. I can handle this."

"Kinda feel like I should be. Just in case you need something."

I nod and fall silent again. It's strange to me that just twenty-four hours ago, Morris was busy marking his territory and all but telling me to get out of town, and now he seems to be taking his cues from me. He wasn't wrong. Most of us in law enforcement, at whatever level, have control issues. I won't deny that about myself. So to see him ceding as much control to me as he has, tells me that he is worried and as desperate to figure out what's happening in his town as I am.

It's a heavy burden of responsibility, but it makes me all the more determined to find justice for this girl, and all of those who came before her and never got the justice they deserved, and to justify the faith Morris seems to be putting in me.

"How many autopsies have you watched?" he asks.

"More than I care to count."

"It's a grim business we're in."

I nod. "That it is. But it's also a business that allows us to change the world around us for the better, I think. We can make a real difference in the lives of some people. We do good work for the people."

"Huh. Didn't have you pegged as an idealist."

"I wouldn't say I'm an idealist," I admit. "I just try to not be a fatalist."

"Fair enough."

I watch Sofia going through the autopsy on the other side of the glass. She's fastidious and precise. She really takes her time and doesn't rush through anything, unlike other ME's I've watched at their work before.

"You've got a good one in there," I say.

He nods. "Yup. Just wish we had less work for her to do," he says, then turns to me. "What are your initial thoughts?"

"Incomplete at the moment."

He frowns. "I know they train you guys to assess everything, right from the jump. I'm not askin' you for anything official just yet. All I want to know is, just based on initial observations, how big is our problem?"

"Well, I'm not going to know how big the problem is until I get through all the files. And that's going to take a bit," I tell him. "But just based on what I've seen so far, there's a problem here."

"Care to elaborate?"

"That girl was dumped there. That wasn't the actual crime scene. There was no blood, no sign of a struggle in the sand around her. She was already dead when she was dumped on the beach," I say.

He nods. "I figured that much."

I let out a breath and turn my attention back to Sofia. The last thing I want is to alarm Sheriff Morris or give him reason to have some crazy knee-jerk reaction. The problem I'm having is that based on the case files I read last night, the problem is widespread. The only commonality between the cases I've found so far is that they resulted in a person being killed. There's no consistent method, no signature, no correlation in the ages or occupations or social status of the victims. It doesn't seem like the work of a serial killer at all.

But I can't shake the feeling that there is something bigger at play here. There's a picture I'm seeing broad shapes of but can't make out just yet. It's like I've turned over the box of puzzle pieces and now I have to figure out how they all go together to form that complete picture.

It's unusual for cities that don't have a gang problem — or

some other situation where the violence is inherent, like organized crime or something — to see spikes of violence this high and this prolonged. Don't get me wrong, as long as there are people, there is going to be violence. In any city. But to have bodies dropping like they do here, it's... not normal.

I think Briar Glen's problem is big, and I think it's only going to get worse before it gets better. And it's only going to get better if we can figure out what's going on in this city and find a way to put a stop to it.

"My initial impression is that the girl in there on that table could be the victim of a serial. I say could be, simply because I don't have enough data to say conclusively just yet," I tell him.

"And what leads you to that thought? The fingernail?"

I nod. "Yeah, that's a big indicator. The fingernail is ritualistic. With an act that deliberate, the killer is not only marking his kill, but he's also trying to communicate something with us."

"And what's that?"

I shake my head. "I don't know yet. That's why I said I don't have enough data," I explain. "I need to go back through the case files and see if there are any other murders that match this MO."

"Nothing stands out to me offhand," Morris says.

I'm not entirely surprised to hear him say that. And I have to remind myself once again that he's not trained to look for the same things I am. If Briar Glen had a detectives department, perhaps they would have gotten the training and knew what they needed to be looking for. Morris and his men are trained to do the basics. Their role is more cleanup and procedural than investigative. They're here to pick up the pieces after a crime, but don't know how to take the steps needed to prevent the next one from happening. Again, not their fault.

"All the same, I need to pore through them to see if there are any others that match this girl," I say.

Inside the autopsy suite, Sofia is waving us in, so we push through the swinging door and walk in. Morris and I stand side by side on one side of the table while she stands on the other. Sofia raises her face and pulls down her mask. Morris is looking pale all of a sudden, like he's on the verge of vomiting. Sofia quickly covers the body with a pale blue sheet, a grimace on her face.

"Sorry, Sheriff. I forgot," she says.

He waves her off. "It's fine. No sweat."

His voice is thick and choked when he speaks. Sofia and I share a small grin when Morris isn't looking. I find it amusing that for such a large man, he certainly has a delicate stomach.

"So what did you find?" Morris asks, trying to reassert himself.

"I won't have toxicology back for a while," she says. "But I'm confident that the cause of death was exsanguination due to a severing of her carotid artery."

"Lovely," Morris mutters.

"I took fingernail scrapings and some other trace evidence like hairs I found, and I've sent them to the lab in Seattle," Sofia goes on. "We won't have them back for a bit either."

I nod. That's standard. It's not like on television, where you get results of tox screens or hair analysis in the blink of an eye. Especially if you don't have an in-house lab who can analyze them. It's not unexpected.

"I can say with some degree of confidence that she was sexually assaulted. Judging by the amount of tearing and bruising to her genital region, I'd say it was by more than one person too," she says, her voice grim.

"I suppose it's too much to hope that you were able to get some fluids," I say.

"Afraid not. There's evidence of spermicide, so the killer was smart enough to wear a condom," she replies.

"Figured," I mutter.

"You said it was more than one person who assaulted her?" Morris said.

She nods. "I can't be one hundred percent certain of course, but that's my gut feeling, again, based on the tearing and bruising," she tells him.

"Jesus," he whispers to himself.

The fact that she was perhaps assaulted by multiple people puts a whole new spin on things for me. It's not often you get a serial killer who works with a partner, let alone a whole team. The signature automatically makes me think serial, and most of those guys are loners. So this is throwing me for a loop.

More than that, I'm left wondering what it has to do with the overall pattern of violence in Briar Glen. Or whether it has anything to do with it at all. Am I simply seeing shadows? Making connections that aren't really there? My gut tells me there's more here. Something sinister is happening in this city. The violent crime rate is just too out of whack for me to think otherwise.

"I need more data. More information," I mutter to myself.

"What's that?" Morris asks.

I shake my head. "Nothing. Just talking to myself."

"So we're looking at a group assault and a murder to cover up the assault," Morris says.

"It's possible," I say.

"You don't sound convinced."

"I'm not. It's the fingernail that's throwing me."

"Why is that?" Sofia asks.

"Because if this was a case of a pack of guys attacking a girl, it would be more frenzied. You'd see more evidence of that kind of bloodlust that comes up in a pack mentality," I say. "The way she was laid out was cold. Calculated. It was methodical. And that fingernail was deliberate. Those aren't the actions of a savage gang rape."

"Is it possible, that nail not breaking was just a spot of dumb luck?" Morris asks.

I shake my head again. "It's also the only one of her nails that was acrylic," I note. "The rest of her nails were natural."

"That's true, Sheriff," Sofia confirms.

"All right. So what does it mean?" he asks.

"I'm not sure yet. That's why I was saying I need more data," I reply. "I need to find out if there are any cases that have matching MOs, and if so, what the disposition of those cases are. I need to know if there are any people who were tossed out as suspects for one reason or another."

"So what do you need from me?" Morris asks.

"Access to your database and all your files," I say. "And also access to Dr. Carville as needed."

"Done," he says. "And I'll even toss in a spare office, so you don't have to work out of that crappy bungalow they have you in."

"Appreciate that, Sheriff."

Silence descends over the room, and all of our gazes drift down to the woman beneath the sheet. Not to speak out of turn, but I get the idea that all three of us feel the weight of responsibility for this woman settling down over us.

It's as if we're all making a silent pact with each other, and with her. She deserves justice, and I'm going to work my guts out to make sure she gets it. I get the feeling all three of us will.

"Okay, let's get to work," I say.

THIRTEEN

Briar Glen Sheriff's Station; Downtown Briar Glen

"Ain't much, but it's all yours as long as you need it," Morris says.

"It'll do me just fine. Thank you, Sheriff."

"I'll have the boxes of files brought in," he tells me. "You can access everything else on that computer."

I give him a nod. "I appreciate all you're doing, Sheriff."

"Like I said, I know my shortcomings, and I'd be a damn fool to turn down help when it's offered," he replies. "On that note, I'll leave you to it. You need anything, just give me a shout."

He closes the door behind him, leaving me alone in the vacant office. The office is in serious need of an upgrade. The wood paneling on the walls looks fifty years old, and the floor is covered with linoleum that's cracked and pitted. There's a large desk in the center of the room with a pair of chairs in front of it.

Against the wall to the left of the desk are two tall four-drawer file cabinets and a long table running beneath the window on the right. There's a large white board on the wall next to the filing cabinets, and a map of Briar Glen tacked to the wall behind it. Except, the map is twenty years old and is sorely out of date. The city has grown quite a bit since that map was drawn up.

I sit down at the desk and fire up a computer that would have been cutting edge in 1990. It probably hasn't been fired up since then, so it takes a few minutes to shake the rust off and boot up. I'm spoiled by the tech at the field office, which unlike this dinosaur, is always state of the art.

When the machine finally finishes booting up, I take a few minutes to get acquainted with the programs and how their system works. I'm no tech genius, but I'm fairly adept at navigating different systems, especially as it pertains to law enforcement databases. They're all usually somewhat similar and it's just a matter of figuring out the small differences. Once you do that, it's pretty smooth sailing.

I call up the search box and start plugging in keywords as I search for similar MOs. The problem I run into is that the Briar Glen PD isn't like us, and they don't break down cases like that. At the Bureau, we log crimes using specific keywords related to those crimes so that we can check for similarities both in the state and national databases. But this department apparently doesn't.

"Damn," I mutter.

I lean back in the chair and quickly realize my mistake as it groans and squeaks ominously, as if it's about to break, so I sit up quickly and glare at it.

"Please. I'm not that heavy," I growl at the chair like it can understand me.

I stand up and pace the office for a moment, deciding on the best angle of attack. I have no other choice but to go old school and dive through the case files themselves. There's a coffee pot sitting on top of the file cabinet that looks as if it hasn't been used since the Reagan Administration, so I'm crossing my fingers that it still works.

I quickly dust it off and carry the pot out of the office, then wander around for a moment before I locate the break room. After washing the dust off the pot and filling it with water, I strike gold and find filters, some ground coffee, and a mug that looks relatively sanitary. After filching enough supplies to get me through the day, I carry it all back to my makeshift office and start getting it ready, making a mental note to stop by a store and stock up on good coffee. Cop shops have notoriously bad stuff. Call me a snob all you want, but coffee is one of those things I don't like to leave to chance. I've got to have a half-decent blend.

It's not long before the office is filled with the scent of coffee brewing. I wait until I have a cup in hand before sitting down at the terminal and bracing myself for the work ahead, which I know is going to be tedious. This is the less glamorous part of the job, but this is the job nonetheless.

I take a sip of my coffee and immediately wince at the bitter brew, half-tempted to spit it out. But I refrain. It's hot and it's got caffeine, and at the moment, that's all I care about. Mostly. I'm not going to drink this swill tomorrow. I look at the computer screen and call up a list of statistics for the previous year.

"Thirty-seven murders in 2017," I say.

Just for comparison's sake, I call up Seattle's stats and find there were only twenty-eight in total. As I toggle between the data sets, I see that so far this year, Seattle is up to forty-nine murders, and Briar Glen is keeping pace with forty-two. But it's only October, so there are still a couple of months to pad those stats.

They're all numbers I'm already familiar with, but it seems

important to me to start at the beginning again. It's an oddity of mine, I know. But when I'm starting from square one, as I'm clearly doing here, I like to physically start from square one. It's like coming to it with a fresh set of eyes for me. I know I'm not, but it kind of seems that way. I remember mentioning that to Paxton shortly after we met and were comparing investigative styles. He said I might be the strangest person he'd ever met. But he also said that whatever I'm doing obviously works because I get results, so to keep on doing it.

So that's what I'm doing.

I call up the crime statistics for this year and immediately remove any that have had an outcome and have officially been closed. That is, any that have resulted in an arrest and a conviction at trial. Those are unimportant. The initial culling leaves thirty-two open-unsolved cases. Which is a lot of case files to go through. Especially when you go through them as thoroughly as I do. But the sight of the woman on the beach, specifically her eyes, flash through my mind, and that's all the motivation I need to quit whining and start working.

I start at the beginning of the year and read every single line of every single case file. Of the thirty-two open-unsolved cases, eighteen were killed by gunshot. Six by manual strangulation. Six by knife wounds, either stabbing, or having their throats cut. And the final two were beaten to death. All of them are grisly ways to go, but there's something about being beaten to death that makes me cringe harder. There's just something so primal and animalistic about it.

"How goes the battle in here?"

I give a start as I look up to see Sheriff Morris standing in the doorway. I'd been so absorbed in the work that I didn't even hear the door open. A rueful chuckle escapes me as I run a hand through my hair, more to give myself a moment to slow my racing heart than anything. I glance at the clock and see that five hours have passed since I first sat down.

"Can't believe it's gotten so late," I say.

He shrugs. "It happens when you get caught up in the work."

"Yeah. That it does. Anyway, I finished with the list of murders so far this year," I tell him. "Gruesome stuff."

He nods. "Tell me about it. The last guy we found, Tyler... Tyler something or other — "

"Salters. Tyler Salters," I say.

"Right. That guy. Cut up like a Christmas goose," Morris sighs. "I mean, I've seen some things, but the way that poor kid was sliced and diced was just inhuman."

I nod and lean back in the chair, recalling what I'd read in the autopsy report for Salters. Seventy-eight cuts and punctures to his body, mainly centered in the chest, neck, and stomach area. The crime scene photos were ghastly, to say the least. Morris walks in and drops down heavily into the chair across from me. I have to bite back the smile that's forming on my lips. His big frame dwarfs the chair and almost makes him look like he's sitting at a child's tea party table.

"It was so bad, it didn't even look real to me," I comment. "Seemed more like a prop out of an Eli Roth splattercore film."

"Splatter what?"

"It's a subgenre of horror," I say. "Focuses more on the grisly aspects of the crime. It's graphic and gory. Horror without limits, is what they call it."

A look of revulsion crosses his face. "I'd call it trash, personally."

I shrug. "It's interesting. From a certain perspective, anyway."

"I'll pass. Give me a good Bogey film any day of the week."

I chuckle. "Humphrey Bogart movies actually suit you. I would have guessed that about you."

"Would it surprise you to know I like period pieces?"

"Let me guess... *Braveheart*? *Gladiator*? No, wait... *Ben Hur*."

"Those are good. Liked 'em a lot," he replies. "But I also liked *Far From the Madding Crowd*. *Elizabeth*. *Quills*. *Pride and Prejudice*. *Shakespeare in Love*. I even liked *Titanic* quite a bit. Good films, all."

I have to keep my jaw from hitting the desk. "You're yanking my chain. Right?"

He shakes his head and chuckles. "Just when you think you've got me figured out, right?"

I smile sheepishly. "In my defense, I haven't been profiling you. Perhaps I should have been."

"Pretty sure you wouldn't find me all that interesting."

"Oh, I don't know about that. We all have quirks I find fascinating," I say. "Your choice in movies would be one of yours."

We share an amicable silence for a moment. But the good humor begins to fade as the dark reality of what we're dealing with starts to settle down over us once more. Morris frowns and looks down at the linoleum.

"You've been Sheriff for what, six years now?" I ask.

He nods. "Yep. My term's up in two years."

"Going to run again?"

Morris runs a hand across his broad face. "Don't know."

"Why not? You're good at your job. And I can tell you care a hell of a lot about this town."

"Yeah, but there's a world of difference between caring and being able to do a good job. You've shown me I've had a blind spot all this time. I've failed this town."

"You haven't failed anything."

"No? How is it you, sittin' all the way up there in Seattle, diagnosed the cancer that's eating away at this town, and I didn't?"

"I think you're being too hard on yourself, Sheriff. I'm trained to look at things like this. You're not," I tell him. "I have a feeling you knew there was something going on here. But without the proper tools and training, how can you accurately diagnose a problem?"

"Shouldn't take a rocket scientist to know when bodies are dropping like they do around here, there may be a bigger problem."

"Why don't you have a detectives bureau here, Sheriff?"

He chuffs. "You should talk to the city council about that. They force us to operate on a shoestring budget, since the city proper doesn't have a police force. We end up having to follow city priorities even if we're technically county level. They cry poverty but go and spend more on their pet beautification projects than the practical things that keep a city safe and secure. Couple years back, they spent half a million bucks on half a dozen fountains for the city. Fountains. That five hundred grand could have put more deputies on the street. Maybe if we had more bodies, we'd be able to head off some of these murders. Maybe that girl on the slab down in Sofia's morgue wouldn't be there."

It's hard to miss the bitterness in Morris' voice. It's unfortunately, a story I've heard more times than I can count when dealing with smaller municipalities. Some of the city councils in these towns get it in their heads that their city is safe and providing more uniformed officers would be overkill. So they allocate their funds to pet projects like fountains.

I've seen it time and time again. It's frustrating and makes life more difficult than it needs to be for men and women like Morris. They've got all the responsibility to safeguard a county, but don't get adequate support or resources from the local political hacks who control the purse strings.

"Anyway, enough of my wailing and moaning," he says. "It is what it is, and there's nothin' I can do about it."

"The one thing we can do right now is solve this mystery girl's murder. And maybe some of these others while we're at it," I tell him. "Maybe if we can close enough cases and show the city and county there's a real problem here, we can get them to pull their heads out of the sand and worry more about the people, than about putting in a new fountain in town. It sure would give you some political capital."

"I hate politics."

I quirk a grin. "So do I. But sometimes you have to play the game to get ahead."

I'm definitely the last person to be talking about playing the game. I abhor politics to the point that I don't even know the rules of the game. It's a game I refuse to play. But for somebody in Morris' position, it's vital that he learns the rules and plays the game. But on his own terms, not theirs.

"I gotta admit, having a little capital would be nice. Real nice," he says.

"Things change quickly, Sheriff. Most normal people, civilians I'm talking about, don't pay attention to things like murder rates. A city council should. And if we show the people the failures of the city council, maybe they'll take it out on them at the ballot box. And maybe, if we're lucky, they'll be replaced by people who care about this town like you do, who will do the right thing."

"Your mouth to God's ear, Agent Wilder," he says. "Your mouth to God's ear."

FOURTEEN

Hikqu State Park; Outskirts of Briar Glen

THE NIGHT AIR IS COOL. Crisp. And the stars overhead sparkle like cold chips of ice in the darkness overhead. My legs and lungs are burning, but I shut out the pain and push on. Running has always brought me clarity of thought, and I need that more than anything right now. After plowing through and organizing another couple years' worth of case files, there's a jumble of information in my head. It's all disparate pieces right now with no common thread that I can see just yet.

Stabbings. Shootings. Bludgeoning's. Strangulation. The victims cut across racial, religious, gender, age, and economic lines. Looking at it from the outside, it simply looks like a whole bunch of random murders. But then there's the woman on the beach. How does she fit into all of this? Does she fit in at all?

The signature, the fingernail, tells me there's somebody out there hunting women. But the idea that she was sexually assaulted by multiple people prior to her death puts a wrinkle in that theory for me. In my experience, that's not how typical serials operate. Her murder, as well as the pile of bodies in this town over the last fifteen years — murders that have never been solved — is confounding me.

My breath comes out in thick plumes of steam, and the steady drum of my footsteps on the soft, packed dirt of the forest trail is in time with the rhythm of the music pumping into my ears. The hard driving guitar and Meg Myers' throaty harmony drives me on as I emerge from the woods that surround my bungalow and into a neighborhood.

It's an upper middle-class neighborhood that like downtown Briar Glen, is a mish-mash of different styles and designs. Victorians are mixed in with Mediterranean, which sit beside both an American and a Spanish Colonial. Further down the street is a Ranch style home, and beyond that, a Craftsman. The one thing they all have in common is that they're well-kept and in good repair.

Some might consider the lack of any coherency in architecture to be off-putting. Some people would look down their noses at the chaotic jumble of competing architectural styles. Personally, I find it charming. It's far better than cookie cutter tract homes, where everything looks absolutely the same, and one house is identical to the next one. And the one after that. And the one after that. To me, all of these different styles in one neighborhood adds depth. Character. And I like that.

It makes me think about my life, with some small part of me wondering if I'm ever going to settle down, or if I'm going to be living in hotel rooms in one city or another for the rest of my life, living out of suitcases full of my own sheets and blankets until I'm too old to settle down.

That, of course, brings to mind my reasons for having such a nomadic lifestyle, and as I scroll down the list of reasons and justifications I've given myself over the years, I arrive at the same realization I came to a couple of years ago. Oh, I've tried to deny it, but I'm not very good at lying to myself. It makes me somewhat envy those people not cursed with a sense of self-awareness.

I prefer living life on the road, as a nomad with no permanent roots, simply because the idea of being bound to one spot terrifies me. It took me a long time to get comfortable living with Annie and Maisey. And although I got good at pretending otherwise, I can say that I never fully settled down in their home. Not because of them. It has nothing to do with them. They were, and are, nothing but supportive and lovely. They welcomed me into their home and treated me not as a strange, distant relation, or an object to be pitied and treated like a glass doll, but as one of their own. It's something I will always appreciate and will never be able to repay them for.

But the fact of the matter is that I've seen firsthand how quickly your home, your sense of safety can be stripped out from under you. I've seen how quickly your entire world can be turned upside down, and how your home can be turned into a house of horrors. It took years of therapy and my own critical self-analysis to realize that deep down, it's like I feel if I keep myself on the move, I can keep myself away from tragedy. If I don't put down permanent roots, my sense of safety can never be shattered, and my world can't be turned on its head. On the move, I'm the one in control and nobody can take that from me.

As the thoughts roll through my mind, they bring with them images of my parents. They bring memories of them lying face down in congealed crimson pools. Gritting my teeth, I push myself harder, run faster, as if I'm trying to outrun my past. Trying to outrun my memories.

A dark-haired woman jogs by, her ponytail bouncing in time with her stride, and gives me a nod as I stop on the corner of a street and put my hands on my hips. I suck in deep lungfuls of breath, giving myself a break for a moment. My mind is still whirling with all the facts of the various cases I've absorbed over the last couple of days. There's something I'm missing. Something I'm not seeing. And I think it's something that will bring everything into a sharp focus. If I can just find that one key, I can make it all make sense.

Unless I'm wrong about it all, of course. That's a thought that's been hanging around in the back of my mind. For all of my number crunching and analysis, I'm human, and as a human, I'm prone to mistakes. Prone to seeing things that aren't really there. It's still entirely possible that this massive spike of unsolved murders in Briar Glen over the last fifteen years are the result of a lot of violent people, and perhaps, helped out by shoddy police work.

Not having trained investigators would, of course, hamper any efforts to bring justice to the victims by closing their cases. That's not the fault of Sheriff Morris and his men, of course. Personally, I'd put the blame on the city politicians who aren't providing adequate support for their police force. But it's entirely possible that the lack of police trained to investigate crimes, and a city council who's apparently blasé about it all, has allowed killers to run free.

The one thing that bothers me about that theory, though, is that from what I've seen, Briar Glen isn't a town that appears to be riddled with crime. It's a relatively affluent place, and there doesn't seem to be a part of this city that could be considered the 'wrong side of the tracks.' There are parts of this city that have been left abandoned after the industry that once sustained it vanished, the buildings left standing empty. But there isn't really a rough side of the town, where crime and violent criminals would normally fester. From what I've seen, Briar Glen is one of those rare, idyllic towns. An upper middle-class utopia.

I hit the button on my ear buds to stop the music as I bend at the waist and put my hands on my knees. I'm still breathing heavily as everything processes through my mind. Clearly, I don't get out and run enough. It's something I need to do more often, and I silently vow to myself that I will. Turning around, I start back the way I came, walking briskly, but not running. I'm not quite ready for that just yet.

The scream echoes through the dark, shrill and filled with terror. I know instantly that it's the dark-haired woman who passed me before. A shot of adrenaline floods my veins, and my heart accelerates once more. Another scream tears through the night, and I take off in the direction it came from, running for all I'm worth.

My pulse pounding in my ears, I push myself harder. I don't know where I'm going exactly, I'm simply heading in the direction the screaming seemed to have come from. The sound of a scream that's cut off, followed by a car door slamming draws my attention.

I turn down a small path that cuts between two large houses. I emerge onto the next street over just in time to see the back end of a dark van tearing around the corner, its tires squealing on the pavement.

I give chase, but it's too late. The van disappears around another corner further ahead and is gone. The dark-haired woman along with it. I pull my phone out of my small pack and call Sheriff Morris, already knowing there's not going to be anything he can do.

FIFTEEN

"No, I was too far away to get a license plate," I say miserably. "Your deputies didn't see anything?"

"Afraid not."

We're both sitting in my temporary office the following morning. After calling Morris and laying out the situation for him, he said he'd have his guys look into it and keep an eye out for the van. After that, he insisted that I go back to my hotel, telling me there was nothing we could do about it and that he'd see me first thing this morning. That we'd go over it together.

I didn't get much sleep. How could I sleep when a woman had been snatched off the street a block away from me, and I could do nothing to stop it? Instead, I pored through the case files I had again, looking at them closer, searching for that one thing I'd missed that would pull it all together for me. I think I dozed off at about four or so, but was back up again at six, ready to get back to work. And to Morris' credit, he got to the station before I did, ready to get to work.

Not that there was much for us to do. We combed through the missing persons reports on file and had no matches to either the woman on the beach, or the woman I saw last night. And nothing new had come in overnight. Whoever the jogger was, nobody was missing her yet, and I wonder how long it's going to be before somebody does. She was a young, attractive woman, surely she's got people in her life who are going to notice that she didn't come home. Hopefully before it's too late.

"Well, it's not like I gave them much to go on," I mutter.

"Don't beat yourself up, Agent Wilder," he says soothingly. "Not much you could have done. Besides, we don't even know for sure it was an abduction. It could have been — "

"No Sheriff. I know the sound of somebody in distress. The scream I heard last night was one of somebody being taken," I interrupt him. "The fear was too raw. Too real. Somebody was kidnapped last night. Right off the street."

"Unfortunately, there's not much we can do until somebody reports her missin'."

"I know," I grumble. "And it's frustrating as hell."

"What in the hell were you doin' out so late, anyway?" he asks. "The world's a dangerous place, Agent Wilder."

"I appreciate your concern, Sheriff... kind of sexist though it may be," I say. "But I like to run at night when I'm working through a case. And I'm a black belt in two different martial arts disciplines. I assure you, I'm quite capable of taking care of myself."

"Two?"

I nod. "Two."

"Huh. That's impressive," he says.

I shrug. "Also practical because, as you say, the world is a dangerous place."

He laughs and sits back in his seat. "That it is, Agent Wilder. That it is."

Thinking of the dark-haired jogger I saw last night conjures images of the woman from the beach, and I can't shake them. I'm half afraid, but half certain we're going to find her in the same condition. Deep down in my gut, I know that her fate was sealed the moment that van took off. Now it's just a matter of waiting for the body to drop.

Feeling agitated, I get to my feet and rifle through the bag I'd brought in with me. I stopped by the store on my way home from the station last night and picked up some essentials. I take out a gallon jug of distilled water and fill the coffee pot and set the dark roast I'd picked up to brew.

"Brought your own coffee?" he asks, arching an eyebrow at me.

"I'm finicky about my morning caffeine," I reply with a small smile. "And no offense, but cop shops always have the cheap blends that taste like they were roasted in a dirty gym sock."

He laughs. "Can't argue with that."

"Grab your mug. Trust me, you'll like this," I tell him.

He nods and goes back to his office to fetch his mug. As I sit behind the desk waiting for him to return, and the coffee to finish brewing, I see the morning shift rolling in. The deputies cast dark glances into the office as they pass by. And I'd have to be deafer than Beethoven to not hear them whispering amongst themselves about me. Though none of them say a word directly to me, it's pretty clear that the deputies are less than thrilled with my presence.

"Your deputies don't seem to like me very much," I mention to Morris when he steps back into the office.

"Nah. It ain't you. They just don't like Feds in general."

I laugh softly. "You didn't either."

"Still don't," he acknowledges. "But you're not a normal Fed, so you're all right."

"You are a smooth talker, aren't you?"

He shrugs. "I try. If any of the boys and girls out there give you any grief, you just mention it to me. I'll take care of it."

The coffee pot chirps at me, letting me know it's ready, so I take Morris' mug from him, fill it, and hand it back to him, then pour one for myself.

"Cream? Sugar?" I ask.

"Black, thanks."

I dose my mug liberally with cream and sugar, then sit back down behind my desk and take a sip, smiling as I feel the contentment spread through my soul. Morris just chuckles to himself then takes a sip.

"What?" I ask.

"Just bringin' your own coffee and fixin's into the office," he says. "Kinda seems like bringin' your own beddin' into a hotel."

I stare at him blankly for a long moment and he seems to pick up on it because he looks down into his mug, a smirk tugging at the corner of his mouth. "Oh," is all he says before taking a sip of his coffee. After another moment of strained silence, Morris looks up at me.

"On the plus side, you're right. The coffee is damn good," he says.

A smile flickers across my lips as I take another drink. But my expression turns sour and my mood darkens quickly as the sound of the woman screaming last night echoes through my mind. I try to shut it out, but the shrill, piercing tone keeps reverberating in my head.

"I hate this," I growl.

"Trust me. So do I."

I'm not good at sitting here, waiting. I need to find something to do. There's a knock on the office door and one of Morris' deputies — Summers is his name — pokes his head in. He's a tall man, with thin dark hair, a square jaw, and dark eyes.

He's built, with wide, sloping shoulders, and biceps as big around as my thigh. He obviously spends an inordinate amount of time in the gym.

"Sheriff, we just got a call," he says, his voice deep and gruff. "Man says his fiancé never came home last night."

Morris and I exchange a look and get to our feet, and I feel a rush of anticipation flowing through me. The deputy hands Morris a slip of paper and the Sheriff looks at it for a moment.

"Thank you, Deputy. Good work," he says, then turns to me. "Let's roll."

SIXTEEN

Murray Residence; Briar Glen, WA

"I HAD to work an overnight at the hospital last night," he says. "And when I got home this morning, Tracy wasn't here."

"Tracy Webster, is it?" Morris asks.

He nods. "Yeah. That's right."

"Jordan, is it possible Tracy is out with friends? Could she have had a few too many last night and — "

"She doesn't drink," he answers.

"Okay, but could she have possibly spent the night at a friend's house?" Morris presses.

Jordan shakes his head. "I've already called around. But she wouldn't have crashed somewhere else without telling me."

"You're sure about that?"

"I'm positive, Sheriff."

I watch as Jordan Murray stands up from the loveseat he'd been sitting on and starts to pace the living room, first folding his arms over his chest, then dropping them down to his sides.

He slips his hands into his pockets and pulls them out again. He's upset. From where I'm sitting, it looks genuine.

The couple lives in a small Craftsman style home. It's one of the smaller homes on the block, and is neat, tidy, and tastefully appointed. This place definitely has young, hip, socially, if not financially affluent couple, written all over it. All of the furnishings, while nice, aren't top of the line or expensive. They're not a wealthy couple, but they do try to make it seem like they are.

I'm sitting on a plush recliner and Morris is perched on the edge of the larger sofa. Both of us are tracking Murray as he walks back and forth, back and forth, fidgeting and unable to sit still. His face is etched with worry and his eyes are red, as if he'd been crying. Murray is doing a decent job of keeping his emotions reined in, but it's a fragile thing, I can tell.

My eyes fall on a photo of Murray and the dark-haired woman I saw last night. She's a beautiful woman with creamy skin and hazel eyes. Her cheeks are naturally flushed, she's got delicate features, and full, pouty lips. She's stunning, and coupled with Murray, who is a tall, lean, athletic, good looking man, I have no doubt they would have made genuinely beautiful babies.

"What is it you do at the hospital, Mr. Murray?" I ask, for no other reason than to give him something to focus on other than his missing fiancée. The more mundane the better. I want to get him calmed down, simply because if his mind isn't occupied with his concern and fear, he might be in a better position to provide us with valuable information that could help.

Plus, it gives me a chance to look for tells. Honestly, my initial sense is that he had nothing to do with it. They say it's usually the spouse or boyfriend, but they're not always right. While it's true that a shocking number of murders are committed by somebody the victim knows, there is still a high number committed by strangers to the victim. It's up to us to determine which kind this is, and what's really going on here.

"I'm a nurse," he tells me simply.

"Do you often work overnights?" I ask.

"No. They called me last night because somebody else had called off and they needed somebody to cover," he says.

"What does Tracy do for a living?" I ask.

"She's a kindergarten teacher," he tells me.

"Did she have any trouble with anybody recently?" Morris asks. "Anybody threaten her or anything?"

He shakes his head. "No, of course not. Everybody loves her. Tracy is a good person. A genuinely good person."

"Everybody has skeletons, Jordan," I tell him.

"She doesn't. I'm telling you, Tracy never had trouble with anybody."

"Does she run the same route every night?" I ask.

He nods. "She's faithful about it. Almost obsessive, really. But it's a safe neighborhood. She's never had any trouble..."

His voice trails off, unable to complete the thought. His face falls and he looks away, doing his best to control his emotions, but I can see that it's taking a real effort on his part to stay calm.

"How long have you been together?" I ask.

He's still bristling at the suggestion that his fiancé is anything but the saint he thinks she is. And maybe she is. But the fact that her abductors knew where she was running, deep inside a neighborhood, tells me that she'd been targeted. They knew where to look for her, and worse, knew what her running schedule was.

"Two years," he says, his voice soft. "We got engaged about four months ago."

"And you're sure that she never had trouble with anybody?" Morris asks.

"I'm positive!" he shouts. "Why are you sitting here asking me all the stupid questions instead of out there looking for her?"

Jordan loses his battle with his emotions and his lips quiver as the tears start rolling down his face. He scrubs them away angrily and tries to reassert his control once more. The tears stop falling, he's breathing heavily, and his face is red. It's a Herculean effort for him, but he's holding on as best as he can.

"Jordan, it may not seem like we're trying to find her but believe me when I say we are. Sheriff Morris is doing all he can," I tell him. "But to find her, we need to gather all the information we can. I know this is difficult, but please try to understand that the questions we're asking are necessary."

"Fine. Ask your questions," he grumbles.

Morris glances at me and I can see his discomfort. Clearly, we're on the same page about the next question and he seems to want me to ask it. I don't blame him. It'll probably be easier coming from me since Jordan may not be as inclined to lash out. At least, in theory.

"Jordan, I apologize in advance because I know how indelicate this is going to sound, but is Tracy seeing anybody else?" I ask. "Do you have any suspicions about her having somebody on the side?"

His eyes narrow and he glares at me hatefully. "Of course not. How could you even ask me that? We loved each other and she would never cheat on me."

On the surface, it sounds like a stupid question to ask. Obviously. I mean, if she had somebody on the side, how would he know? On the other hand, him finding out she had a side piece would absolutely be motive for murder. So asking him the question isn't so much because I think we'll get a straight answer from him, it's because I want to see his reaction to it. I want to get a read on him and see if I get the idea that he knew about it. And if I get the slightest hint that he knew, I'll have no choice but to consider him a suspect.

As I study him closely, reading his micro expressions and body language, I can tell that if she were stepping out on him, he had no idea. The look on his face and the outrage I'm seeing in his expression all point to a man who believes, down deep in his soul, that Tracy was faithful to him. And maybe she was. That will all come out the deeper we dig into her disappearance. But for all practical purposes, although I can't entirely exclude him as a suspect at this point, I think I can fairly safely move Jordan to the back of the list.

So that brings me back to the question at hand — how did Tracy's abductors not only know where to find her, but when she would be at her most vulnerable?

SEVENTEEN

Burt's Burgers; Briar Glen, WA

WE'RE SITTING at a patio table, soaking in the sunshine. The afternoon is cool, but not cold, and there isn't a cloud in the sky. It's a perfect day, weather-wise. After spending a few hours talking to Jordan Murray about his missing fiancé, Morris decided that we needed to stop off for lunch, so he decided on Burt's, claiming it had the best burgers in town.

The waitress comes out and drops off our plates: a bacon cheeseburger and fries for me, a double bacon and barbecue burger and onion rings for the Sheriff. My mouth starts watering at the sight of the still sizzling grease and hot cheese oozing out from under the bun and onto the wax paper beneath the burger. I pick up a fry and pop it into my mouth, enjoying the crunchy texture of the outside that surrounds a softer middle.

"You know, it's a good thing I enjoy a good burger, or I might have been offended by you choosing this place for us," I remark.

Morris smirks as he takes a bite of his burger. A rivulet of grease spills down his chin, so he sets his burger down and grabs a napkin, quickly wiping it away as he chews.

"It's a good thing I know you're not the type who's easily offended," he replies.

"And how would you know that?"

He chuckles. "You're not the only one who can read somebody, you know. I may not be a fancy profiler like you, but I can read people well enough."

"Okay first of all, I'm not a fancy profiler. I'm not part of the BAU," I say with a laugh. "Maybe someday, but I'm not there yet. But I've got a pretty good understanding of psychology, and of people in general. I just use everything I learned in getting my degree in my work."

"All right, fair enough."

"And second, I never said you couldn't read people. I imagine as a cop, you actually have to be pretty skilled at it."

"I do my best. As for my read on you, I know you're not easily offended because you're made of tougher stuff than that. You ain't one of these people who get offended by the slightest thing that can be perceived as politically incorrect," he says.

"Not bad," I reply. "But I admit that I can be a bit touchy about dealing with sexist crap. Just because I'm a woman, it doesn't mean I'm less than anybody."

"And I'd never say you are. In fact, if I'm bein' honest, some of the toughest people I know are women. Smartest too."

"That's a pretty enlightened attitude, Sheriff. I don't see much of that around the hallowed halls of the FBI."

"I hear it's an old boy's club."

"That's an understatement."

He chuckles. "I think that's pretty common in law enforcement. You look hard enough, you'll see it in my department too," he admits. "But I've got more female deputies in my shop than we've ever had in the town's history. So I'd like to think I'm makin' progress on that front."

"I'd say so," I tell him.

I look at him for a moment as I cut my burger in half, then take a bite of it, studying him closely to see if there's a punch-line coming. But I judge that he's being sincere. Which means I'm the one who's a jerk here since I've been making assumptions about him since I got into town. I let his big, gruff, country demeanor lead me to assumptions about everything from his taste in music, his taste in movies, and his attitude toward women. I've been wrong about everything about Sheriff Morris, which has been humbling, to say the least.

I chew another bite of my burger, which I have to say, is actually pretty good. I guess it's just another thing Morris is right about. As we eat our meals in a companionable silence, my thoughts turn to the woman on the beach, and of course, to Tracy Webster. Her abduction has started to clarify some things in my mind. But at the same time, I'm still a bit confused. And sadly, the only way my theory is going to pan out is if we find her body.

I'd much rather be proven wrong, to be honest. Being wrong, I can deal with. Having to look into those hazel eyes that looked so full of life in that photograph, dulled and glazed over in death would be unbearable. I understand it's an aspect of the job, but it doesn't make it any easier. I take a small piece of every person whose had their life stolen with me. They're in my heart and always will be.

Some consider that a liability. Some stress the need to keep a distance from the victims, to not personalize things, and keeping your heart cold, just to maintain our own sanity. It's a philosophy I disagree with. I think part of what makes me good at my job is that I do take these crimes personally. Seeing these people, whose lives have been stolen from them makes me want to hold somebody accountable. It drives me to seek justice for them. And I don't think that's a bad thing.

"So, I'm thinking Jordan doesn't have anything to do with it," I start.

Morris nods. "I agree. Poor kid's all torn up."

I nod. "And even though I want to be wrong and desperately want to find her, I'm pretty sure we're only going to find Tracy when her body is dumped somewhere."

He sighs. "I had the same thought. Which would be a damn shame. To say the least. But what's cookin' in that big brain of yours? I can practically smell the smoke from here."

I frown for a moment as I consider my words. "I don't have anything concrete just yet, I'm afraid."

"But you've got some ideas. I can see it on your face."

"It's just... the woman on the beach, and now Tracy," I say. "Did you notice how similar in appearance they are?"

He sits back in his chair, munching on an onion ring as he ponders my words. He obviously hadn't noticed the similarities in their appearance.

"They're both young brunettes. Similar body types — thin but curvy," I say. "Both very pretty."

"And does that mean something? I mean, it could be a simple matter of coincidence. Availability."

"Possibly. But I think it's more than that."

He smirks. "I feel some of your profiler voodoo comin' on."

I laugh softly. "Hardly. Just observational work. But it could be that what we have is a preferential offender."

"A preferential offender?"

I nod. "Yes. And in this case, our unsub prefers curvy brunettes," I say. "It could be that these women are substitutes for a curvy brunette who did him wrong at some point in his life. And by killing these women, he's symbolically killing her."

"That's an interesting take."

"It's also not certain yet. There are certain things that still aren't making sense to me."

"Like what?"

"First, I'm looking at this as a serial. But the multiple offenders who assaulted the woman from the beach argues against that. And last night, when Tracy was snatched, the use of a van suggests to me that there were multiple offenders at that scene as well."

Morris purses his lips. "What makes you say that?"

"If this was a single offender, he'd be a lot more circumspect about taking her. He'd use stealth and speed. I doubt that a single offender would risk snatching a woman out in the open like that. And the use of a van suggests to me, there was at least one man in the cargo area who did the snatching, as well as a driver. I believe we're looking at two offenders. At least."

"How could you possibly know that?"

"The time between the sound of the door slamming and the van taking off was too fast for anything else," I explain. "So I believe we're looking at multiple offenders. Which makes no sense if this is a serial since they don't typically work and play well with others."

I sit back and take another bite of my burger and wash it down with some soda. I go over my words and all of the facts I have in my head for the millionth time. There are so many things that are starting to come into focus, but at the same time, so many more questions are forming in my mind.

"But I won't know whether my theory holds water or not until we find Tracy. If she's returned without harm, I'm wrong —"

"But if she's not, you'll be able to put together a profile."

I shake my head. "I'll have another data point to start a profile. There's still a lot I don't know. A lot I need to figure out first before I can give you the most accurate profile I can put together."

"So how do these preferential offenders who snatched Tracy work in with the other murders you're looking at?" he asks.

I shake my head. "I don't know that they do, to be honest. There's still a lot I'm trying to figure out, Sheriff. But I'm hoping to find answers in all of the case files I'm sifting through. I have to say though, Briar Glen is a complicated, confusing place."

He chuckles. "You don't even know the half of it."

"It's a good thing I like riddles and puzzles."

A rueful smile touches his lips that looks sort of nostalgic. Like his thoughts are forcing him to look into a fonder time in his past. But in a way, he also looks somewhat sad.

"Penny for your thoughts," I say.

"I was just thinking that police work sure has changed over the years. It used to be easier back in the day. I'll admit, it was a lot sloppier and less precise. But easier," he tells me. "I came up in a time when we didn't have all these psychological considerations. And Briar Glen isn't exactly the kind of place that fosters that sort of forward-thinking police work. But I can see it has its uses."

"Maybe once this is all over, we can work on getting you a federal grant to get some investigative training. If we can secure you the grant, you'd be able to bypass the city council altogether, since it's not coming out of the city's general fund. If you're interested in something like that anyway."

"That sounds terrific to me. I'd sure appreciate that," he says.

"Then we'll see what we can do," I tell him. "But first, let's get everything here sorted out."

"Sounds like a plan to me."

EIGHTEEN

Briar Glen Sheriff's Station; Downtown Briar Glen

It's just after seven the next morning and I'm sitting at my desk in my borrowed office, immersed in the case files. As I laid in bed last night, unsuccessfully trying to get some sleep, a thought occurred to me. So after a few fitful hours of sleep, I made my way down to the station to get to work on seeing if my idea bore fruit. And so far, after a couple of hours sifting through the case files — the crime scene photos in particular — I feel the twinge of excitement pulsing in my belly.

As I stand to refill my coffee mug, the door bangs open and the square-jawed deputy from yesterday steps in lugging a couple of boxes with him. He drops them on the floor in the corner, flicking a dismissive glance at me. I pour my coffee and turn to him, irritation in my eyes.

"Excuse me, Deputy Summers, but have I done something to offend you?" I ask.

His smirk is the embodiment of arrogance. "As a matter of fact, yeah. I found you walkin' into our station pretty offensive," he sneers. "And I find you tryin' to make Sheriff Morris look bad even more offensive."

"With all due respect, Deputy, I'm not here trying to make anybody look bad. I'm trying to help clean things up here."

"What makes you think we need help? Things seem to be workin' just fine to me," he says.

"If you think the astronomical murder rate, not to mention the sky high open-unsolved percentage in Briar Glen to be things working just fine then, I don't actually know what to say," I reply. "If you can't see there's something strange happening in this town, I can't help you, Deputy."

"Maybe I don't need your help."

I shrug. "Maybe you don't. But thankfully, you're not the one who gets to make that call."

He scoffs and gives me the up and down elevator eyes, a sneer on his face. This is a man I have no doubt has no compunction about putting hands on a woman. I don't need to be a psychological expert to profile this guy. He's a cretin and a chauvinist, probably suffering from a touch of narcissistic personality disorder.

"You Feds are all alike. You think you walk on water," he spits. "You think you can just roll into town and act like we should be grateful. Like we should roll over and thank our lucky stars you're here to save us from falling all over our own feet," he growls.

I drop down behind my desk and set my mug down, letting out a hearty chuckle. Summers' face darkens and he glares at me like he wants to beat me bloody here and now. But he's given himself away. Now I know his secret. His hatred of Feds — any Fed — and the vitriol he's spewing can only come from one place.

"So when were you rejected by the Bureau?"

His jaw is clenched so tight, he looks like he could shatter stone between his teeth, telling me that I scored a direct hit.

"Let me guess, you didn't pass the psych eval," I press. "Am I right?"

Summers opens his mouth to reply, but wisely bits off his words. Instead, he turns and stalks out of the office, slamming the door behind him, no doubt going to go trash-talk me to some of his buddies. Which is fine since I don't really care what somebody like him thinks of me.

With him gone, I get back to work, calling up the next case file and immediately scrolling to the crime scene photos. This is one of the homicides in the city from a couple of years back, a guy named Donald Landry. I'd been so busy trying to glean whatever information I could from the case files themselves, I never stopped to thoroughly study the crime scene photos. Now that I'm taking the time to thoroughly examine them, I'm seeing the threads of my theory starting to come together to form one intricate tapestry.

Or at least, one of my theories. I'm not sure how it dovetails with the other, or if it does at all. It could be that I'm looking at two entirely different situations unfolding that may coincidentally be overlapping with one another. I've never been a big believer in coincidences. However, that's a song for another dance. Right now, I need to ensure that my first theory holds water.

"One thing at a time though," I quietly remind myself.

I blow up the images of the Landry crime scene and carefully look them over, then look at the notes in the crime scene report and see they don't match one another. Next, I call up the crime scene photos from one of the more recent homicides, that of Tyler Salters. Same thing. No blood at the scene, and it's not noted on the report either, adding another brick to the wall of my theory.

There's a knock at the door, and I look up to see Sheriff Morris standing there. He gives me a grin and walks in, coffee mug in hand, and immediately fills up. When he sits down in the chair across the desk from me, I give him a grin.

"I thought the cop shop swill was good enough for you," I tease.

"I dwelled in darkness, but you have shown me the light," he replies.

We share a laugh, but it fades quickly as my thoughts turn back to the matter at hand. And once again, I feel that tingle of excitement in the pit of my belly I get when I'm onto something and the momentum of a case begins to accelerate.

"So I've been going through the case files. Studying the crime scene photos and all," I begin. "And I'm noticing a trend among the victims — "

"Which victims are we talkin' about here? Is it the brunette women, or is it the non-brunette women kind?"

"The non-brunette woman kind," I clarify. "Although, there is an interesting commonality. But I'll get to that in a bit."

"The floor is yours," he says.

"Let me just say up front that this is hardly definitive. At the moment, it's little more than anecdotal," I explain. "But it's an interesting place to start. See if we can build out the theory from there."

"All right. Noted."

I take a drink of my coffee and give him a nod. "So anyway, I've picked out half a dozen cases from different years. And in those six cases, the photos from the crime scene show no pooled blood," I tell him. "But it's not noted on the original ME's report. That's why I didn't see the link between these cases before."

"Let me be clear on this. You're sayin' the lack of blood at the crime scene is a link between different crimes, from different years?"

"You don't?"

"Well, I admit, it's an awfully big coincidence, but — "

"I'm not a big believer in coincidences, Sheriff. These six bodies I've found so far, and who knows how many more I'm going to find, were all dumped," I say. "Killed at a secondary location and dumped. And for some reason, the initial crime scene reports don't mention that fact. Don't you think that's a bit strange?"

"Well, when you put it that way, it does sound strange," he says.

"Tell me something, how long has Dr. Carville been the ME here?"

"Oh, I guess it's got to be about ten years or so now," he frowns, and then his eyes widen. "You're not sayin' you think she's mixed up in this somehow, are you?"

I shrug. "I'm not saying anything yet. But of the six cases I've pulled so far, she's the name on all the reports. She analyzed the crime scene but didn't see fit to note that the victims were killed at a different location. To me, that's a curiosity."

"I've known Sofia for a good long while now, and I can tell you firsthand the woman wouldn't hurt a fly," he says, his face suddenly red. "There ain't no way she's mixed up in this. God, I've known her for years. I don't believe that."

"And that may be, Sheriff. Like I said, right now all I'm doing is gathering information and trying to see how the puzzle pieces all fit together," I say.

That seems to mollify him somewhat, and he sits back. The sudden heat in his voice as he defended her is interesting to me. It suggests a personal relationship between the two. A relationship that isn't strictly professional. Not that I'm judging them for it. Not at all. My only concern is that it could cloud Morris' judgment when it comes down to it, if the pieces do actually fall the way they're suggesting to me right now.

I'm troubled by the fact that as the city's one-woman forensics unit, Sofia can paint a picture of a crime scene any way she wants without being contradicted. And the fact that in these six cases, across six different years, all fail to list the obvious fact that it was a body dump bothers me. It definitely sets my radar pinging.

"Sheriff, I need to know that no matter how this all shakes out, that you're with me. That you're committed to getting at the truth," I say.

His expression darkens and he glares at me with actual heat in his eyes. He hasn't looked at me with that much anger in his expression since the day I walked in. That further bolsters the idea that he and Sofia are more than just colleagues.

"You can say whatever you want about me, Agent Wilder. Call me an ignorant yokel. Call me an idiot for not bein' the kind of cop you are, what with all your fancy degrees and education. I don't give a damn," he says, his voice low and menacing. "But don't you ever sit there and question my integrity. Ever."

"I'm not questioning your integrity, Sheriff. I would never do that. All I'm saying is that I know how difficult it is to believe that somebody we care about could be involved in something so... shocking," I say as delicately as I can. "I know how our personal feelings and our relationships to others can cloud our thoughts. Believe me, I've been there. That's all I'm saying."

He sits back and I watch as the heat and anger melt away, his expression turning to one of surprise. He runs a hand over his face and that's when I see the worry crossing his features.

"How'd you know?" he asks. "About Sofia and me?"

"It's my job to be observant. To pick up on the subtle clues."

His laugh is rueful. "We've been discreet. Nobody knows about us. Can't know about us," he says. "It's improper, and in the case of Briar Glen, illegal for me to be having relations with a subordinate."

"How is she your subordinate?"

"Because accordin' to our charter, the ME's office falls under the auspices of the office of the Sheriff," he says. "They could fire me. Jail me for a bit, if they're feelin' vindictive. They'll sure as hell strip me of my pension."

"The city council?"

"Nest of vipers. Yeah, them," he says. "The mayor and the council sometimes like to make examples of civil servants who displease them. And I've displeased them more than once, so they're lookin' for reasons to take me behind the woodshed."

I lean forward and pin the Sheriff to his seat with my eyes, letting him feel the intensity of my gaze.

"Nobody will ever hear it from me, Sheriff. I give you my word," I tell him, mustering every last drop of sincerity I can.

He looks at me for a moment, then nods. "I appreciate that, Agent Wilder."

A grin touches my lips. "Are you ever going to just call me Blake?"

Morris' chuckle is a deep rumble that starts in his belly and works its way upward. But I can see the relief in his face, knowing I'll keep his secret. It might be a moot point though, if the pieces keep falling into place in the direction they're going. It makes me wonder if Sofia would keep their secret or use it as leverage against him to either avoid any responsibility, or to cut a deal that benefits her. I hope we never have to find out.

There's a knock on the door and Summers sticks his head in again. He glares balefully at me while Morris' back is turned, but when the Sheriff turns, his expression morphs to one that's far warmer and friendlier. The shift is so sudden, I almost laugh as I think about how badly he must have failed Quantico's psych eval, which I can guarantee he did. Just for giggles, I make a mental note to look it up.

"Sorry to interrupt, Sheriff," Summers says. "But we've got a body."

Morris and I exchange a look, both of our expressions darkening as the full implication of it hits us.

"Damn," I mutter.

NINETEEN

Widow's Bluff; Briar Glen, WA

"Couple of hunters found her and called it in," Morris says.

"Why is it called Widow's Bluff?" I ask.

"If you believe the old stories, back in the day, women who'd just lost their husbands would come out to this point and throw themselves off," Morris replies.

I step to the edge and look at the waves crashing against the rocky shoreline a hundred feet below and shudder, then quickly step back. I'm not much for heights. Especially when there's tall, jagged rocks waiting for you below.

Turning around, I watch Sofia kneeling down next to the body of Tracy Webster, scratching out notes and observations in her notebook. This time, I'm looking at her with a more critical eye, watching everything she's doing, looking for any sign that would confirm my theory. Or refute it. From the corner of my eye, I catch Morris watching me scrutinize her. His face tightens and he steps away but says nothing.

On the ground, Tracy's body is staged just like the other woman's. She's been wrapped in a thin, muslin robe, her hands folded over her chest. And just like the other woman, she's got one white acrylic fingernail with a red cross on it, which confirms one of my theories. There is a serial in play here.

It's a good thing, and a bad thing. On the plus side, it will help me refine my focus. With two bodies now, I can start putting together a profile. And in the negative column, of course, is the fact that somebody is hunting women in Briar Glen.

"Looks like you're right."

Sofia's voice cuts into my thoughts and I look down at her. There's part of me that wants to believe Morris is right about her, that she wouldn't harm a fly. But my experience has shown me that some of the worst monsters hide behind the sweetest faces. You just never know what darkness lurks in the hearts of people.

But as I look around at the terrain, I know for certain that if Sofia is involved with this, she's not working alone.

I squat down on the other side of the body. "Right about what?"

"That we've got a serial killer in town," she says, pointing to the nail. "The signature."

"And the robes," I note. "Very ritualistic."

She nods. "This girl took a beating. Look at the bruises on her face, and those you can see on her body."

Like the first woman, the cloth is thin enough that it's nearly see through. I can see not only that she is nude, but that she is covered in bruises.

"Sadistic bastards," Sofia mutters.

Her tone suggests genuine outrage to me. That could argue that she's sincere in her shock and anger. Or that she's a very good actress.

"You studied forensics at Washington, right?" I ask.

She nods. "I have a dual degree in internal medicine and in forensic science from U-Dub. Go Huskies," she says with a small laugh. "I've also studied a little criminal psychology and profiling techniques. Nothing like you of, course. I'm definitely not profiler material, but I find it, and what you do, fascinating."

I laugh politely but add that bit of information to the pile growing in my mind. If she's got education in profiling techniques, she would know how to plant evidence or remove it based on potential profiles. And her training as a medical examiner means she'd have access to crime scenes, and the authority to make final reports. She'd know to make the appropriate determination about dump sites versus primary crime scenes in her reports. It rules out the possibility that this was just sloppy police work, which is another damning brick in the wall I'm building around her.

There is still a lot that isn't adding up in this scenario, of course. But the signs I'm seeing are pointing to Sofia's involvement, in some fashion. It could be that her role is simply limited to falsifying reports. It makes her no less culpable, of course but it does make me wonder who she could be covering for. Who could she possibly be willing to risk going to prison for the rest of her life for.

My eyes find Sheriff Morris. He's standing with a couple of his deputies, gesturing to the area around them, obviously giving them orders to sweep the area for evidence and clues. But could he be ordering them to look for things he knows aren't there? I don't want to believe it, and everything inside of me is resisting the idea, but I have to consider the possibility that Morris is involved as well.

There have been cases of men and women working in tandem to commit serial murder. Paul Bernardo and Karla

Homolka come immediately to mind. Back in the nineties, Bernardo and Homolka worked together to rape and murder teenage girls, including Karla's younger sister. So it's not unprecedented. But what's throwing me is Sofia's assertion that there are multiple offenders.

It makes me wonder if perhaps she threw that out there as a red herring, knowing it would muddy the waters. If she's studied profiling, she would know how to throw a monkey wrench into the gears. Her knowledge of forensics, crime scenes, and profiling makes her a very dangerous person. It also puts her near the top of my suspects list.

What I don't have is motivation. What would Sofia get out of this arrangement? Karla Homolka claimed that Bernardo abused her mentally, physically, and sexually, breaking her down and eventually forcing her into the series of rapes and murders they were convicted of. Karla claimed that his abuse had stripped her of sense of self, and that she had lost her ability to think and act independently.

But as I look at Sofia, then at Morris, I just can't see it. I understand that my growing fondness for the gruff old sheriff could be clouding my vision, but I just don't get the sense that he's the type of man who would ever lay hands on a woman. Much less coerce her into a series of rapes and murders. He doesn't read sociopath to me, which he'd have to be to commit these atrocities.

But then, sociopaths are adept at hiding their true natures and mimicking normal emotions. I like to think that I've been educated and trained well, not to mention that I have a natural ability, and can see through the BS. I like to think I'm intuitive enough to see through a person, see whether their emotions are genuine, or whether they're simply faking it. And Morris doesn't ping my radar.

That doesn't exclude him, of course. Standing back and

looking at this objectively, there is no way I can exclude him. Not now. Not after what I've learned so far. But I want to think it's unlikely. Time, and the evidence, will tell. What I do know for certain is that I need to be on my guard around them both, and I need to view them through an entirely dispassionate and objective lens.

As Morris approaches me, I get to my feet and give him a nod. "Ritual's the same. Condition of the body seems the same too."

He nods. "Don't need to be a profiler to see that. Initial thoughts?"

"Whoever did this is young. Strong. Fit."

Morris looks around and nods again, turning to look at me pointedly. I can already see his mind working and know exactly what his next words are going to be.

"Terrain would make it tough for anybody but a strong, fit man to hike out here carrying a body," he says.

And that much is true. The path through the woods is steep in places, and rocky. It's tough to get to and lugging Tracy Webster's one hundred and twenty pounds of dead weight would make it even more difficult. His implication, of course, is that Sofia couldn't have done it. But I look him in the eye, holding his gaze firmly.

"Not necessarily. It could be that somebody smaller and physically weaker had help hauling Tracy Webster up here," I offer. "We may be looking at multiple offenders, after all."

Morris grinds his teeth so hard I can practically hear them cracking. I'm not sure if he's more upset that I won't rule Sofia out as a suspect, or if that I'm basically implying that he's involved. Could be a mixture of both. He leans forward, moving closer to me, and when he speaks, he pitches his voice low so that only I can hear.

"Be careful what you're accusin' me of, Agent Wilder."

"I'm not accusing anybody of anything," I reply, my voice just as low. "I'm simply stating the facts as I see them. Which is what I thought you wanted me to do."

He takes off his Smokey the Bear hat and runs a hand through his short, gray hair, then puts it back on. He's flustered and upset. I can see that plain as day. I probably would be too if somebody was implying that I was a serial rapist and murderer. But at the same time, I can also see that he's hearing my words, and though he doesn't like them, he has to grudgingly respect them, since I am presenting facts as I see them in an unbiased way.

He looks at me for a long moment, then leans forward again. "I can tell you unequivocally that I'm not involved with this. And I know for a fact that Sofia wasn't either. We were together last night."

A wry grin touches my lips. "You know as well as I do that doesn't prove anything, Sheriff. Co-conspirators can't provide alibis for one another since they tend to be less than reliable. I mean, co-conspirators kind of have a vested interest in protecting each other."

He smirks, knowing I'm right and that his words were foolish. He nods and glances over at Sofia, who's still hard at work processing the body. I feel bad for putting him on the defensive like this, but it's my job. This is what I do. I dig and keep digging until I'm able to ferret out the truth.

"For what it's worth, my gut instinct tells me you're not involved. I can get a feeling about a person sometimes and let me just say you're not setting off the warning bells in my head. But I have to follow the evidence where it leads me," I tell him, then add pointedly, "Wherever it leads me."

He nods and grits his teeth, obviously not wanting to continue this out here, which I don't blame him for.

"Listen, I need to get back to town. I need to notify her

fiancé. I'll have one of my deputies drive you back when you're ready to go," he says, obviously not wanting to be around me right now.

"That's fine," I reply. "I want to spend a little more time out here anyway."

"All right then. I'll see you back at the station later."

I watch Morris walk off. He's still tense and angry, but he's not trying to deter me from what I'm doing. I can see it's taking a toll on him, which doesn't seem unreasonable, given how everything seems to be unfolding.

I don't actually believe that Morris is involved. And I don't want to believe that Sofia is either. The odds of two sociopaths meeting and joining forces like this are long. At best. But as Paul Bernardo and Karla Homolka showed the world, it's not impossible.

And like I said before, we never truly know what darkness is inside somebody's heart.

TWENTY

Pacific Crest Motor Court; Briar Glen, WA

I WALK to the edge of the hotel lot and stare out at the Pacific. The sun is slipping toward the horizon, setting the sky a Lame in vivid shades of orange and red. The vast and endless ocean in front of me shimmers, re Lecting the colors in the sky like it's a pool of fire. A cool breeze blows in, rustling through the brush and making the trees of the forest that surround the hotel groan mournfully.

I slip the Bluetooth ear bud in and press the button to make the call, then drop my phone into my pocket as I wait for the call to connect.

"As I live and breathe, it's world-renowned monster hunter Blake Wilder on my phone. It's like having Publisher's Clearing House show up on my doorstep with one of those giant checks. Whatever did I do to earn such an honor?" Astra gasps, feigning breathlessness.

Despite the dark mood that's settled down over me, I laugh.

"Have you always been this big of an ass and I've just never noticed before?"

"Yeah, pretty much," she chirps brightly. "Being observant was never really your strong suit, babe."

I like that no matter how bleak my mood, Astra can usually get me laughing and lighten my mood. She's a bright spot in my life, for sure.

"So how are things down in southern hickville?" she asks.

"Complicated. Getting more complicated by the minute?"

"Really?"

"Indeed."

"Like, good complicated, as in you found yourself a rich, gorgeous man and you've decided to run off to the Maldives with him?"

I laugh and kick at a stone near the toe of my boot. "Fortunately for me, it's not that kind of complicated."

"I don't know what's fortunate about that," she replies. "I mean, that's the dream. What about this sheriff you're dealing with? Small town sheriffs are known to be super-hot. I think it's that Old West cowboy vibe or something."

"Oh, Sheriff Morris is great. He's a smart, tough, and good-looking older man," I tell her. "I bet he'd fit right in with your daddy issues perfectly."

Astra's burst of laughter is so loud, I can feel my shoulders moving up towards my ears as if to protect them.

"That was a nice shot, Blake," she says. "I hate you for it, but that was a good one. And they say you're a goody two shoes, uptight prig of an ice queen who doesn't have a sense of humor."

"I see you attended Grant's latest TED talk about me."

"I just got the Cliff Notes version," she replies.

My laughter and the good cheer she inspired in me tapers off as I stare out at the ocean, thinking about everything that's happening. And right on cue, the darkness that's been hovering at the edges, kept at bay by Astra's humor, crawls back in and settles down over me.

As I stand there, I feel a prickling on the back of my neck. A sensation like a finger of ice sliding down my spine makes me turn around and scan the grounds around me. I'm certain I'm being watched. But I don't see anybody lurking about. I look at the forest that surrounds me, peering into the shadows, looking for the slightest movement, but still see nothing.

I'm not one given to fits of paranoia. My instincts are usually spot on. I learned to trust them completely a long time ago, and right now, my instincts are telling me that somebody's watching me. I can't see them, but I know somebody's out there. I'd bet my life on it.

"So what's up, girl? Why do you sound so tense?" she asks.

"Hang on a sec," I reply.

The unsettling thought that somebody's watching me through a rifle scope steals over me. I suddenly feel exposed. Vulnerable. Silhouetted against the backdrop of the fiery colored ocean behind me, I'm sure a blind man could drop me with a shot. This is hunting country, after all, and everybody is armed.

Moving with a purpose, I walk back to my bungalow and go back inside, shutting the door behind me. I turn the locks and quickly retrieve my sidearm. I chamber a round and turn out the lights, sidling over to the window and peeking around the curtain. Nothing outside moves and I still see nobody. But the feeling of being watched doesn't diminish.

"Blake? What's going on?" she asks, her voice suddenly as tense as I feel.

"Nothing," I reply. "Maybe I'm just getting jumpy in my old age."

She scoffs. "You're the least jumpy person I know. Are you in danger?"

"Unclear at this point," I respond. "But I'm pretty sure somebody's got eyes on me."

"That's my best friend Blake, always making friends and influencing people wherever she goes."

If somebody was going to take a shot at me, they probably would have done so by now. God knows I presented them with a perfect target outside. I'm not going to ignore it or write it off. Somebody was definitely out there and they were definitely watching me. I'm sure of it. But I back down the threat level in my head, thinking that perhaps it was kids. Or some random hunter passing through. Or somebody with no nefarious intent.

I set my sidearm on the table and sit down, keeping my eyes trained on the grounds outside. It never hurts to be vigilant. But I turn my attention back to my phone call when Astra snaps me out of my head and back to the present.

"Blake?"

"Yeah, I'm here," I sigh. "Sorry."

"You're freaking me out, babe."

"It's fine. I'm sure it's nothing," I tell her. "I'm just wound pretty tight right now. For such a small city, there's a lot going on here."

"Lay it out for me," she says.

And so I do. I lay out the facts as I know them, including my observations and conclusions, and give her my theories as to what I think it all means. She listens to me patiently, and knowing Astra as I do, she's analyzing it all. She's a lighthearted goofball and a free spirit, but she's a damn good agent and truly one of the smartest people I know.

"Wow," she says when I'm finally done. "There really is a lot going on there."

"There is. And I could really use your help," I say. "I need your brain, Astra."

"Sure, what do you need me to do?"

"Honestly? I need you to pack a bag, grab your gear, and get your butt down here," I say. "I'll clear it with Rosie and Potts."

"Road trip. Excellent," she says.

"I'm going to send you some files and if you don't mind looking over them tonight, I'd really like to hit the ground running," I say. "I need you to analyze some things for me. I need independent corroboration."

"You got it," she says. "I'll do my homework tonight, and head out first thing in the morning."

"You're a life saver, Astra."

"Yeah. I really am."

I laugh and shake my head. "Great. I'll see you then."

I disconnect the call and set the earbud down next to my sidearm, then turn my attention back to the window and the grounds beyond it. But the feeling of being watched has dissipated. Whoever was out there is gone, but the disquiet I feel about being watched in the first place lingers.

TWENTY-ONE

City Morgue; Briar Glen, WA

THE NEXT MORNING, I called Rosie and Potts first thing and got them to sign off on lending Astra to me for a while. I made sure to leave her a key to the bungalow and instructions with the manager to let her in. I left a message for her in the room, telling her what I needed her to start with.

After that, I headed down to the morgue. I wanted to be there for Tracy's autopsy. Well, *want* probably isn't the right word. I felt like I owe it to her to be here and to bear witness. It's not a pleasant way to spend a morning, but it serves to reinforce my determination to get justice for this woman.

"Cause of death is manual strangulation," Sofia observes, using her stylus to point to bruising around Tracy's neck that are definitely shaped like fingers. "Her hyoid bone is also broken."

Tracy Webster, the beautiful vivacious girl in the photos in her fiancé's home, is pale, cold, and lifeless on the slab in Sofia's morgue. She's covered in bruises and more than two dozen cuts and stab marks by my count. Her face is still swollen, and there is a large indentation in the side of her head, as if somebody beat her with a baseball bat.

Her hands, like the first woman's, are torn and ragged. They're covered in defensive wounds, cuts, and abrasions. Her nails are cracked and torn, and there are two missing altogether. And there is, of course, the one pristine acrylic. It tickles something in the back of my mind, but I can't quite figure out what it is just yet, so I file it away for more thought later.

"She's also got four broken ribs, a fractured skull, and... a lot of other wounds," Sofia continues, shaking her head and looking miserable. "All of the damage you're seeing was inflicted antemortem."

"Jesus," I whisper.

"Oh, I'm pretty sure he wasn't there. I doubt he would have let this poor girl suffer like this," she replies. "But wait, there's more."

Sofia points to a video screen on the wall and uses her remote to call up images from her computer. They're pictures of Tracy's back and my eyes widen at what I see.

"Please tell me those aren't whip marks," I say softly.

"Certainly look like it to me," she replies.

I step closer to the monitor and force myself to look closely at the wound patterns. They're not like a normal whip that leaves singular lash marks. These look to be grouped together, but the flesh is so ravaged, it's hard to tell for sure. Shaking my head, I turn around to Sofia.

"Looks like a cat o' nine tails maybe," I say. "It's definitely not a regular whip."

"I agree."

"And the first girl didn't have these wounds, right?"

She shakes her head. "Definitely not. I would have mentioned it."

Like you mentioned some of the vics we're looking into were killed elsewhere before being dumped? The thought makes it to my lips, but I bite it back, not wanting to put her off, or put her on alert that I'm looking at her, just yet.

"Are these wounds antemortem?" I ask, afraid I already know the answer.

"Most assuredly," she replies. "This girl suffered enormously. And she too, was assaulted by multiple people. I've found bite marks, Agent Wilder. I'm not a forensic odontologist, but they look to have been made by different mouths. I'm going to send them to somebody for analysis, but I'm certain she was bitten by different people as she was being assaulted. The rectal and vaginal tearing and bruising is consistent with our first victim."

I turn away from the screen, wanting to get the visual out of my mind, but I know it won't be easy. The poor girls back looked like raw hamburger. That's not something that's easily unseen. I've seen all kinds of degradation visited upon innocent people. I've seen all manner of horrors people can inflict upon others. But this has to rank up there with the worst of them.

"What kind of person can do this to another?" Sofia asks quietly.

"It's not a person. It's a monster."

She nods, but says nothing, her expression sober and a touch sad. Sofia sounds sincere, like she's earnestly trying to understand, but can't quite grasp the answers she's searching for. But there's that piece of my mind that wonders if this is all an elaborate act. Wonders if she's simply engaging in a bit of theater to keep the waters muddied and deflect my focus. It's cynical, but I keep coming back to the fact that her reports have been altered.

In most cases, that would be enough for me to pull her in and have a sit down with her. But I'm hesitant to pull the trigger on dragging her into an interrogation room just yet. Partly out of deference to Sheriff Morris. I want to have more than just altered reports to hit her with when I do have that conversation with her. I know that if she really is this clever, and this good at playacting, I'm going to need it.

If she truly is this sociopathic murderous mastermind I'm starting to think she is, she'll be able to find some way to explain the discrepancies in her reports away. And without further proof to bolster my case, I'll be left grasping at air. I won't get a second bite at that apple, so if I'm going to go at Sofia, I need to have everything lined up just right, so I can go at her hard, box her in, and give her no wiggle room she can use to escape.

That's part of the reason I called Astra. She's great at analyzing data. I need the fresh eyes, just to make sure I'm not barking up the wrong tree. She'll tell me if I'm off my rocker, or if there really is fire underneath all the smoke that's surrounding Sofia right now. I need her perspective and insight.

"What are you thinking, Agent Wilder?" Sofia asks. "Do you have any suspects? Any leads?"

I shake my head. "Not yet. I'm still gathering information. There are a lot of moving parts here, and I like to be thorough before I do anything."

She nods soberly, but she looks at me as if she can see that I'm withholding. She's a smart, observant woman, so I need to watch myself around her. The last thing I'm going to do is lay out my theories or thoughts any more than I already have with her, lest I tip her off that I'm looking at her involvement.

That she's probing me and trying to glean information tells me that Sheriff Morris hasn't said anything to her about where my thoughts are leading. I know it can't be easy for him to keep that to himself. He cares about her quite a lot, and I'm sure it's killing him to remain silent as I zero in on the woman he loves.

To me, that shows Morris' strength and character. It also

leads me to think he's not involved. If he were her co-conspirator in this, he would have told her, if only so they could make plans to throw me off the scent. Or perhaps make plans to just kill me outright so I stop digging into things they'd rather keep secret.

That option would likely bring scrutiny they wouldn't want, but it's something I need to remain cognizant of in any case. It seems a small thing, him not telling Sofia that I'm circling. But it makes me think even more highly of Morris than I already did. It shows his integrity to me.

I walk to the edge of the table and look down at Tracy. She looks peaceful. Like she's at rest. But I know what she endured before her death and it hurts my heart for her. It makes me angry. As I stand before her, I silently pledge to find the monsters who did this to her and make them pay for it. I've never been the religious type, but I hope wherever she is now, she can hear me.

As I look at her, something in her hair catches my attention. I bend down and look at it closely.

"What is it?" Sofia asks.

"Something in her hair," I reply. "Do you have a pair of tweezers?"

Sofia quickly hands me a pair of long handled tweezers and a specimen jar. I latch onto it and pull the object out of her hair and hold it up, scrutinizing it.

"It looks like red wax," I say. "Candle wax."

I drop it into the specimen jar and hand it to Sofia. She examines it for a long moment before she nods.

"I think you're right. Candle wax," she says.

"Nothing she could have picked up in the forest," I muse. "It could have come from the primary kill location."

"Agreed."

I don't know what it means yet. Although I'm inclined to

say it's evidence from the primary crime scene, I can't say it definitively. For all I know, she got it at home. It's unlikely. I don't recall seeing any used candles in her home when we were there. But since I wasn't exactly looking for candles, let alone taking an inventory of them, it's still possible she picked it up at home.

"Could be nothing," I say.

She smirks. "I remember you saying that everything is something when you're dealing with a crime scene."

"I believe I said most everything is something," I respond. "This could be one of those things that's not."

"Well, I stand corrected then," she says.

The air in the room seems to grow thicker around us and a sense of anticipation is hovering overhead. Anticipation of what, I don't now, but it's there all the same. There's a lot to consider, so I want to get out of here and get back to the hotel to see if Astra's there yet, and if so, what she's been able to turn up.

"I appreciate you letting me sit in, Dr. Carville," I say. "But I should get going. There are some things I need to attend to."

"Of course. And if you need anything, anything at all, just give me a shout."

"I'll do that. Thank you."

I walk out of the morgue, a million different thoughts spinning through my head. There's something percolating in the back of my mind. I need to give it some time and space to breathe and form into something coherent. Perhaps even something that can blow this wide open for me.

TWENTY-TWO

Briar Glen Sheriff's Station; Downtown Briar Glen

I POP BACK into my office to grab my bag and a few of the files I want to take a closer look at. After packing it all up, I sling my bag over my shoulder and head out. I can feel the eyes of the deputies milling about the bullpen on me. The male deputies, anyway. It makes me chuckle to myself as I realize how much it doesn't feel like I ever left the field office. All I need is a counterpart to Grant here trying to impugn and degrade me at every turn. Summers can probably fill that role.

I don't know what it is about guys in positions of authority. It's wrong to generalize like I am, but most of the guys in law enforcement, be it local or federal, are arrogant jerks. They always look down their noses at female cops or agents. It's like they think having a penis somehow makes them genetically and professionally superior. It's like these Neanderthals haven't gotten the message that we're living in the twenty first century yet and women are the majority in this country. Won't be long before we're running everything. It's a thought that pleases me.

As I pass by Morris' office on my way out of the building, I see his door standing open. He's sitting behind his desk, a scowl on his face. The man sitting in the chair before him is dressed in a nicely tailored three-piece suit. He's a tall, thin man I'd say is in his mid-fifties, with a long aquiline nose, light hair that's cut short and parted on the left. A pair of round, rimless glasses are perched on the end of that patrician nose of his, and the way he's sitting there, his back ramrod straight, a pinched look on his face, tells me this a man is one of privilege and entitlement. Which I'd guess would probably make him one of the city's politicians.

"Special Agent Wilder," Morris calls. "Can you come in for a minute?"

I'd rather not, but the way he said it made it sound less like a request than an order. Not that he thinks he can order me around. I think he's just looking for somebody to save him. So I slap on a smile and a pleasant expression, and head inside.

"What can I do for you, Sheriff?" I ask.

"Agent Wilder, this is Mayor O'Brien," he introduces.

The mayor doesn't stand, and for a moment, he simply looks me up and down silently. After he's taken my measure and asserted his dominance, he finally extends his long, obviously well-manicured hand to me. I take it and give him a firm shake.

"Nice to meet you, Mayor O'Brien," I say.

"So, you're the FBI Agent that's come to save us all from the murderous hordes, are you?" his voice is high and reedy and seems to fit with his face.

"Guilty as charged, I suppose."

"Tell me, Ms. Wilder, was your assistance requested?"

I exchange a glance with the Sheriff and in his eyes, I can see the disdain he has for this man. And just based on my brief interaction with him, I'd say that distaste for the mayor is well warranted. I turn back to him and put on my best FBI face.

"First of all, it's Special Agent Wilder. Or simply Agent Wilder if you prefer," I start. "And second, no. My assistance was not requested. My presence was a surprise to Sheriff Morris as it is to you."

"Well, if your presence and assistance weren't requested, what are you doing here?"

I have to fight to keep my mouth from falling open. The sheer arrogance of this man is stunning — and coming from the FBI where they practically teach classes in arrogance, that's saying something.

"With all due respect, Mayor, you not only have two young women who have been brutally murdered — with more to come, I assure you — but you have an overall violent crime rate that's astonishing," I say, fighting hard to keep the anger out of my voice. "I would think that as the mayor, you would be concerned with the fact that you have killers roaming free in your city. And judging by the amount of bodies stacking up, you have a lot of killers."

"Yes, well, I was just speaking with the Sheriff about that very subject," he replies coolly. "Specifically about the fact that his police department seems ill equipped to close these cases and take these killers off the street."

"It would certainly help him do that job if he had the proper resources and equipment. If he had the support of the city council, I guarantee you that you wouldn't be having these problems," I say. "Sheriff Morris is an excellent cop."

O'Brien stares at me balefully. "You have quite the nerve to stand here and lecture me about how to run my town."

"Somebody has to. For a city this size, it is unconscionable that you don't have a detective's bureau," I fire back. "Or at the very least, have not provided the police department adequate investigative training. There is only so much Sheriff Morris can do when he's handcuffed by the bureaucracy in this town."

"It's easy for you to stand there and judge me, isn't it?"

"Yeah, it actually is."

"You don't have the first idea what it takes to run a town," he says. "I have to worry about things like tourism and home valuations, as well as — "

"Are you even kidding me? You have a possible serial killer loose in your town, and you're worried about tourist dollars?" I shoot back. "I'll tell you what kills the tourism industry faster than anything — having killers in your town. When bodies are dropping as fast as they do here, people tend to look elsewhere to spend their vacation dollars."

That internal voice is screaming at me to stop. To shut up. It's telling me that this is exactly why Potts is hesitant to send me anywhere to do my thing. This right here. But I've got no tolerance for those who play politics with other people's lives, and even less for those who pass the buck when their failures are exposed. Once I start this train rolling, there's no stopping it, and it has most definitely left the station.

"How dare you," O'Brien says. "Who do you think you are?"

"I thought we covered that already. It's Special Agent Wilder, in case you forgot already."

"Sarcasm won't win you any points with me, young lady," he growls. "And since you were not asked for assistance, I would like you to leave Briar Glen."

"Let's get something straight. I don't need your permission to be here. I'm with the Federal Bureau of Investigations. Federal supersedes state, and it most certainly supersedes municipality, in case you didn't know," I spit. "And your inaction on an alarming number of murders over the years, warrants an investigation. Not just of all these homicides, but of you personally, Mayor O'Brien. By letting these killers roam free, I'm quite sure Director Wilkins can make a pretty compelling case that your failures have violated people's civil rights. He could perhaps even have the Attorney General charge you with negligent homicide to boot. And do you know what happens to people convicted of civil rights violations?"

O'Brien seems to shrink back into his seat, his eyes widening slightly behind his spectacles. The haughty expression on his face has melted away and has been replaced by one of fear, and he doesn't speak, so I answer for him.

"Civil rights violators go to prison for a very, very long time. We in federal law enforcement take that kind of thing seriously," I go on. "So unless you want me to contact the FBI Director, I'd shut my mouth if I were you. More than that, I'd see about getting the Sheriff's department the proper training and equipment ASAP. Otherwise, you're going to have a lot more people just like me in the streets of Briar Glen."

Without a word, O'Brien gets to his feet and stumbles to the door, clutching his briefcase to his vest like a shield. Before he leaves, I stop him.

"One more thing, Mayor O'Brien," I say, making my voice as intimidating as possible. "If I hear of you taking this out on Sheriff Morris, or retaliating against him in any way whatsoever, my first call will be directly to the AG. Understand?"

O'Brien hustles through the door and disappears, making me laugh to myself. I look down at Morris who's looking back up at me with a stunned expression on his face. But he clears his throat and quickly recovers.

"Well, I'd say that was less cordial than he's used to," he says.

"Yeah well, I'm not the type to kiss anybody's ring."

"Clearly," he chuckles. "But tell me something... can you really bring civil rights violation charges against him?"

I bark out a laugh. "Honestly, not a chance. But he obviously doesn't know that," I say. "And knowing he's going to be up all night Googling whether I can or not gives me a brief bit of joy."

Morris laughs out loud, but it soon fades, and then a moment of silence stretches out between us and I can feel that tension creeping back into the air. I know it's a tension that will not evaporate until I stop circling his girlfriend, which means it's going to linger for a while.

"Anyway, I should get going," I say.

"Yeah well, thanks for saving me from O'Brien," he replies. "I hate dealing with that guy."

"I can see why. He seems to have some screwed up priorities."

"To say the least," he says. "Anyway, you did me a solid, so thanks."

"Anytime, Sheriff. Anytime."

Unless, of course, that solid means giving a pass to his possibly murderous girlfriend. But I'm not going to say that and hope it's implicitly understood. Not waiting for a reply, I walk out of his office, then out of the station and head back to the hotel.

TWENTY-THREE

Pacific Crest Motor Court; Briar Glen, WA

"You're really livin' the high life out here," Astra says as I walk through the door. "What is the motif here? Trailer park chic? Honey, the Bureau gives you a hotel allowance. Why not use it?"

I laugh. "It keeps me humble."

"If you were any humbler, you'd be sleeping in a doorway using newspapers for a blanket."

"It's got running water, heat, and a soft bed to sleep in," I say. "That's really all I need to do the job."

She gives me a smirk and picks up my pillow. "But just think... if you used some of that hotel allowance on a better room, maybe you wouldn't feel the need to bring your own sheets."

I close the door and shake my head, my grin stretching from ear to ear. "Astra, I could be staying at the Waldorf Astoria, and I'd still bring my own sheets. You ever seen a set of hotel sheets under a UV light?"

Her laugh is rich and sultry. "I think I'm part of the reason you should never look at sheets under a UV light."

"You are awful," I say. "Truly awful."

"That's not what the boys say."

I roll my eyes and set the bags of food down on the night-stand, and my bag on the bed, since there's no room on the table. I have to admit, seeing Astra in this room is kind of like seeing a swan in a crappy, scum-filled duck pond. But then, she presents herself a lot better than I do. She's a high-class woman, while I'm a bit more down to earth. She's champagne to my six pack of beer. But that's one reason I think we're so close. We provide each other with a much-needed balance.

I see that she's already got a white board set up in the corner, and she's taken over the table. Her laptop and a lot of files are scattered across the top of it. Astra postures as a high society woman, unaffected by life and above it all. But deep down, she's every bit as driven and determined as I am. She may not be as outwardly enthusiastic about it, but she wants to see monsters brought to justice every bit as much as I do. It's yet another reason she and I have been so close from day one. We get each other.

"When did you get in?" I ask.

"About nine," she replies, looking down at the papers in her hand.

As I look out the window and see the sun sliding toward the horizon, I realize she's been cooped up in this room literally all day long. I've been down in the offices at the Sheriff's depart-ment, but at least I wasn't cooped up in a tiny bungalow. But she doesn't seem to even notice. She's shuffling through the papers, reading everything carefully and processing all the information.

"Come on," I tell her. "Drop the papers. Let's go and get you some air."

"I thought you brought food?" she asks. "I smell something greasy and I'm pretty sure it's not you."

I laugh. "Not this time. But you have apparently been locked in here, hammering away all day. You need some air. And a drink."

She instantly drops the papers in her hand, and I watch them flutter to the ground at her feet. A wide smile stretches across her face.

"Now you're speakin' my language, Wilder."

"So what do you think?" I ask.

"I think it's a good thing you brought me down here," she replies. "Like you said on the phone, this thing is really complicated."

I nod. "Right? It's like we've got two things happening at once. First, we have this serial killer. Except this serial killer operates with a team, and he allows this team to sexually assault and beat their victims. It makes no sense," I say. "But second, we apparently have another serial killer running around murdering all of these other people with no preference at all. He doesn't adhere to racial, religious, gender, or socioeconomic lines."

"He's an omnivore," she remarks.

"Exactly. And you can't profile omnivores accurately."

Our server arrives and takes away our salad bowls, and once the table is cleared, sets our entrees down in front of us — salmon with a white wine and lemon sauce, with grilled asparagus for Astra, a rare ribeye steak and french fries for me. I order another round of wine for us, and we both tuck into our meals, taking a few minutes to enjoy the food in silence. It's kind of our unspoken agreement that we don't discuss the more disturbing and bloody aspects of the job over a meal. It's nothing we arranged, we both just kind of fell into it a long while back, and we've never questioned it, and it's just second nature to us now.

"Why is it you refuse to eat a baked potato?" she asks. "Whenever we go out, you always order the same thing. You always get the steak with french fries, and never a potato."

I hold up one of the fries, admiring the golden color and crispy texture. "This is the only acceptable form of a potato," I tell her. "Hashed browns are fine, so long as they're so crisp, they're almost burned."

"What's wrong with a baked potato?"

"Just don't like them. Never have," I shrug. "My parents, and then my Aunt Annie all tried to get me to eat one. I'd never do it. I just don't like the taste or texture of it."

Astra is grinning wide and shaking her head at me. "Wilder, you have more idiosyncratic quirks than most of the nutcases we put away. You do know that, right?"

"I'm aware. I like to think it gives me character."

"It gives you something."

I laugh and take another bite of my steak, relishing the char on it, as well as the way it nearly melts in my mouth. I'll say one thing for Briar Glen... they certainly know how to make good food here.

"How's your fish?" I ask.

"This might actually be the best salmon I've ever had," she groans with pleasure. "I may have to marry the chef. Or maybe I'll just give him the best night he's ever had in his life."

"Incorrigible."

"That's why you love me."

We make small talk, chatting about inconsequential things as we finish our meals. Eventually, the waitress arrives and clears the table, leaving a dessert menu behind when she goes.

We both look through it for a little while. The waitress comes back, takes our orders, and hustles away again.

"So anyway, as I was going through everything today, I had a thought," Astra says. "What if, you're not dealing with two different groups of people, but one group that's committing all the murders?"

"I thought about that, but it doesn't add up in my mind," I reply. "The signature on these two women — the fingernail — is specific, and it's something that's missing from the other murders."

She purses her lips, as if she's thinking. "What if it's a different faction from the same group?" she asks. "I mean, the odds of two different groups of serial killers operating in the same city at the same time, is remote."

"Yeah, I know. It's unheard of," I admit, letting out a long sigh. "I just can't help but think I'm missing something huge here. I feel like it's staring me in the face and I just can't see it."

"Because you've got that big brain of yours working. It complicates things that are simple. You know, like finding yourself a boy toy. That's as simple as it could be, but you overcomplicate it," she says with a laugh.

"How did I know you'd find a way to work that into the conversation?"

"Because you know me so well."

"Better than you know yourself."

The waitress arrives and drops off our cappuccinos and desert. I'm having tiramisu while Astra opted for the chocolate molten lava cake with vanilla ice cream. We dig in and fall silent for a few moments, both of us lost in thought. Our moratorium on shop talk only covers dinner, not dessert. As I mull everything over, I come to the realization that I've been so focused on the bigger picture and trying to figure out how everything connects, that I indeed have allowed myself to lose sight of the forest for the trees.

"I think you're right. Exactly right," I say. "I need to go back to the beginning and simplify this. We need to look at the basics."

"Probably the best place to start," she tells me.

"You're a genius."

She smiles wide. "I know."

I laugh and take a bite of my dessert. I love this woman. She keeps me grounded.

TWENTY-FOUR

Pacific Crest Motor Court; Briar Glen, WA

"ALL RIGHT," I say, slamming the door behind me. "Wakey wakey, time to work."

Astra pulls the pillow off her face and looks at me through one squinted eye. "Do you have any idea what time it is?"

"Five after seven."

"How are you awake and so energetic?"

"I went for a run at five."

She groans. "What in the hell is wrong with you?"

"That is a very long list, and we don't have time to go through it all today."

Astra flops back on the bed and pulls the pillow over her face again. I laugh as I throw open the curtains, letting the morning light filter through and brighten up the room. After that, I walk over and yank the pillow away from her.

"I'm on vacation," she groans. "I get to sleep until nine when I'm on vacation. It's the law."

"Pretty sure it's not actually a law," I say. "And just because you had a couple more shots at the bar last night than you should have doesn't mean you're on vacation."

"I'm not hungover," she argues. "I just like to sleep."

After dinner, we found our way to one of the town's main watering holes. Astra claimed it was scientific research and she wanted to observe the Briar Glen locals in their natural habitat. That of course, led to one drink. Which turned to another after a couple of guys noticed her and started to ply her with more. I pulled the pin before she did and reminded her that we're working and that I needed her to have a clear head. To her credit, she stopped drinking and didn't flirt with the guys who were buying her drinks, let alone go home with one of them. Or both of them.

"Up. Shower," I order her. "And after you get out, we'll have food and coffee."

"I'll have coffee now."

"Sorry, you don't get coffee until you're showered and ready to party."

"You suck," she groans. "And this is hardly a party."

That much is true, and I concede the point as she rolls out of bed and heads for the shower, grumbling the whole way. She closes the door and a moment later, I hear the shower start up. Experience tells me I've got a good twenty minutes or so before she emerges, so I busy myself while she's in there.

I grab the dry erase pen and go to the whiteboard, drawing a line down the middle of it, separating it into two columns. At the top of the first column, I write "Omnivore Unsub," and underline it. At the top of the second, I write "Preferential Unsub," and underline that. Then in that column, I write the name Tracy Weber, and the first woman, who I learned, was named Stephanie Helton.

Stephanie's roommate Casey finally appeared down at the Sheriff's station to file a missing persons report. According to

Casey, it wasn't unusual for Stephanie to take off for a day or two, but when she still hadn't turned up after a few days, she began to worry. She'd called around and nobody had seen Stephanie, so half out of her mind with worry, Casey finally came to the station to report her missing.

I make a mental note to speak with Casey myself, then step back and look at my handiwork and nod to myself. That done, I tidy up the table and lay out the food I brought back with me. After my run, I stopped by the Sheriff's station on the off-chance Morris would be there. He was, and he filled me in on the ID.

I told him I likely wouldn't be in the station today and left, picking up some of those delicious smelling breakfast burritos he'd had the first day I popped into his office. And by the time I got back to the hotel, I was filled with a renewed sense of purpose and determination. Astra's comments last night, and the realization that I'm definitely complicating things, really struck home.

The shower turns off and I have to wait a few more minutes for Astra to emerge in a cloud of billowing steam. Her hair is tied up in a bun, and she's got no makeup on. Not that she wears much to begin with when she's out on assignment. But even in yoga pants and an oversized, baggy sweatshirt, she still looks ready for the catwalk.

"You look entirely too pleased with yourself this morning," she remarks as she drops down into the chair across from me.

"And you finally look alive," I reply, sliding one of the cups of coffee over to her. "You may have coffee now."

"You are a benevolent god."

"I am actually."

I hand her the burrito and some breakfast hash browns, and after a moment of looking at it, then sniffing it suspiciously, Astra tears into hers. As she eats, groans of pleasure escape her mouth that, even muffled by her food, sound wholly indecent. I'll admit, the burritos are really good, but I certainly don't think they're *that* good.

When we're finished, I clean up and throw everything in the trash can, then retake my seat. I stare at the white board as I sip my coffee, focusing on the two names I scrawled out.

"Basics," I announce. "What's the first thing we're taught to look at? The most basic thing we're told to focus on?"

"Victimology," she says.

"Correct," I say. "Why this person at this time? What is it about these victims that attracted their killer to begin with?"

"Basics," she says with a smile and a nod.

"Doesn't get any more basic than that."

"So, if I'm reading you right, you want me to do a deep dive on these two women," she says.

I nod. "Also, I want you to go back through the old case files and find more victims. Throw out any case where the body was found at a primary crime scene. If there's blood on the ground, toss it. I only want cases where the body was dumped. And you may need to look closely at the crime scene photos for that. You probably should anyway, just in case. If you find a case that meets that parameter, write their name in the first column."

"Anything else?"

I nod. "Then I need to know what's linking all of these people. I need a background on them. It doesn't have to be too deep just yet. But I need to know the basics," I say. "There's a reason these people were picked by the killer. I want to know what it is."

She sketches me a small salute. "Aye, Aye, Cap'n. I'll get right on it."

"Good. Thank you." I get to my feet.

"Where are you going?" she asks.

"Shower, and then I have a couple of things I need to follow up on."

"Lead?"

"Possibly," I nod. "Hopefully. I'm getting tired of spinning my wheels and waiting for bodies to drop. I want to get out ahead of this. I want to figure out what in the hell is going on in this town."

"I don't know much. Not yet. But based on what I've read so far, there's a lot of bad things happening here."

I laugh. "That's very true. On so many different levels."

TWENTY-FIVE

St. Bernard's Midnight Mission & Food Bank; Briar Glen, WA

HAVING SPENT a couple of hours interviewing Casey, Stephanie Helton's roommate, I got nowhere. Not that I expected it to yield any answers. According to Casey, Stephanie was a good person, did good works, never had trouble with anybody, and didn't have any enemies. Stephanie was studying to be a social worker and child advocate. She was passionate about caring for children.

After talking to Casey and poking around Stephanie's room, I retreated to a coffee house to regroup. I spent some time on my laptop, going through the digitized case files, looking for something, some direction to run in. In the file for the Tyler Salters murder, I found the name of a witness who'd come forward, saying he saw Tyler being taken off the street. According to the log, it's a man named Louis Vuitton.

My first inclination was to brush it off, just as the deputies who interviewed him had, simply because the name is obviously fake. A play on a popular fashion designer Louis Vuitton.

And also because the account he gave seemed rambling and incoherent. Mr. Vitton spoke of angels and demons taking Tyler away. I figured talking to him would just be more pointless wheel spinning.

But I have nothing else. No other leads. And in the end, I know I have to do my due diligence. One thing I feel separates me from a lot of my colleagues is that I don't cut corners. I run down every lead, no matter how outlandish it might seem. No stone left unturned and all that. You just never know what might be hiding underneath that last stone you're tempted to ignore. I must have said it a million times to myself: there's nothing I hate more than things getting missed.

So I figured I might as well try to track down Mr. Vitton to see what he has to say for himself. I mean, he did come forward and all. Maybe I can cut through the angels and demons and decipher what it is he's really getting at. I reason that he wouldn't have come forward about that specific case if he hadn't actually seen something.

That led me to St. Bernard's Midnight Mission and Food Bank. After asking around, I learned that because they've got such a relatively small homeless population, this is the only shelter in all of Briar Glen. And if Louis Vitton is going to be found anywhere, it's probably going to be here. Especially as the nights continue to grow colder the closer to winter we get.

The mission is located in the warehouse district of the city. It's a little dingy and grimy, but it's not nearly as bad as some of the run-down sections of Seattle. It's largely abandoned, but there are still a few places trying to make a go of it. I see a small packaging company, as well as an auto restoration shop. A few restaurants and other businesses still maintain a warehouse here as well. And despite the numerous derelict buildings, I still don't see many homeless people.

I park in the lot beside the building, which looks like an old warehouse that's been rehabbed and repurposed to accommodate its new purpose. It's definitely still industrial, but it's been cleaned up, had a new coat of paint slapped on it at some point in the last decade, and looks fairly well kept.

I walk to the front door, passing between a marble statue of an angel in armor, holding a fiery sword on one side of the walk, and another of whom I assume is St. Bernard himself. He's dressed in the bulky robes of a monk, and he's holding a staff that's topped with a cross in one hand, with a Bible in the other.

There are a few people milling about outside the doors and they all turn to look at me as I walk by. I get the feeling I'm being sized up, the way a predator measures his prey, deciding whether or not it's worth giving it a shot. One thing my father always told me was to walk confidently and carry yourself with purpose, even if you're scared. Perhaps especially if you're scared. He said carrying yourself with confidence will always make somebody think twice before having a go at you.

I haven't been genuinely scared for a long time, knowing I can take care of myself if it comes down to a scrap, but that advice has always stuck with me. I think there are some people who will always underestimate me and think they can roll me. But they're few and far between, simply because I do walk with my chin up and chest out, just like my dad taught me. Projecting strength and confidence.

It apparently makes the guys outside the doors think twice, because they turn away from me and go back to their conversations. I pass through the thick haze of cigarette smoke and into the mission itself. In front of me, I see a couple dozen cafeteria-style tables arranged in neat rows. There are about twenty-four people or so sitting at the tables eating.

Beyond them is a row of banquet tables covered with large soup tureens and warming dishes full of food. There are several people walking down the line, letting the volunteers behind the tables dish up their food. Once served, they walk over to the tables and find a seat.

On the far end of the cavernous room a makeshift church has been set up. There's a tall, curtained backdrop that's adorned with a few religious tapestries. A small dais sits in front of the backdrop with a pulpit situated on top of it. A series of wooden benches sit in front of the pulpit, serving as their pews. There are currently no services being held.

"May I help you?"

I turn at the sound of the voice to find a diminutive woman standing behind me. Her smile is warm and welcoming. She can't be more than five-two, if that, and probably doesn't weigh more than a hundred pounds. Despite her small stature, there is a presence about her that commands attention and respect. She is one of those people who definitely seem larger than their body.

She's dressed in a drab gray dress with very sensible leather shoes and black stockings. Even if she weren't wearing the head covering traditional for nuns, I would have guessed she was a Sister anyway. There's just something very spiritual about her. It's comforting. A silver cross dangles around her neck, and I would guess that she's in her mid to late fifties.

"Hi," I say lamely. "I'm Blake. Agent. Wilder. Special Agent Blake Wilder."

Inwardly, I slap myself silly. I'm not somebody who makes a habit out of tripping over my own tongue, and I don't know why I am now. I take a deep breath and exhale slowly, giving myself a mental slap upside the head.

"Sorry," I say. "Let me try that again. My name is Special Agent Blake Wilder and I'm with the FBI."

A look of worry crosses her face, but her smile never falters. "My name is Sister Catherine," she replies. "I guess you could say I'm the caretaker here."

"How long have you been here, Sister?"

"Please, just call me Catherine. Or just Cat," she says, waving me off. "I've never been one for formalities."

"Me either," I say, giving her a smile. "It's nice to meet you, Cat. Just call me Blake."

"Has something happened? Has somebody done something?" she asks.

"Do you think somebody's done something?"

Her smile is beatific. "It seems a logical deduction, since I can't say I've ever had the FBI in my mission before."

Her wit is disarming and makes me laugh. She's a clever woman, and a very likeable person. I can also see the sharp intelligence in her eyes and know that she's got a formidable mind. I know I should keep my distance, but I like her almost immediately.

"How long have you been here, Sister?" I repeat my question.

"Oh, I guess about twenty years now. Though, it's getting to the point where our services don't seem needed as much," she says. "It used to be overflowing in here every night. Now, the population of homeless and lost souls has been dwindling over the years. Praise the Lord."

What she sees as a cause of celebration and thanks, I see in a very different, sinister light. Either I'm just cynical, or something is really rotten in Briar Glen. Homeless populations don't just spontaneously dwindle. Sure, sometimes cities enact programs to help them out of poverty and off the streets. But judging by Mayor O'Brien's attitude, I don't think that's the case in this city. He didn't even seem to care that young women are being butchered.

The idea that the homeless have somehow been lifted out of poverty enough to get off the streets and build new, prosperous lives seems about as likely to me as Bigfoot riding a unicorn through the front door right now. It puts the case files sitting back in my hotel room in a whole new light for me.

The one thing I didn't check on was their living situation. When I go back and check through the files, if these open-unsolved homicides are majority homeless, then it turns the case on its head. Suddenly, my theories start coming together. This could really be the one thing I've been missing to bring the whole picture into focus.

Even though adrenaline is flowing through my veins like a raging river, I force myself to calm down. I don't want to get ahead of myself and end up falling flat on my face. It's happened to me before, and that was such an unpleasant experience, I have no desire to repeat it.

Stick to the basics, I tell myself. I've got to walk before I can run, and I need to remember why I'm here.

"I'm looking for a man, Sister."

I bite back the laugh that threatens to bubble up and out of my throat as I listen to the words in my head and realize how it might sound. I really am hanging around Astra far too much. I look at Sister Cat and immediately feel my cheeks flush with heat as I think about her reading my thoughts and disapproving mightily. I clear my throat and try again.

"He could be a witness to a crime. A very bad crime, and I need to speak with him," I say.

"Who is it you are looking for, Agent Wilder? And why do you think he's here?"

"Please, call me Blake. And my understanding is that the man I'm looking for is homeless, so I'm just kind of putting two and two together here," I explain. "I'm hoping he's here, or that you know him and can point me in his direction. He's not in trouble, Sister. I just need to speak with him."

I can see she's very protective of her flock, which makes me like her even more. She is a true champion for the downtrodden and actually lives the faith she preaches, unlike so many others I know. I respect that about her.

"I don't know, Agen — Blake," she corrects herself. "The people who come to me, come in search of peace. Solace. They come to get away from the horrors of their lives. I don't know that I can betray their trust."

"I understand, Cat. I truly do," I say. "But this man came forward voluntarily. He spoke with the police of his own accord. I just need to speak with him about his statement. I swear to you that I'm not looking to hurt him."

She sighs and tugs on the cross around her neck, as if seeking divine input or something. Her lips are compressed into a tight line, and I can see she's struggling with the decision. I just need to give her a push to topple her over that edge of indecision.

"This man I'm looking for may have witnessed a murder, Cat," I tell her. "This is as serious as it gets, and I really need his help."

She fixes her blue eyes on me, seeming to have come to her decision. "What is his name? This man you're looking for?"

"I don't know his real name, but I'm hoping that since you're familiar with the less fortunate, you might," I say. "The name he gave the police was Louis Vitton."

A smile flickers across her lips and she shakes her head. She knows him. Sister Cat looks up at me and grins.

"His real name is William Turner," she says. "Sergeant William Turner. He's a veteran and has some issues. He's also got an affinity for fashion designers. William likes to tell people his name is Ralph Lauren, or Giorgio Armani. My favorite was when he insisted his name was Diane von Furstenberg. That went on for a couple of weeks. But he's much better when he takes his meds. He's lucid. Stable. Doesn't run around telling people he's Gianni Versace."

"Do you know why he does that?" I ask.

She shakes her head. "I have no idea. It's just one of his eccentricities, I suppose," she says. "You can't go to war and see the things he saw, or do the things he did, and not come back a little... different."

"That's so true," I say. "I've known plenty of vets who've been changed forever by war. I can't imagine."

"I tell you that so that you know he's delicate, Blake," she says. "I understand you need whatever information he might have, but I beg you to please be gentle with him."

"You have my word, Cat."

"Then that's good enough for me. I can see you're a good and trustworthy person," she says. "That's the only reason I'm going to help."

"And I appreciate that more than you know."

"I'll put out the word that I need to see him," she tells me. "Come back tomorrow around lunchtime. I'll be sure to have him here."

I take her hand and give it a squeeze. "Thank you. Thank you so much," I say. "I'll see you tomorrow."

TWENTY-SIX

Industrial District; Briar Glen, WA

I GET up from the bed and get myself dressed, my eyes never leaving her. She's curled into a ball on the mattress, her bare back to me. She's hugging herself tightly and sobbing wildly. I've soundproofed the walls in this room. In theory, she can scream all she wants and nobody will hear her. I'd prefer she didn't though. It would irritate me.

When my people joined me in this mission, I rebuilt this room in the old family factory. I paneled the walls and made it a comfortable bedroom, bringing in a large, soft bed and other furnishings. This is where the ritual takes place. This is where we purify our souls and consecrate our bodies.

"Be still. Stop crying," I command.

She tries to choke back her cries but can't. I reach for the cat o'nine tails on the nightstand, running my hands up and down the long, smooth, leather handle. The feeling of my tool, my instrument, my weapon, my holy totem, sends shivers and purpose running through me. I smile, content in God's light.

"I said be still, child. You are being purified. Your body consecrated. And your sacrifice sanctifies us all," I say. "Your sacrifice blesses our work. So do you not see? There is nothing for you to cry about. You are doing a good thing, child. You are helping us cleanse this world of evil."

She continues to sob, but it's quieter than before. Even still, her crying irritates me, so I lash out with the cat o'nine tails. She screams and arches her back as the welts from the studded leather braids bite into her flesh.

"Mortification of the flesh has been used to purify ourselves for centuries. For thousands of years," I tell her. "We rend our own flesh to purge the evil within us. To cleanse ourselves."

I'm tempted to lash her again, just to get her to stop crying, but I don't want to mark her up too badly. The others have not had their turn just yet. This is part of the ritual. Part of the cleansing and purification of ourselves, and the renewal of our bonds to both, our mission, and to ourselves.

I walk over to the oak highboy and pick up the candle, then turn and carry it back to the bed. I tilt it and watch as a thin stream of wax spills over the side and splashes onto her flesh. The girl screams as if I've just used a hot iron to brand her and writhes on the bed in front of me. I chuckle to myself and return the candle to its place.

"Why are you doing this?" she whimpers.

I turn to her, surprised to hear her speak. The candlelight glows softly on her creamy pale skin, and glints off eyes as green as jade. Dark hair frames her lovely face, and my eyes are drawn to her full lips. My gaze travels lower, taking in the swell of her breasts, and curve of her hips, and I feel my arousal growing again.

I push it away though. I've purified myself. To partake of her flesh again would be gluttonous. Lustful. It would be wrong, and so I must deny myself. But she is such a beautiful woman and reminds me so much of my wife, who has been gone from this world for a long while now. In a way, they all remind me of her. But the woman on the bed before me looks so similar, she could be related, and the thought of keeping this one drifts through my mind.

The knock on the door draws my attention and pulls me out of my thoughts. Thankfully. Those were abhorrent thoughts. Dangerous thoughts. Entertaining the idea of keeping this woman for my own is wrong. It goes against my teachings and would be an affront to my people and our ways. It would endanger our mission and disrupt our good works.

"No, I can't think of keeping her. I won't keep her," I mutter to myself.

Turning away from her, I slip into my robes and slide my mask down over my face. Only then do I walk to the door, unlock it, and open it up to the next of my flock.

"My heart has been purified," I give our traditional ritual greeting. "My body has been sanctified. My bonds to you, to our faith, and to our good works have been renewed. How do you enter?"

"I enter seeking to be purified and sanctified," he replies. "I enter seeking to renew my bonds to you, to our faith, and to our good works. Nos servo fidem."

"Nos servo fidem," I repeat. "So may you enter."

I step out as he goes in and closes the door, locking it behind him. She is the third of our seven. I have the next four picked out already. As usual, our ritual is running smoothly. Once we have all purified ourselves, we will then purify her through mortification of the flesh. We will send her to God as pure and innocent as a newborn. And my people and I will be sanctified for the next seven years.

My footsteps echo around the empty corridors, and my torchlight flickers and jumps upon the walls like living animals as I make my way toward the stairs. His voice stops me before I get there.

"Brother," he calls.

I turn to him. "Brother," I reply. "I believe your turn to purify yourself comes next."

"It does," he replies. "But I wanted to speak with you first. I have concerns."

Of course he does. He always has concerns. Of my people, he's the jumpiest. He's always on edge and worried about something. He wasn't always this way. But over the years, he's grown more skittish. It makes me wonder whether he is still a true believer or not. If he still believes in our mission and in our works.

That I have to question it at all disturbs me. I will need to address this at some point, because if he cannot be trusted, he is a danger to our entire flock. I hate to think of it like that. I've known him for thirty years and consider him one of my closest friends. But I can't have him endangering our work.

"What are your concerns?" I ask.

"The FBI Agent," he says. "She found her way to St. Bernard's."

"I know this already."

"And you're not concerned?"

"Why should I be? Sister Catherine knows nothing," I tell him. "There is nothing to tie St. Bernard's to our works."

"Are you sure of that?"

"Of course I am," I assure him. "If I wasn't, I would share your concerns. As would everybody else. We all have the same skin in the game, Brother."

He shifts on his feet, still radiating tension and fear. In truth, I'm merely saying what I have to in order to calm him. I don't know for certain what this FBI agent can find at the mission, but I don't think there's much there to find. It's slightly worrisome, but I don't really think it's a big deal.

It's true, our group was founded there. It was where we first shared our grief. Shared our stories. It's where the seeds were planted and nurtured. Our names are on records somewhere in there, but unless you knew exactly what you were looking for, there is no way to connect us.

"She's clever, this Fed woman," he continues. "Smart. Worse than that, she's determined. And relentless."

"Be calm, Brother," I implore him. "I truly don't think there is anything to worry about. I think you are working yourself up for nothing."

"I wish I could believe that. But we have so much to lose."

Reaching out, I put a hand on his shoulder and give it a reassuring squeeze.

"Be at ease. We have all already lost everything that was precious to us," I tell him. "There is nothing in this world that can be taken from us that's worse than what's already been taken. It is only our work that frees us. Am I right?"

He hesitates, but nods. "You are right. As always," he says. "I'm sorry for my doubts, Brother. Forgive me."

"There is nothing to forgive. We all have fears. We all have doubts," I say. "If we did not, we would not be human. Nos servo fidem."

"Nos servo fidem."

He gives me a nod, then turns and walks away. He says all the right things, but I know he's still scared. On the one hand, I can't blame him. I have no desire to spend the rest of my days in prison either. That would be a fate worse than death. On the other hand, we expect total commitment. Our work demands it.

Faith is all we have. Faith in each other, and faith in our work. Without faith, we are nothing and we might as well not do our good works. We might as well sit back and let the degenerates and evildoers have run of the world.

But I will not have it. My people will not have it. God demands faith and he demands justice. If there is something at St. Bernard's that must be dealt with, we will deal with it. Just as if we have somebody who is losing their faith and breaking their bond with us, we will deal with that too.

Nos servo fidem. We keep the faith.

TWENTY-SEVEN

Pacific Crest Motor Court; Briar Glen, WA

"So we have a witness?" Astra asks.

"I'm hoping so. I have to go back to the mission at noon tomorrow to meet with him," I tell her.

Astra leans back in her chair and looks at me. "A witness would be good. Really good."

"It would be. But I have to be honest, I have my concerns about him," I say. "In his initial statement to the police, he was talking about angels and demons kidnapping this kid Tyler. Plus, Sister Catherine said he's delicate. So I'm not entirely sold on this guy yet."

"Probably suffering from PTSD."

I nod. "That was my thought too," I tell her. "It might not hurt to see if we can get him into the VA."

"If he'll go."

"Yeah, there is that."

I drop down into the chair across from her and turn my attention to the white board. She's got twenty-three names in the "Omnivore Unsub" column, with dates, and brief descriptions next to them. I note that there are men and women on the list. White, Black, Asian, Hispanic. Again, it cuts across all normal demographic lines, staying true to the omnivore profile.

"There are undoubtedly more. This is just over that uptick in the last four years you had me look at," she says, noticing me looking at the list. "But those were the ones I've found so far that were dump jobs. And none of the ME's reports back that up. It's only in the crime scene photos that you can tell."

"And let me guess, Dr. Sofia Carville was the ME listed on all the reports?"

"The one and only."

"This is looking worse and worse for her," I mention.

Astra nods. "But here's the weird thing. Originally, I couldn't find the crime scene photos from these case files. They'd been deleted."

"Deleted?"

She nods. "Yeah, like physically deleted."

"So how'd you dig them up?"

"I called a friend of mine who's pretty good with computers and he was able to... recover them."

I look over at her, a smirk on my lips. "Do I want to know how your friend managed to recover them?"

"No, definitely not."

"Fair enough," I grin. "Ignorance, as they say, is bliss."

"Especially if it keeps you out of prison."

"Absolutely," I reply.

We both fall silent for a moment as I continue to scan the list on the white board. I think back to my conversation with Sister Catherine and the idea that took root in my head at the mission.

"Tell me something," I say. "Is there any way for you to tell if the names on the Omnivore list were homeless?"

"I looked at that and they all have addresses listed," she replies. "And get this, here's another commonality that we can't overlook. Those twenty-three people all had previous brushes with the law."

"Brushes?"

She nods. "None of those twenty-three were ever convicted of anything, but they were all charged for one thing or another at some point," she says. "But, like the crime scene photos, their charging records were all deleted."

"Well, if they were never convicted of anything, they wouldn't have a record."

"That's not what I mean. When you're charged and booked, you generate paper. Charging documents, mugshots, the whole works," she says. "And those papers get stored, whether you're convicted or not. But it's like somebody went into the database where those papers are stored and plucked them out."

I tug on the end of my hair, thinking about it and know that she's right. Charging documents and all don't just magically disappear when your case is disposed of. It's not an open case, of course, but those records are definitely kept in a database somewhere. The fact that they were erased is intriguing. To say the least.

"Okay, so who would have access to do that?" I ask. "Who could go into a court database and delete things?"

"Anybody with a password. This isn't a federal database, babe. It's a local municipality. They maintain their own records," she tells me. "So anybody from the mayor, to the city attorney, to your Sheriff could possibly have access. You also have to wonder if former employees still have access. If the city isn't diligent about changing access protocols and passwords, there could be an even bigger group of people out there who can do it."

"Yeah, but don't they leave fingerprints?" I ask. "I mean, if it's a login database, they surely have to have a record of who went in and removed the files."

"Had my friend check that too, and whoever it was, knew to cover their tracks," she tells me. "They used a system admin login. There's no way of telling who it was."

"Well that should narrow the suspect pool some."

"Sure. Assuming the people who have system admin passwords haven't given them out," she says.

"This just gets better and better," I sigh in frustration. "Okay, I think the first thing we need to do is get a list of people who have system admin passwords currently. We can cull through those and find a possible suspect that way. Or at least somebody we can squeeze until they squeal."

Silence descends over the room again as we lose ourselves in our thoughts. This whole thing is beginning to take focus, and the picture it's revealing is a lot uglier than I ever anticipated it would be. If all of this theory pans out, we're looking at a possible conspiracy to commit mass serial murder inside the city's government. To pull off something like this, it would require multiple people. One person couldn't do this alone any more than Sofia could have carried Tracy Webster out to Widow's Bluff all by herself either.

It's not lost on me either that the uptick in the last four years happens square right in the middle of Morris' term as Sheriff.

It sounds absolutely crazy. Like something out of a Grisham thriller or something. It's a plot that doesn't sound like it can be real. The idea of multiple members of a city government conspiring to murder their own citizens sounds beyond outlandish. Preposterous. And yet, here we are, all the same.

I frown as the pieces in my head start to fall into place. "So, stop me if this starts to sound too insane — "

"Stop," Astra says with a laugh. "Trust me, I've been looking at this all day. I've been looking at it from every possible angle, and it gets more and more insane the more I think about it."

"You're not wrong. But I need to talk this out," I tell her. "So, we have somebody inside the city government, we'll call them unsub A, who has an axe to grind with people who are charged with crimes but are never convicted."

"It could be multiple unsubs, but we'll go with A for expediency's sake."

"Good. That works. Okay, so unsub A, enraged by the system failing to send people who, in their view, are criminals, to jail, murders them," I go on. "And once he carries out his sentence, he then uses his access and goes into the appropriate databases, police and court, and removes records, photos, and everything else, to cover his tracks. How am I doing?"

"Oh, it still sounds outlandish as hell, but you're doing fine," Astra says. "Go on."

"That's where I stop," I reply. "Because I'm still trying to figure out how Tracy and Stephanie fit into this picture."

"Let's assume for a moment they don't," she says. "Let's just take them off the board for now and forget about them. Let's focus on the omnivore."

I stand up and start to pace the room, needing to get my body moving to activate my brain. If we want to catch the omnivore, I'm going to need a working profile. The problem is, the omnivore is multiple. And how do you profile a group of people?

"Back to basics," I mutter to myself. "Let's get back to basics."

Pausing to look at the white board for a moment, I read the list of names again, committing them to memory. I know it's only a partial list, and I dread knowing just how many will be on it by the time we're done. Fifteen years, at least, is a long time to kill, and the pile of bodies he, or they, have racked up has got to be prodigious. It's a heavy weight on my shoulders.

"So, we know the unsub has a proficiency with crime scene. He uses forensic countermeasures," I say. "We also believe he's a mission-based killer. He thinks he's righting some wrong. In this case, he believes he's picking up the slack of the court system. Handing out the sentences he feels they deserve for their crimes."

Astra snorts. "Execution seems a little extreme for shoplifting."

"You think?" I reply with a grin. "But to this unsub, it's perfectly reasonable. He's handing out justice. He's fervent in this belief."

"And what do we know about mission-based killers?" Astra asks.

"That they won't stop. That they have to be stopped."

"Right. And they will usually go down in a blaze of glory, preaching the righteousness of their cause with their dying breath."

"Which means, this will probably get worse before it gets better."

"Exactly," she says.

"That's not the worst of it."

"No?"

I shake my head. "Now take that profile and apply it to a group," I tell her. "What do you get when you have a group of mission-based killers who fervently believe in their brand of justice. They're in lockstep all the way and are willing to die for their beliefs. What do you have?"

Astra's eyes widen slightly as she considers my words. "A cult."

TWENTY-EIGHT

St. Bernard's Midnight Mission & Food Bank; Briar Glen, WA

I SIT in Sister Catherine's office in the St. Bernard's dormitory, which is located behind the combined chow hall and church. The dorm is actually another, smaller warehouse, connected to the chapel/chow hall by a short hallway built out of plywood and sheetrock with a slab of paint slapped on. But hey, it's functional.

The dorm is lined with bunk beds, all in militarily precise rows. Or, in the sort of precise rows one might see in prison. It's a thought that makes me shudder. Sister Catherine's office sits in the corner of the dormitory and is built in the same fashion as the hallway that connects the two buildings.

To say it's austere would be an understatement. She's not one for adding personal flourishes to her workspace. But then, in a dorm full of people who might very well walk off with your things, I might not be either. Perhaps she doesn't want to tempt these people to ignore their better angels.

I'm sitting in the chair behind her desk, a large battle-scarred affair that's definitely seen better days. There's a single chair on the other side of the desk, and to my right is a bookcase filled with mostly religious texts. Though on one shelf, I see the Big Book that belongs to AA, and the texts for various other Anonymous help groups. I guess groups like AA and NA would be big in a setting like this. Makes sense.

As I sit waiting, I think about everything Astra and I went over last night. The idea that there is a cult running around Briar Glen, a cult that counts some of the city's leaders as members, is a frightening thought. But the fact that they have possibly been running rampant and killing with impunity for the last fifteen years is downright enraging.

It's still a theory, of course. I have no proof to back it up just yet, but I'm hoping to rectify that situation. I'm going to need to have a very frank and uncomfortable conversation with Sheriff Morris when I'm done here with William Turner. I need to figure out whether he's part of this cult or not. And if he's not, I'm going to need his help in figuring out how to flush them out.

As if my thinking about him summoned him, the door to Sister Cat's office opens up and a tall, African American man steps in. He's built a lot like Sheriff Morris, though he's a bit softer around the middle. He's got a wild, unkempt beard shot through with gray, and dark eyes that smolder with intensity. I get to my feet and walk to him, extending my hand.

"Sergeant Turner," I greet him.

He backs up and puts his hands up, trying to keep as much physical distance between us as he can. I take the hint and move back to the chair I'd just abandoned and take a seat, laying my palms flat on the desk before me. He stands near the door, his eyes flitting rapidly around the office, seeming as if he's deciding whether to stay or bolt out of here.

I can see the toll not just the war, but life on the street has taken on him. His face is etched with deep lines, and he looks ragged. Worn. Frayed around the edges. There's a wildness about him I imagine has to come from having to be on guard and looking over your shoulder twenty-four-seven. His eyes are slightly jaundiced and there's an air of unhealthiness about him.

"I appreciate you taking the time to talk to me, Sergeant," I say.

I use his rank one, as a sign of respect for his service, but two, to try and anchor him to reality. I need to keep him connected to who he actually is, rather than let him float away into his fantasies of being Coco Chanel. I wish I understood what his fascination with designers was, because it's another tool I might have been able to use to establish a rapport with him.

Unfortunately, I myself am not a fashion plate, nor do I keep up with the latest trends. I wear what's comfortable. That's the most important quality to me. Second is that I wear what I think looks cute on me. It's an admission I'm sure will result in my woman card being revoked permanently. So be it.

"Sergeant Turner," I say again. "I'd like to speak with you. I just have a couple of questions for you. Will you have a seat?"

He looks at me as if just realizing I'm there and moves into the corner of the room, pressing his back into it. He watches me like I'm a snake, coiled and ready to strike at him, for a few long moments. I don't make any moves, nor do I say anything else. I want him to come take a seat in his own time, when he feels comfortable. The last thing I want to do is scare him anymore than he already is.

Slowly, I see him start to shift. His eyes change and that look of a wild animal that's cornered and ready to fight fades, and he seems to be coming back to himself. He straightens up and keeps his gaze on mine. He looks lucid and alert, and I have to wonder if Sister Cat gave him something to help keep him rooted to reality with his lunch and that it's just now kicking in. If so, I'd like to know what she gave him.

"Who are you?" he asks, his voice a deep, booming bass.

"My name is Blake Wilder," I tell him. "I'm with the FBI."

"FBI? I haven't done nothin'," he starts, that wild look quickly returning to his eyes.

"I know you haven't. And you're not in trouble, Sergeant," I assure him, trying to keep my voice soothing. "But you gave a statement to the police recently about the abduction of Tyler Salters. Do you remember that?"

He chuffs. "Of course I remember. You think I'm an idiot or somethin'?"

"That's the furthest thought from my mind, actually."

He watches me warily as he crosses the room and drops into the seat in front of me. Turner is a man who looks haunted. I bet he hasn't had a night's sleep free of the nightmares of his wartime experience in a very long time. It breaks my heart for him. Him and the countless thousands of others who've come back from the war... broken. And to a system that doesn't support them well enough. It's an injustice that infuriates me to no end.

"So what do you want to know? I told the cops everythin' already and they laughed at me. Called me an idiot," he says, his voice colored by bitterness.

"You're not an idiot. They are — "

"Lady, I don't mean no disrespect, but don't patronize me," he cuts me off. "Ask your questions 'cause I got to go. Sister Cat's bakin' cookies and if I don't get some warm ones, I'm gonna be pissed."

"That's fair," I nod. "Okay then, I just want you to tell me, in your own words, what you saw the night Tyler Salters was taken."

"Who else's words would I use?" he scoffs. "Like I told the

cops, I was sittin' on a stoop. I remember that I scored some money panhandlin' that day, so I got some McDonald's for dinner," he starts. "Anyway, I'm sittin' there eatin' and I see Tyler — I know him on account of we help each other out now and then, but he ain't my friend or anything like that. We just do business together sometimes."

I'm tempted to ask him what sort of business, but decide it's not really relevant to anything, so I let it go.

"So yeah, I'm sittin' there and I see him walkin' toward this dude on the street. I can tell Tyler's clockin' the guy and is lookin' to roll him, so I don't say nothin'. Ain't my business," he goes on. "Anyways, I see this other dude come up behind him and grab him around the neck in a chokehold. He sticks somethin' into Tyler's neck and before you know it, my boy is out cold. A van rolls up and these two demons throw Tyler into it and take off. I wanted to say somethin'. Maybe do somethin', but I ain't afraid to admit I was scared of what would've happened if I did. I didn't want to be injected with somethin' and thrown into a van. And you know what?"

He looks at me, clearly expecting me to give the appropriate response, so I do. "What?" I ask.

"Turns out, I was right to be afraid and to not do nothin'," he says. "Look what happened to Tyler."

I nod. "You were definitely right to keep yourself safe, Sergeant," I say. "Tell me something. In your statement to the police, you said something about angels and demons? What did you mean by that?"

He snorts and waves me off. "Man, those fools weren't listenin' to me. They think I'm crazy anyway, so they wasn't listenin'," he says. "What I told them was that I called the cats who threw Tyler into the van were demons. I called them demons. I wasn't sayin' demons did it."

"All right, I can see that," I reply. "But what about the angels? Where did that come from?"

"The van, lady," he tells me. "It had an angel logo on the side and back doors. And some writin'. It had some writin' on it, but I couldn't make it out."

"An angel logo?"

He nods. "Yeah, the outline of some dude with wings and a halo," he goes on. "He was holdin' a sword or a staff or somethin'."

The description immediately brings to mind the statues out in front of the mission. And the back end of the dark van I saw carrying Tracy Webster to her death. I make a note to check to see if the mission owns any dark vans, though I can't make myself believe Sister Cat would be involved with this.

"Is that it? Anything else?" he asks me impatiently. "I smell the cookies."

He's right. As I inhale, I catch the distinct scent of chocolate chip cookies in the air. It makes me smile.

"Just one more question, Sergeant," I say. "I'd like to get you some help. Would you be willing to go to the VA in Seattle — "

He shakes his head. "Nah. I ain't goin' to the VA. They don't do nothin' anyway. They don't want to help people like me. They don't care."

"Sergeant — "

"I said no," he snaps. "Now, beggin' your pardon, I got to get into the kitchen or I'm gonna miss out. And you don't want me to miss out. Trust that."

He gets up and leaves me sitting behind Sister Cat's desk, going through everything he just told me, trying to make sense of it. He certainly was a lot more coherent than the initial report made him out to be. It sounds to me like they let their bias creep into their report. So unprofessional.

And yeah, he might be a little off, but clearly, when he's on medication, he's not crazy and can function like a normal human being. I just need to find a way to get and keep him on some medication. That's the trick. And it's made all the more difficult by the fact that he doesn't want to comply. It's his right of course, I just hate to see somebody who sacrificed so much for this country get left behind and tossed away.

I sigh and get to my feet, walking out of the office. There are a few people scattered about the dorm, huddled together, talking quietly. And when I walk by, all conversation ceases and they follow me with their eyes, watching me suspiciously. I take a tour of the grounds around the mission, looking for dark vans, but come up empty.

"Did you get everything you need, dear?"

Sister Cat startles me, and I have to physically restrain myself from jumping. I turn around and look at her, a rueful smile on my face.

"I think we need to get you a bell to wear alongside your Crucifix," I say. "You're silent as a cat."

"I'm sorry. I didn't mean to startle you."

"It's fine. I'm only kidding," I say. "And yeah, I got most everything. I do just have one question though. Does the mission own any vans?"

She nods. "We have four. But only one of them is working," she tells me. "We use them for our Meals on Wheels program. We take food to seniors and those incapable of leaving their home."

"That's very charitable."

"The Lord smiles upon those who are," she says. "But what made you ask about the vans?

"Oh, just something Sergeant Turner said to me," I say, and then change the conversation, not wanting to answer any more questions. "He's a remarkable man. Sergeant Turner. I wish he'd go to the VA and get some help."

"I do too," she says. "It breaks my heart to see him this way."

"Mine too, Sister. Mine too."

I want to get a look at those vans, but I don't want to alert her — or anybody else. Which means, I'm either going to need to come back at night or find some other means of viewing them. I'll figure it out.

"Thank you for everything, Sister," I say. "I really appreciate it."

'You're very welcome. I hope you learned something you needed to learn that will help you in your investigation."

"I do believe I did," I reply. "You have yourself a good day, Sister Cat."

TWENTY-NINE

Pacific Crest Motor Court; Briar Glen, WA

I PULL into the parking lot and stop just outside the bungalow, quickly cutting the motor, and jump out of the car, then hustle to the room. I was on my way to have my showdown with Sheriff Morris when I got a frantic call from Astra, saying she had some big news that couldn't wait. So I turned around and beelined for the hotel. My conversation with the Sheriff can wait a little bit.

I burst into the room and find Astra glued to her laptop. The room looks like a tornado ripped through, scattering boxes and paperwork everywhere. I see she's taken the framed picture that had been hanging on one wall and has started taping pages and pictures to it instead. She's definitely hot for something right now, and I'm suddenly curious what it is.

I close the door and she gives a start, as if she'd been so engrossed in what she was doing that she didn't realize I'd walked in. I know how that is. I get like that sometimes. She looks up at me in a daze and gives herself a little shake.

"You all right?" I ask.

She nods. "Fine. Just immersed in some of Briar Glen's sordid history," she replies. "It's fascinating reading."

"Have you been out of the room at all today?"

She shakes her head. "Nope. Been squirreled away in here like your dirty little secret all day."

I laugh. "Come on then. Clean up and let's go get you some food. I don't want you telling Rosie I starved you or she might not let you tag along next time."

"Tag along?" she sputters. "Please, I'm adding culture and style to your investigation by being here. I am definitely the Watson to your Sherlock."

"That analogy doesn't work, since most people think Watson was the real brains behind that duo, and we know that's not true in this case."

She laughs as she gets up and stretches, then starts to get ready. I do what I can to clean up the aftermath of Hurricane Astra as she does, stacking files and papers into neat piles, and getting everything off the floor. She gets ready quickly, and ten minutes later, we're on the road. Ten minutes after that, we're pulling into the Sunnyside Up Diner. I look over at her skeptically as I cut the engine.

"What? I like having breakfast for dinner sometimes," she chirps. "And look at it this way... this place probably doesn't serve booze so there's no chance of me getting tanked."

"Doesn't mean you'll be any more pleasant to wake up in the morning."

"That is true. But that is your cross to bear, my friend."

We laugh as we walk into the diner and take a booth near the window. The diner isn't anything exceptional to look at, but Astra assures me they have very high Yelp ratings. For whatever that's worth. It looks like every other breakfast diner in Anytown, USA. Lots of white and black tile, and chrome fixtures. It's bright and cheery, which is the exact opposite of most people, including my friend, first thing in the morning. But I will say that the aroma in here is heavenly.

A girl who can't be more than eighteen or nineteen with midnight black hair and the perfect, smooth complexion, and naturally firm, curvy body that only comes with youth, bounds over to our table. She's got a wide smile on her face that makes her sapphire-colored eyes sparkle. She's wearing a red and white vertically striped uniform dress that falls halfway to her knees, white athletic shoes, and a white apron around her waist.

She's petite, feminine, perky and she's cute... and she immediately makes me think of the first two victims of the Fingernail Killer, as Astra and I have taken to calling him. I push away the thought and chastise myself for being so morbid. Aside from the obvious and ghoulish resemblance to two homicide victims, there's something familiar about her. I know I've never met her before, but something about her strikes a chord with me for some reason.

"Welcome to the Sunnyside," she greets us. "What can I get you to drink?"

"Orange juice for me. Tall one," Astra says. "And a coffee."

"Ditto that for me," I say.

"Great. Comin' right up," she smiles. "I'll take your orders when I come back."

"Perfect."

We watch her flounce off, then I turn to Astra. "You do realize that was you not all that long ago."

"Please. My chest wasn't quite that perky."

I pointedly look at her chest. "It still is."

"Wonderbras are miracle workers. Better breasts through engineering."

We share a laugh as I peruse the menu. I look up to find Astra staring at me, an incredulous look on her face.

"What?" I ask.

"Why do you even bother looking at the menu? As long as I've known you, whenever we go for breakfast, you always get the same thing."

"I like to keep my options open," I reply.

"You mean pretend to keep your options open since you never, you know, exercise any of those options."

"You never know," I say. "I may surprise you one of these days."

"I won't hold my breath."

The waitress comes back and sets our drinks down in front of us, then takes her pad out of her apron pocket.

"What can I get you?" she asks.

"I'll take the blueberry waffles," Astra says. "With eggs over easy, and sausage on the side, please."

"Excellent," she says. "Is there anything better than breakfast for dinner?"

"Oh, I can think of a few things that maybe I'll tell you about when you're older," Astra says seductively.

"Astra," I snap, fighting hard to keep the smile off my face.

"What?" she replies, feigning innocence.

The waitress gives her a knowing smirk and a wink. Clearly, the girl is advanced for her years if she's picking up on Astra's vibe. She turns to me, apparently as amused by my discomfort as Astra is.

"And how about you?"

"Country fried steak. Hash browns, extra crispy, two eggs, over easy, and sourdough toast please."

"Fantastic. Let me get your orders started," she says and dashes off.

Astra is staring at me with a smirk flickering across her lips. "I guess that day you're going to surprise me isn't today, huh?"

"Doesn't look that way. Maybe tomorrow. Check back with me then. That is, unless you're too busy corrupting the youth of Briar Glen."

"Funny girl," I say. "That girl absolutely understood what I was saying. We're not all sexual wastelands like you, Wilder. Some of us enjoy our bodies and like what they can do."

"As you've told me many times over," I respond with a laugh. "Anyway, food's not here yet, so lay it on me. What's this big, earth shaking discovery?"

Astra glances around the diner, then leans forward, obviously not wanting to be overheard. Her expression shifts from glib to sober in the blink of an eye, and I can tell that whatever it is she found, it's serious.

"The discovery is that exactly seven years ago, there was a similar string of murders here," she says. "A string of seven murders, to be exact."

I sit back in the booth, feeling like she just knocked the wind out of me. It makes perfect sense though, since I posited that these two murders we're looking at weren't the Fingernail Killer's first. They were too smooth. Too polished. There was none of the sloppiness you see in a killer's early work. The Fingernail Killer has an MO, has a signature, and is efficient with his kills. I knew he'd been operating in the shadows for some time.

"So this first series of seven, were they all good-looking brunettes? Were they all young?" I ask. "Did they bear a resemblance to Tracy Webster and Stephanie Helton?"

"You know they did."

"The fingernail — "

"Was present in all seven," she says. "White nail, red cross."

"Jesus."

"I told you I was gonna rock your socks off."

"I think you rocked my pants off along with them."

"We might need a few drinks for that. But hey, I'm game if you are."

I look at her for a long moment, not comprehending at first. And when I do, my cheeks flare with heat and I burst into laughter. Astra's smiles at me like the cat that ate the canary, feeling mighty pleased with herself that she's embarrassed me so thoroughly.

Slowly, my laughter tapers off and I regain control of myself again. My mind immediately shifts from mirth to somber as I contemplate what she just told me. There are so many layers to this and it's only growing more complicated as we go. It's like every answer we find turns up a hundred more questions.

The waitress comes over and drops off our plates with a smile, then leaves us to it. We tuck into our meals in silence for a few minutes, then Astra looks up at me.

"I say we suspend our moratorium on shop talk while we eat just this once," she says. "This is important, and we need to talk about it."

"I agree. I feel like this case is gaining momentum and we need to get a hold on it before we get run over by it."

"Agreed."

"Good. So walk me through what you found."

"I was just perusing the case files, looking more for the omnivore side of the board when I stumbled across this string of cases," she says. "Same deal. Crime scene photos had been erased, and the ME's report didn't match. But there was one name attached to all seven of the cases. And you're not going to like it."

"Morris."

She nods. "He was the responding officer for all seven," she tells me. "And apparently, he never connected the cases. Which tells me he's either a really lousy cop, or he's covering something up."

I take a bite of my gravy smothered steak and chew as I think about it all. I don't want to believe it. Not of him. But the fact that he covered up seven murders forces me to rethink how I see him. Add to that, the fact that his girlfriend, Sofia, is altering her reports to cover up certain aspects of the current series of murders, and I think it speaks for itself. And what it's saying is really depressing.

I truly believed that, at heart, Morris was one of the good guys. Seems I put my faith in the wrong person. Not that it's the first time, and probably won't be the last, but it still feels like I've been kicked in the gut by somebody with a steel-toed boot.

"Well, I think we have our connection between the Fingernail Killer, and the omnivore," I say. "Sheriff Morris is at the center of both strings of killings. As is his girlfriend, the town ME."

"I don't understand why they'd do it," she says.

I shake my head. "I have no idea. I mean, I can guess that in Morris' case, as a lawman, he probably does get sick and tired of seeing people beat the system. Gets tired of not seeing justice served," I say. "I get that, but I'd never take it to that extreme."

"And the girls?" she asks. "Got a reason for that?"

"Sexual sadist, maybe. Gets off on the power and control," I reply. "I was actually thinking of it like a Bernardo and Homolka type situation. He and his girlfriend enjoy torturing and killing together."

"Will this world ever run out of sick ways sick people can kill innocents?"

"I think that's probably a big no," I reply. "But there's one thing that's still bothering me. Sofia claims that both Tracy and Stephanie were raped by multiple men. If this is the sort of situation I think it is, it should only be the two of them engaging in it. There shouldn't be a group."

"But if we're positing a cult type deal going on here, he might give these girls over to his followers once he's done with them," she offers.

"Yeah, I suppose that could be. There's no doubt that Morris is a charming and charismatic man," I point out. "I suppose I could see him using those powers for evil."

"We've seen it before."

"True enough."

We eat in silence for a little while, each of us processing our thoughts. I only eat because I know I need the fuel. The food itself lost its taste for me a while ago. I might as well be spooning gruel into my mouth for all the pleasure I'm taking out of my meal. I want to be wrong about Morris. I really do.

"You know, as a representative of the Federal government, you really should attempt to be a little more professional."

O'Brien's voice pulls me out of my thoughts, and I look up at him, a sneer on my lips already. Astra looks from me, to him, then back again.

"Who is this walking turd?" she asks.

I bite back my laugh as his expression turns to one of pure outrage. He opens his mouth but before he can say anything, I jump in.

"Astra, this is Mayor O'Brien," I introduce him.

If she's impressed by his title, she doesn't show it. She simply looks him up and down, her distaste for him clearly painted on her features. He turns away from her and his eyes latch onto mine.

"You are causing a disruption in this city. And I'll have you know, I did my research, and the Attorney General cannot bring charges against me," he spits. "I have not, and am not, violating anybody's civil rights."

I can't stop the laugh as it bursts from my throat as I imagine him frantically Googling the question. It's then he seems to pick up on the fact that I knew that all along and was only yanking his chain. His face darkens and he looks ready to explode with anger.

"I'm going to call your supervisor and let him know how you've behaved in my city," he growls in that high pitched, reedy voice. "I'm going to tell him what an incredibly horrible person you are, and just how irresponsible you've been."

"That's fine. It's not like he hasn't heard that before," I say. "And his name is Potts. Special Agent in Charge Potts. Did you want me to write that down for you?"

"How dare you," he says, sounding positively scandalized.

"You meet the coolest people, Wilder," Astra remarks.

He stands there for another minute, seemingly deciding whether to launch another tirade or not, but opts for the latter. Turning on his heel, he storms out of the diner and into the night. Our waitress is standing in front of us before the doors even close. I look at her and realize I know why she looks familiar. It's the nose. I should have seen the similarity before.

"I'm sorry about my dad," she says. "He's a dick, but he's pretty harmless. For the most part anyway."

"Well, I'm sorry he's your dad," Astra replies.

She smiles wide at Astra, laughing like it's the funniest thing she's ever heard as she walks away. Astra turns to me.

"Cute kid," she says. "Poor mom, though. Can you imagine having to go home and sleep with that guy? And pretending to like it?"

"Not on a bet. I wouldn't screw him if I was borrowing your body," I reply.

"Thanks. I think."

I give her a small smile. "You know he's definitely going to call Potts, right?"

"I do. And I can't tell you how much I'm looking forward to having that conversation with him."

"You and me both. Should be a lot of fun."

I sit back in the booth and poke at my food, trying to keep my thoughts from turning too dark and too inward. Which is not easy to do when you're dealing with what we are right now. Most of all, when I'm dealing with the level of disappointment I feel toward Sheriff Morris.

But I'm trying. I need to keep my head in the game.

THIRTY

I'M SITTING across from Sheriff Morris, watching his micro expressions and body language carefully. He's tense. I can see the anger bubbling below the surface like a volcano. That magma chamber of rage is quietly pushing its way toward the surface and if I say the wrong thing, it's going to burst and trigger an eruption that will likely make Krakatoa look like a party favor.

But I did tell him at the outset that I was going to follow the evidence. And I stressed that I would follow it wherever it led. I told him that I would follow it regardless of who it implicated. I just personally never expected that it would lead back to him.

"So, do you want to tell me about the girls?" I ask.

"What girls would those be, Agent Wilder?"

We're back to Agent Wilder instead of Blake now, I see. Well, this is off to a great start. But then, what did I expect, knowing what I'm about to drop on him? The problem is, I need to tread carefully. Everything I have is circumstantial, and unless Astra and I can dig up some actual physical evidence, I'm going to need a confession. Which is why I'm currently wired, and Astra is sitting in the car outside recording this entire conversation.

"Seven years ago, seven girls were murdered in Briar Glen," I tell him. "And all seven of them had the same acrylic finger-nail that both Stephanie Helton and Tracy Webster had when they were killed."

He cocks his head and looks at me like I'm suddenly speaking Chinese. He looks at me like he's not understanding a thing coming out of my mouth. It's a good thing I came prepared. I pull the file I put together last night out of my bag and hold it up for him. It's a crime scene photo of the first girl in the series.

Everything is identical to Tracy and Stephanie, from the white robes, to the physical torture, to the sexual assault, and of course, to the fingernail. I hold the photo, allowing him to see it, but he still looks confused.

"Amanda Fisher," I prompt him.

He shakes his head, looking confused as I drop the picture on his desk and pull out the next one.

"Jennifer Betts," I say, then pull out the next one. "Jamie Pitzer."

He still shows no sign of comprehension, so I toss the folder onto his desk. It lands in front of him and he picks it up, thumbing through all of the pages inside of it. And when he gets to the reports section of my presentation, he pauses. He picks it up and looks at it closely for a long moment before dropping the page and looking up at me with a look of shock in his face.

"You can't possibly think I had anything to do with this," he says.

"Isn't that your name on the responding officer's report?"

"It's my name, but I didn't write it."

I look at him incredulously. "So that's what you're going with? You're being framed? Really?"

"Don't take my word for it."

He grabs a random folder off the corner of his desk and tosses it to me. I catch it and open it up. On top is a requisition form with his signature on the bottom. I compare his signature on the form to the report I brought and see that they're not even close. I frown as I look at them, then turn my gaze back to him. I close the folder and toss it back to him.

He sounds sincere. I want to believe him, but in the absence of a better explanation, I can't make that turn yet.

"So who's framing you?" I ask.

"And I would know that how?" he shoots back. "Isn't that the nature of a frame? You don't know who's setting you up?"

He has me there on logic. But it still doesn't explain it all away for me.

"So are you really expecting me to believe that seven girls were murdered and despite your name being on the report, you know nothing about it?" I ask.

He shrugs. "It's the truth. Sure, I was a deputy back then, but I didn't take every call. There was a lot that went on that I knew nothin' about," he says. "Sheriff Montez compartmental-ized a lot. He thought things ran more efficient that way."

"Okay, let's shift gears for a minute then," I say. "What about Sofia's crime scene reports? I've been through them all and she's been falsifying them, Sheriff. Pertinent information has been left out."

He shakes his head. "I can't believe that she's falsifying anything. That's not her way," he says. "She's a straight shooter."

"I can show you the reports, Sheriff," I say. "I can show you her reports and let you compare them to the crime scene photos. You can see for yourself they don't match. And this has been going on for a very long time."

He sits back in his chair, looking flabbergasted. I'm dropping a lot on him all at once just to see how he reacts. I'm watching his face and his body language closely, looking for the slightest tell. But so far, I see nothing. So I ratchet up the heat.

"And then of course, there are the other murders. What we've uncovered so far is pretty damning," I say. "Deleted records, deleted evidence."

"What are you talking about?"

"The murders in your town aren't random. They're very purposeful, in fact. They're executions," I tell him. "We've uncovered twenty-three over the last four years so far. These twenty-three people have been charged with crimes but were never convicted. And yet, they mysteriously end up murdered. And all court documents related to the case suddenly disappear. They're physically deleted."

"How is that possible?"

"Somebody with system admin access to both the police and the court databases is logging in and deleting the records," I inform him.

With each new revelation I drop on him, Morris has a physical reaction, like he's taking a body blow every time. He's stunned and staggered, and at the moment, doesn't seem to know up from down. I watch him closely and judge his reactions to be genuine. I don't detect any deception. And I don't think he's that good of an actor, which means he might actually be innocent of all of this. He might actually be the victim of a frame job.

"Does Sofia have system admin access to the city's databases?" I ask.

"She's the ME. Of course she does," he replies. "But I'm

telling you, she's as innocent of anything as I am. If her reports are being altered, she's being framed as well."

"I need a list of anybody, past and present, who's had that sort of access," I say. "Even if you don't think they're involved, I need them on that list, Sheriff. This is not the time to be holding anything back. I've got enough to convene a grand jury as it is, and if I do, it's going to go really badly for you."

"I told you before that I don't like being threatened."

"It's not a threat. It's just a fact," I say. "All of the evidence I have — "

"Is circumstantial," he interrupts me.

"Be that as it may, it will be for a grand jury to decide its merit," I say. "And I have to tell you, all of the evidence I have, circumstantial or not, points to you and Sofia right now. And believe me when I tell you, I've seen grand juries vote to indict on a lot less than what I have. Is that a risk you want to take, Sheriff?"

He lets out a long breath of frustration as the reality of the situation settles down over him. Morris suddenly looks weary and older than his years, and I feel a pang of guilt for coming down on him so hard. But he has to know what he's up against. Has to know the precariousness of his situation and the severity of the consequences.

Deep in my heart, I don't believe he's guilty. I just can't see this man, who I think is good, murdering innocent people. And I don't see him as the leader of some fanatical, justice-seeking cult. But I've been wrong about people before.

"I need you to put together that list, Sheriff," I tell him. "If for no other reason than to find another suspect. If you say you're being framed, that's fine. Let's prove it. Together."

His eyes linger on mine for a long moment, but he finally nods. "I'll put a list together," he says. "But I have to tell you, I may not know everybody that has the sort of access you're talkin' about."

"We'll cross that bridge when we come to it," I tell him. "Right now, we just need a starting point."

"Fair enough."

THIRTY-ONE

Pacific Crest Motor Court; Briar Glen, WA

"You listened to him," I say. "What did you think?"

She shrugs. "Honestly, I don't know. He sounded sincere, but it's hard to say when you can't see their facial expressions and body language," Astra says. "So the better question is, what do you think?"

"I think if we're wrong, we just tipped our hand and could be in for some real trouble. If Morris is our guy, and he knows we're onto him, he's either going to run, or he's going to make sure his loose ends are handled," I tell her.

"We're his biggest loose ends."

"Yeah, I know."

"You're not making me feel real comfortable here."

Night has fallen outside, and the darkness is absolute. I stand at the window for a moment, looking out into the night beyond, recalling the feeling I had of being watched. Could it have been Morris out there, perhaps contemplating tying up his loose ends? Or was it somebody else? With as many feathers as I've ruffled since I got here, it's tough to say.

But as I stand here gazing out into the abyss, I get that familiar tickle along my skin. I feel the goosebumps marching up and down my arms as a finger of ice slides down my spine. Somebody's out there again. Watching. I quickly draw the curtains closed and glance at my sidearm that's sitting on the table. Not wanting to alarm Astra, I leave it where it is, but sit in the chair, keeping it within easy reach.

She's sitting cross-legged on the bed munching away on her salad. After gorging ourselves on pure crap food the last few days, she insisted on getting something reasonably healthy. I opted for a burrito, arguing that I'd go for a run later to burn it off. Honestly, I just need some fresh air and the burn in my legs and lungs. I need that almost Zen-like state I fall into when I run.

"Do you think he had anything to do with it?" she asks.

I shake my head. "Honestly, I really don't. He seemed genuine to me. And nothing in his face or body language made me think otherwise."

"I've learned to trust your instincts. Maybe you should too," she says. "If you don't think he's involved, he's probably not."

"But that takes us back to square one."

"Not exactly. We've got a mountain of information," she says. "We just need to figure out how all the different pieces fit together. Once we do that, we'll have our bad guy and life will be rosy again."

"Yeah, but figuring out how they fit is the problem."

"Don't dull my shine here," she says. "I'm trying to keep it positive."

I laugh softly. "Sorry. I'm feeling kind of pessimistic."

"Understandable, given everything going on," she says. "Let's see if we can make some pieces fit. Maybe it's like a jigsaw puzzle and if we figure out one small section of it, the rest of it will fall into place."

I open my laptop and fire up the search engine. With everything else going on, I almost forgot that I need to check something out. When my system's ready to go, I call up the website for St. Bernard's and get back a bunch of links. I scroll my cursor down to the mission's website, but something draws my attention and I click the link. A page comes up with the likeness of the man I saw in statue form outside the mission. And when I read a bit on the page, I feel my stomach clench as the adrenaline hits my system once more.

I quickly flip back to the page for the mission and find the link for their Meals on Wheels program. As it comes into focus, I see photos of their fleet of black panel vans with the emblem of St. Bernard's Mission emblazoned on the side — the angel with the sword in one hand, and a shield with the Templar cross with a B in an elegant script intertwined with it in the other.

"Angels and demons," I mutter to myself.

"What's that?" Astra asks.

"Just something Sergeant Turner said."

As far as I'm concerned, that confirms Sergeant Turner's story, so I flip back to the page that drew my attention before. And the more I read, the more adrenaline I feel pouring into me. I feel a few more pieces of that puzzle falling into place, just like Astra said a moment ago. It's not much, but it's something. A direction to go in. And as I contemplate what it is I'm reading, it opens up a whole new avenue of thought for me. It's giving me a different perspective on this case and the motivation behind it all.

As I look at the image of St. Bernard of Clairvaux, I feel like that one thing that's been staring me in the face the whole time, the thing I couldn't see before, suddenly becomes visible.

"Did you know Bernard of Clairvaux was the patron saint of the Templar Knights?" I ask.

Astra looks over at me, an incredulous expression on her face. "Thinking of becoming a history professor or something?"

I turn to her, growing more and more excited as the connections start snapping together in my mind. I don't know yet how it all fits together in the bigger picture, but I know in my heart of hearts that this is relevant. And that this is huge.

"Think about it for a minute, Astra," I say. "What did the Templar Knights stand for? What was their thing?"

"I didn't realize there was going to be a pop quiz. I didn't study, sorry."

I laugh softly and toss a balled-up piece of paper at her. "They were the grail knights, according to some histories. The knights who protected the Ark of the Covenant in others," I explain. "But there are a lot of stories out there that describe the Templars as the deliverers of God's Justice. They were fanatics about their faith and about delivering justice to the people."

"And by justice, I'm guessing you mean they cut the heads off a lot of people," Astra notes wryly.

"That they did. Their battles against the Muslims, especially during the Crusades, were infamously bloody," I tell her. "But they believed they were following God's will, which was to deliver His justice upon those who'd broken His law."

"Okay, I can see the fanatics angle here, but why does this Templar thing have you so hot and bothered? There are fanatics of every stripe out there."

"Yeah, but not all of them are dropping bodies with acrylic nails painted with a Templar cross on it."

I call up the crime scene photos for both Tracy Webster and Stephanie Helton, pulling up the photos of their hands, adjusting them so they're side by side. Astra gets off the bed and sets her salad down on the nightstand, then walks over to me. She leans down and looks at the photos of their nails, and when I feel she's fully taken them in, I pull up a picture of a Templar knight. She gasps when she looks at the rendition of the Templar tunic — white with a blood red cross down the center of it. But she quickly gathers herself and looks at me.

"Okay, that's impressive and all, but what does it mean?" she asks.

"That I've been looking at this all wrong from the jump. Religion plays a massive role in this whole thing. Religion may be the driving force," I say.

"How do you figure? I mean, they could have just as easily picked that symbol because it looks cool."

"True. But there's more. The number seven is considered a holy number," I add. "It's considered the number of perfection by many religious folk. And you found seven victims, seven years ago."

Astra purses her lips and ponders my words, but I can still see she's skeptical.

"Trust me, this feels right," I say. "And this is a good thing."

"Okay, let's assume you're right and that religion is a factor in all of this. What does it prove, and why is it a good thing?"

"Because, it narrows down our suspect pool even more. There can't be that many religious zealots in town. They'll stand out to other people," I say. "We just need to figure out the right people to ask. And consider this, aren't most cults based in some sort of religious faith? Sure, it may be abhorrent to all of us, but to them, it makes perfect sense."

"But what about the revenge angle?"

"Not revenge. Justice," I say. "God's justice. They wouldn't sully themselves with something as petty and worldly as man's revenge. Like the Templars, they'd consider them-selves harbingers of God's justice. And by punishing those who escaped judgment, they believe they're carrying out God's will."

Astra whistles low then frowns. It's a lot to take in, I know. And I understand why she's skeptical. It sounds crazy to me too. But the thing is, believing that these guys see themselves as some modern-day Templar Knights is no more outlandish than a conspiracy inside the city's governmental body designed to murder its citizens.

She looks over at me. "This whole thing just took a turn for the darkly weird that I was not ready for."

"Well, buckle up. I've got a feeling this is going to get really bumpy from here on out."

THIRTY-TWO

Miller's Beach; Briar Glen, WA

ANOTHER DAY, another lonely stretch of beach that's totally uninhabited, and another body of a beautiful brunette. Business as usual in Briar Glen. Astra and I stand side by side, watching Sofia working with the body, taking measurements and jotting down notes. I eye her critically as she works.

It's getting harder to not voice my suspicions to her, but I hold myself back. If Morris is being framed, it stands to reason she could be too. So until I have more evidence, I'm going to hold off on dragging her into an interview room out of deference to the Sheriff.

Speaking of the Sheriff, he walks over to us and looks at Astra curiously. "Y'all are multiplying now?"

"Sheriff, this is my partner Astra," I say, then turn to her. "Sheriff Morris."

She shakes his hand and exchanges pleasantries with him. A gust of wind rips down the beach, making the both of us shudder and pull our coats around us a little tighter. The surface of the ocean is dotted with whitecaps, the wind creating a lot of chop on the water.

Miller's Beach is even more remote and isolated than Rhodes. And since it's not known for its exceptional waves, few surfers come out this way. It was a man walking his dog early this morning that found the body and called it in. Sheriff Morris called just after daybreak with the news, and I told him we'd meet him there. I figured it was time he met my better half. Mostly because I want her unbiased take on both the Sheriff and on Sofia.

The victim is wrapped in the same muslin robe as the others, has dark hair and pale skin. From where I'm standing, I can see the acrylic nail with the Templar cross on it. After the rush I got last night making the connection, I've backed off, slowed down, and am now trying to look at this with logic and a critical eye.

If this cult, for lack of a better word at this point, running around Briar Glen is all about delivering God's justice, why is it they've now killed three women, who by all accounts, were good and decent? What was their crime? I'd had Astra run backgrounds on the first two vics and nothing popped. No mysteriously deleted files, no record of arrest anywhere, and no trouble in their lives.

And when we get this woman's identity, I'll have Astra do the same, but I'm already fairly certain the result will be the same. So why did they have God's justice visited upon them? That's where this connection starts to fray for me. It doesn't fall apart completely, simply because it fits too well with the other murders. It feels right when I spell it out.

But as I go back to basics, I ask myself again, why these three women? Why now? What did they do to earn this punishment?

"I don't see any drag marks," I mention to Morris. "Somebody had to have carried her out here."

He nods. "That tracks."

As Sofia continues to work, snapping pictures now, I pull Morris to the side. Astra and I then go over everything we learned last night, laying out our theory about the Templars and the religious motivation behind the killings. Astra is watching him closely, as am I, searching for any tells. Once again, he gives nothing away. Nothing that would indicate we'd struck a nerve, or that he was surprised we put it together. Nothing but genuine interest.

"So, you're thinkin' it's religion at the root of all this?" he asks once I've finished.

"We think so. It fits. The religious iconography. The number seven. The Templar cross on the fingernails of the three female vics," I tell him.

"All right, supposing I buy this, what is it these three women did to earn this wrath of God or whatever it was?" he asks.

"God's justice. Not wrath," I correct him. "As for what our three did, I have no idea. I need to think on that some more to see if I can find a connection. But the Templar cross on the nails is the link to the other killings. Those victims all had God's justice delivered to them for whatever offenses they were never convicted of."

"So now we're thinking it's one group, a cult I think you called 'em, running around town, thinking they're doing God's work by killing people? How does that make sense?" he asks.

I shrug. "It only has to make sense to them. In their mind, they're doing as God commands."

"When in truth, they're doing what one narcissistic, egomaniacal, murderous sack of crap is telling them to do," Astra chimes in.

We're both looking at him closely as her words wash over

him. Astra isn't normally that aggressive when questioning people, so I know she did it for the shock value. She wanted to see what Morris would do if she impugned his character. Wanted to see if he'd react at all, even unconsciously, to her verbal salvo.

But he doesn't even flinch. Doesn't bat an eye. He simply stands there, his mind working, and doesn't react at all. Astra and I exchange a look with each other and I can tell we're both on the same page about Morris. Neither of us are inclined to think he's involved with this. Either that, or he's got the most remarkable self-control of anybody on the planet.

"You know, I've been standin' here thinkin'," he muses. "You told me ritual was big for these people, right? That everything they did was ritualistic?"

I nod. "Absolutely. The condition the bodies are left in strongly suggest their ritualistic nature."

"What if these three women are part of that ritual. Or, what I mean is, what if they're a ritual unto themselves?" he asks.

I cock my head and look at him. "What do you mean?"

"Just that... we had the seven women before, seven years ago, right?"

I nod. "Right."

"What if their ritual, for whatever reason, is to murder seven innocent women every seven years?" he wonders. "I mean, I don't get it, but like you said, it only has to make sense to them."

"And the rest of the year, they deliver God's justice to those who escaped earthly punishment," Astra says, picking up on his train of thought. "Maybe this seven-year cycle is their way of like, renewing their faith."

I nod as I catch onto where they're headed with this. "Or maybe it's their way of bonding themselves all together, making sure any new members have just as much skin in the game by forcing them to participate in this kind of ritual," I say.

Morris scratches his chin. "They all get together and have a mass rape and murder fest to make sure everybody's got blackmail material on each other, so if you implicate somebody else, you're also implicatin' yourself. That's twisted."

"What's even more twisted is that they've perverted religion enough to make their sick little fantasies fit the narrative," Astra says. "They hide what they're doing and commit atrocities behind the veil of religion."

"So they use whatever criteria they use to determine somebody's guilt, and then kill them," I say. "And then every seven years, they choose seven innocents to murder and call it faith. Twisted doesn't even begin to cover it."

"Okay, but why the preference for the brunettes?" Morris asks. "I know you said there's a woman in the past who hurt this guy and all. But if we're dealing with a cult, rather than just one man, how does the preferential offender bit work? I mean, there's obviously still a preference."

"It's because whoever is leading this cult is the dominant personality," I say. "It's his will that's imprinted on the group."

"But they believe his will comes from God," Astra adds.

"Right. But because he's the dominant, his preferences win out," I tell him. "When they select their victims for this renewal ritual or whatever it is, it's this dominant man who selects them. And he selects them based on something in his past. He must have some connection with a woman who looks a lot like these victims."

"So it's still like you said, that he's killing that woman over and over by killing these women in her place?" Morris asks.

I shake my head. "I thought so at first, when I thought we were dealing with one offender. But now that we've shifted to a cult dynamic that focuses on God's justice and righting wrongs,

I'm changing that opinion," I say. "Given that these people believe they're avenging injustices, my theory is that these cultists were touched in some way by injustice themselves. They probably suffered a tremendous loss, perhaps the loss of a loved one, and had to sit back and watch the system fail them. That's what I believe has spurred this group. And I believe this leader, the one choosing the victims, must have lost someone who looks like her. Maybe his wife?"

Morris nods and Astra looks at me, a mischievous smirk on her lips.

"Damn girl, that was deep. Made you sound real smart. Smarter than I ever thought you could be," she says, making me laugh.

He tries to stifle it, but even Morris laughs at that. The laughter is a good palate cleanser. With so much tension in the air, it's like pulling a pressure release valve.

"Okay, so we just need to find a man who lost a brunette wife or significant other at some point, who suffered some sort of injustice, and is religious," Morris says. "Should be simple."

"I think it's a lot simpler than you think, Sheriff. First of all, our suspect pool is pretty narrow, all things considered," I say.

He barks laughter. "Right. Anybody who, at any point in time, had system admin privileges to the various city databases."

"Probably still a smaller pool of humanity than if we had to rule out everybody in the city."

He gives me a lopsided smirk. "Touché," he notes.

"It'd be helpful if we knew where these people first crossed paths," Astra says. "Knowing the origin of the group might help us find the individual members, as well. Especially if they're not inclined to help us."

"I actually have an idea about that," I say. "We need to take a little ride."

THIRTY-THREE

St. Bernard's Midnight Mission & Food Bank; Briar Glen, WA

"WELL, THIS PLACE IS CERTAINLY CHARMING," Astra says. "It actually makes your bungalow look like a room at the Four Seasons."

I laugh. "They're a homeless shelter. It's not big on frills and unnecessary ornaments. They're here to serve people, and that's it. And from what I've seen, they do a great job of it, so cut 'em a little slack."

"That's fair," she says.

The tables are only half full, but all eyes turn to Astra when we walk into the mission. Good thing I'm used to it from our countless excursions to the bar, or my feelings might be hurt, since the only attention I drew was from guys deciding whether or not they could roll me.

I see Sister Cat approaching us and give her a friendly wave. She smiles in return.

"Sister Cat, nice to see you again," I say.

"Lovely to see you again as well, dear."

"This is my partner, Astra."

They shake hands and then Sister Cat turns to me. "I'm afraid Sergeant Turner isn't here today."

"Oh, that's all right. I actually didn't need to see him. He was very helpful," I say. "I actually came to talk to you."

"To me?"

I nod. "The other day, you'd mentioned you had a fleet of vans for your Meals on Wheels program?"

"Yes, but as I mentioned, only one of them is working right now, unfortunately. We just haven't had the money to get them repaired."

"That's all right. I was wondering if I could have a look at them."

"Oh, well, I suppose that would be all right," she says. "They're around the back, behind the dormitory. I'd take you out there myself, but I'm right in the middle of lunch service."

"That's fine, we can find them ourselves," I say and give her a warm smile. "I appreciate your help. Again."

"May I ask why you need to see the vans?"

"It's part of our investigation. I'm afraid I can't say much right now, but as soon as I can, I'll fill you in."

She looks a little concerned, but hands me a ring of keys anyway. Then she offers me a weak smile and a nod before turning away and heading back to the serving tables to finish up with the lunch service, leaving Astra and I to our own devices. So we head out to the parking lot behind the dormitory and find four dark panel vans, each of them emblazoned with the St. Bernard's insignia.

"You don't really believe that sweet old nun has anything to do with this, do you?" Astra asks.

"Of course not. I think that somebody is taking advantage of her," I reply. "Or to be more specific, is taking advantage of her vans."

"How so?"

"Sergeant Turner told me he saw a dark panel van with an angel on the side being used to abduct Tyler Salters, who as you know, later turned up dead," I say. "And the night Tracy Webster was abducted, I saw the back end of a dark van. I didn't see the insignia, it was too far around the corner for that, but it was definitely a dark panel van."

"And the puzzle pieces keep falling into place."

"That they do. And hopefully the picture they're forming is the right one."

We check out the vans, and as Sister Cat reported, three of them look like they haven't moved from their spots in a year or more. They're coated in a thick layer of dust, there are cobwebs hanging from the wheel wells, and two of them have flats. The fourth van, though, looks freshly washed and detailed.

I use the keys to open the rear doors and am immediately assaulted by the acrid punch of bleach.

"Wow," I note. "Somebody really wanted to cover something up in here."

I step back, my eyes watering from the fumes. Covering her mouth, Astra hops up into the van and looks around. She squats down just behind the driver's seat and looks at the floor paneling closely.

"Looks like they missed a spot," she calls back.

"What do you have?"

She climbs out of the van and steps away, taking a few deep breaths to flush out the stench of the bleach. She looks at me and grins.

"I think we have a crime scene," she says.

I'm tempted to call Morris and have him send Sofia down here with a luminol kit just to see if she can pick anything up. I'd hate to jam up Sister Cat by taking her one good van out of commission, but I don't know that we have much of a choice.

There might still be evidence inside the van. Of course, I'm still not convinced that Sofia isn't part of it, so if I call her down here and she turns out to be part of this cult, she'll destroy whatever evidence is in there.

But I think there's another way.

"I have an idea," I say.

"Oh man, I hate it when you say it like that," Astra replies. "That usually means we're going to get into some trouble."

"I thought you liked getting into trouble," I say with a grin.

"Very different kind of trouble," she says. "Very different."

We close up the van, and I slip the keys into my pocket. We walk back into the mission and we both head over to the serving lines and offer to help. We work the rest of the lunch shift, then help clean up when it's over. After that, we grab a can of soda and sit down at the table to wait for Sister Cat. She comes over a few minutes later and sits down with us.

"Well, I certainly do appreciate you helping us out today, ladies," she says. "We were a little busier than usual. It was nice being able to help so many who needed it."

"It was," I reply, and actually mean it.

"So, can you tell me why you were looking at the van?" she asks.

"Sister Cat, are you aware of all the murders going on in the city?" I ask.

She nods, a look of sadness in her eyes. "I am aware. And it's terrible. Such a waste of life. It just breaks my heart."

"Mine too. And that's what we're here trying to stop," I tell her.

"That would be a wonderful thing."

"The problem is that we believe your van was used in commission of at least one of those murders," I say.

Sister Cat's face blanches as she looks at me. Her mouth opens and closes, but no words come out. I think the look of disbelief on her face is genuine, and I don't pick up any sense of falseness or deception in her. I quickly glance at Astra, who gives me a subtle shake of the head. She agrees with my assessment.

"How could that be possible?" she asks. "The van is only used to deliver food to people who need it."

"Have you ever given out spare keys?" Astra asks.

She shakes her head. "Absolutely not," she replies. "It's not that I don't trust people, but those vans, or rather that van, is all we have. Without it, we wouldn't be able to run the Meals on Wheels program. So no, I haven't given spare keys out."

Astra and I both nod, but it's my turn to ask a question. "All right, so who does your regular driving for the Meals program?"

"That would be David," she says. "He's a lovely young man. Strong in his faith and dedicated to helping the needy. There is absolutely zero chance that he is involved with something like a murder."

"That's wonderful to hear. And I'm sure he is a lovely," I say. "I'm going to need to speak with him, though."

"I don't understand," she says, sounding heartbroken.

"I'm not saying that David was directly involved," I say. "But that van has been implicated in two abductions that resulted in murders now, Sister Cat. If David isn't the one doing this, we need to find out who he's loaned the van to."

"We're terribly sorry to upset you like this, Sister Cat," Astra says. "My partner and I don't do delicate or subtle very well. But it's vitally important that we speak with David..."

Astra lets her voice trail off, obviously wanting Sister Cat to supply the last name. Which she does. Grudgingly.

"David Whitscomb," she says. "And he works at his father's hardware store. Whistcomb and Son. Please, go talk to him. You'll see that he doesn't know anything about any abductions or murders. I promise you that."

"Thank you, Sister Cat. We really appreciate your help," Astra says. "And I hope you're right, that he had nothing to do with it."

"Thank you, Sister Cat," I say as I climb to my feet and give her shoulder a reassuring squeeze. "And don't worry. Everything is going to be all right."

We leave her sitting at her table, her keys still in my pocket, looking utterly miserable. Like a woman who just turned her own child into the secret police. I hate to jam her up, but the van is a crime scene, after all.

THIRTY-FOUR

Whitscomb & Son Hardware; Briar Glen, WA

With Home Depot and Lowes elsewhere in town, Whitscomb & Son is one of the last independent hardware stores left in the city. And they're making a good go of it, as business seems flush. Astra and I wait by the door, chatting amongst ourselves as we wait for the crowd to thin.

We spotted David right off. He's a tall, gangly kid with a full head of dark, wildly curly hair. It's the kind of hair women pay hundreds of dollars to get. He's pale, too thin for his height, and has black horn-rimmed glasses. He's dressed in blue jeans, a plaid short sleeved shirt, black Chucks, and of course, the company apron around his torso.

As the crowd finally thins and there's a lull in the crush of humanity, David spots us and walks over, a wide smile on his face.

"Anything in particular I can help you ladies with?" he asks.

"Actually yes, David," I say. "You can tell us who you lend Sister Cat's van to."

If he grew any paler, he'd be translucent. David works his mouth, obviously trying to work up a little spit to get it working again. His eyes are wide behind his spectacles and his face is etched with fear.

"I — I don't know what you're talking about," he stammers, though it sounds more like a question to me.

"Look kid, lying to FBI agents is a crime," Astra replies. "You do know that, don't you?"

He shakes his head as dots of perspiration form on his brow. "I'm not lying," he tells us. "And you're not FBI."

Moving in unison, Astra and I both flip out our credentials, and when he sees them, I'm half-convinced he's about to wet himself. He somehow manages to maintain control of his bladder, which I find impressive.

"Who did you loan the van to, David? We know you loaned it to somebody because neither of us think you're capable of murder," I state. "But, if you continue to deny it and insist you didn't loan the van out, I guess you're taking the full weight of a murder rap all on your own."

"Do you know what happens to guys like you in prison?" Astra says. "Let's just say you wouldn't walk right ever again."

I shrug. "Wouldn't matter because he'd be spending the last of his life behind bars. They won't mind if he walks funny."

"Oh, they're going to love you in prison, David. I mean really love you."

"Nightly," I say.

"Sometimes more than once a night."

"Stop it. Just stop it," he hisses. "You're both lying. I'm not going to prison."

"Afraid you are," I press. "Unless you tell us who you loaned the van to."

He sighs. "He paid me a hundred bucks every time he used it," he stammers, careful to keep his voice low. "It was his idea, and I didn't kill anybody. I swear it."

"And who is he, David?" Astra growls.

"Highsmith," he says. "Tony Highsmith. But please don't tell him I told you. He'll kill me. Like literally."

"And where do we find Tony Highsmith?"

"He works at Roland's Garage," he says. "Now, if you don't mind, I need to get back to work."

Without waiting for our reply, David turns and all but sprints off. I turn to Astra and grin.

"He'll never walk right again?" I ask. "Kind of morbid, don't you think?"

She shrugs. "But effective."

"Too true," I reply.

We turn and walk out of the hardware store, bound for Roland's Garage.

"Tony Highsmith?" Astra asks.

The man underneath the car doesn't say anything. With as loud as the music is in here, he may not have heard her, so I walk over and turn it off. The shouting and cursing coming from underneath the car is enough to make a sailor blush. He rolls out from underneath the car on the rolling creeper and jumps to his feet.

He's a large man with wide shoulders and biceps as big as my thighs. He's got blonde hair, green eyes, and grease covering most of his face. He's not a pretty man, that's for sure. And his demeanor only makes him even less attractive. Tony Highsmith is a man who swings first and asks questions later. If he bothers asking questions at all.

"Who the hell are you?" he growls.

Astra and I flash him our creds and his expression goes from righteous indignation to terrified in the blink of an eye. That tells me right off that we're on the right track. But then he turns and dashes out the back door, quick as a rabbit. Astra and I have just enough time to share a look of irritation before we take off after him.

I'm first through the door and have just enough time to register the steel pipe coming for my head to throw myself to the side. I feel the wind from the pipe brush past my face, missing me by scant inches. But I hit the ground and shoulder roll, popping back up to face him. He comes at me, his face twisted with rage, gripping the pipe with both hands like a baseball bat.

"Tony, stop," I say. "We just want to talk."

But Tony doesn't stop. Instead he takes a home run cut, one that very likely would have knocked my head clean off my shoulders if he'd connected. But his swing is sloppy and he's off balance, so I sidestep it easily, throwing my elbow back with as much force as I can muster. The connection with his face sends a jolt up my arm and into my shoulder that hurts like hell. But I feel his nose give way with a satisfying crunch that makes it all worth it.

When I turn, I find him bull rushing me again, blood streaming down his face, and murder in his eyes. The man is a lumbering ox who doesn't know the first thing about keeping your balance when you fight. Obviously. But it works to my advantage. He's probably used to his size intimidating people into backing down from a fight. And though he is a frightening looking man, I don't back down from a fight.

As he closes in on me, I feint as if I'm going to spin to the left. Tony bites on the move, so I spin around to the right and drive my foot into the back of his knee. I hear something pop and then his leg buckles under him, sending him sprawling face first into the dirt. He howls in agony and clutches his knee as he rolls around on the ground, reminding me of a soccer player.

I step over to him, careful to stay out of range of those long, thick arms and give him my sweetest smile.

"You know, this all could have been avoided if you'd just talked to us," I tell him. "But now you're going to jail for the attempted murder of a federal officer."

"Screw you," he hisses, his voice tight with pain. "I don't answer to the laws of men. Only God can judge me."

"Well, I'm pretty sure that's not how our judicial system works, so roll onto your belly and put your hands behind your back," I say.

He glares at me, pain etched into his every feature. "You broke my knee."

"That's entirely possible. But if you roll over onto your belly and let me put these handcuffs on you, we can see about getting you some help for that knee."

He hesitates but finally complies. I move in quickly, planting my knee in the middle of his back, and clap a pair of handcuffs on him, saying a silent word that this gorilla of a man doesn't snap them.

I get to my feet and dust off my hands to find Astra leaning against the doorway, her arms folded over her chest, a broad grin on her face.

"Thanks for the help," I say.

"Help? You had the situation well in hand," she offers. "It was impressive. Really. The guy is like four times your size and you destroyed him. I was too in awe to help, to be honest."

I laugh. "Shut up and call it in. I think we're going to have to take him to the hospital before we question him," I say. "I heard something in his knee pop. Probably tore some ligaments or something."

"Well maybe if you weren't such a brute..."

I laugh and turn away as she pulls her phone out of her pocket and walk back over to Tony. I squat down in front of him, my expression suddenly dropping.

"Tell me about this little murder cult you're part of," I say. "Who else is a member? Who's in charge."

"We are Manus Domini Dei. We are legion, and we do not answer to the laws of men — "

"Yeah, I got that the first time you said that," I cut him off. "But who's your Jim Jones? Who's leading this cult?"

"I want a lawyer," he spits.

"You don't answer to the laws of men, but you want a man who practices the laws of men, to defend you from having to answer to the laws of men? Is that about right? Is that what I'm hearing?"

"Lawyer. Now."

"Who's your leader, Tony? Who gives the kill orders? Who picks out the targets?" I ask.

"Are you deaf, woman? I said get me a lawyer," he demands. "Get me a lawyer now. That means, stop asking me questions."

I sigh and get to my feet, looking down at him with contempt. "Well, shockingly, you're not as dumb as you look. Unfortunately."

THIRTY-FIVE

Pacific Crest Motor Court; Briar Glen, WA

DARKNESS HAS FALLEN by the time we finish up at the hospital with Sheriff Morris. Tony got his public defender who promptly shut us down and kicked us out, citing his client's emotional and physical exhaustion as a reason to postpone the questioning. Said his client would not be answering any questions under duress, and not until he was feeling better. He even hinted at filing a lawsuit against me for excessive force as the cherry on top.

I'm frustrated. I feel like we're so close to cracking this case. All we need to do is crack Tony. But that's something I feel might be easier said than done. I have a few cards up my sleeve to play though. I just need to get into his room to play them.

"We'll get him. Don't worry," Astra says. "The guy is going to fold."

"I wish I had that kind of confidence," I mutter, keeping my eyes on the road ahead.

"He will. We're going to make him fold."

"We will," I say, but without much conviction in my voice.

"Oh hey, I meant to tell you. Dr. Carville is off the hook," Astra says. "I heard from my friend and he found evidence that her records had been tampered with after she'd keyed them into her computer. My guess is that if you look at her handwritten notes, they won't match what's in the system."

"Great. Another apology I owe Sheriff Morris."

She shrugs. "Look at it this way, you've had enough practice that you should be pretty good at it by now."

I laugh. "Shut up."

We ride in silence for a few minutes, each of us thinking about today, and what it means. Snatching up Tony could be the key we need to turn the lock that opens this thing and gives us a look behind the curtain. He could be the key to figuring out who's calling the shots and taking him down.

"I'm beat," I sigh. "I need a shower. And some sleep."

"You and me both."

"So how do we attack this guy? I'm not sure threatening him with prison is going to help. Pretty sure he's been there before and it doesn't scare him anymore," I say.

"I don't know. The thought of spending the next, oh I don't know, lifetime behind bars might be enough to sway him to give up his leader."

"I wouldn't hold my breath," I say. "That guy is ride or die with his little murder cult. I saw it in his face. He'd rather cut out his own tongue than rat on his boys."

"Well, we could always give him that option, of course."

I laugh as I take the turnoff that leads into the parking lot of our luxurious home away from home. I cut the engine and climb out, still pondering how we're going to attack this guy and get him to fold.

I'm already heading for the door when I hear the sharp

crack of the shot. I yank my sidearm and throw myself to the ground, then roll back behind the car.

"Astra," I call out. "Astra, answer me."

I don't hear her. Panic floods through me, but I shove it down. No time to freak out. I have to respond. I get to my knees and raise my head just over the hood. The crack of the rifle repeats, forcing me back down behind the car again. There's a hard thump and I see splintered wood flying as the bullet tears through the column that fronts the bungalow.

"Astra! Call out, dammit! Astra!"

That she's not answering can't be a good sign. That ripple of fear only surges even faster in my veins. Who in the hell is out there shooting at me? A dozen different names go through my head, including Sheriff Morris tying up loose ends. I want to doubt it, but right now I don't know anything other than the fact that I'm taking fire and I'm positive that my best friend's been hit.

I need to get to her to see how severe her injuries are. I need to get her to the hospital. But before I can do anything, I need to get rid of that shooter. I raise my head again and hear the report of the rifle followed by the heavy thud of a bullet slamming into my car. I quickly jump to my feet, assume a shooter's stance, and start firing off rounds in the direction the rifle shot came from.

I empty my clip and squat down to reload when I hear the crashing through the undergrowth of the forest. I slam the magazine home, chamber a round, and get to my feet again. No shots come, but I can still hear somebody crashing through the shrubs and trees out there, running away as fast as their legs can carry them. It's a shame. I much rather would have put him down.

Rushing around the car, I fall to my knees beside Astra. She's not moving. I lay my hand against her and can't feel a pulse in her neck. My heart is thundering in my chest and my stomach is turning over on itself. The taste of bile is strong in the back of my throat and my vision is obscured by the shimmering quality of tears that are streaming down my face. But I push it away. No. Not now. I can't panic.

I flip her on her back and immediately start CPR on her chest.

"Somebody help!" I cry out.

Suddenly remembering that my phone is in my pocket, I pull it out and call emergency services. Once the bus is on its way, I call Sheriff Morris and tell him what happened, still frantically pushing, compressing, checking for a pulse, listening close for a heartbeat. He's not out of breath from running, nor does it sound like he's outside, so he couldn't possibly be the shooter.

I'm still performing CPR when the bus rolls in, its lights rotating, creating a wild, strobing light around the motel grounds.

The EMT's run over and try to pull me away, but I can't force myself to let go of Astra's hand, cold and clammy though it is.

"Ma'am, you have to let go of her."

A second EMT grabs me by the shoulders and pulls me away as they go to work on her. Slowly and reluctantly, tears still streaming down my face, I get to my feet and step back, watching in horror as they tend to her wound. There's just so much blood — too much blood — and I instinctively know it's not good.

I sink to my knees, tears streaming down my face, my hands covered in Astra's blood, saying a silent prayer to anybody who might be listening for her to make it. For her to live.

THIRTY-SIX

Industrial District; Briar Glen, WA

THE ROOM IS FILLED with our brethren. There is fear and tension in the air for the first time. We've donned our robes, and torchlight gleams off all of our masks, but there is no celebration to be had tonight. Our ritual of purification and renewal has been interrupted by the rash and foolish actions of two men. Everything we have worked for – the utopia we have made of this town – has been jeopardized, if not outright destroyed, by two stupid men.

He stands in the middle of the circle, all eyes fixed on him. He's not in his robes or mask, and his eyes are wide and filled with fear. As they should be. I step forward, pulling the cowl of my robe down, and take off my mask. I glare at him with every ounce of contempt I can muster as I step to him, our faces scant inches apart.

"What have you done?" My voice is low, but it echoes around the vast open space of the factory floor.

"I did what had to be done," he replies, his voice quavering.

"We couldn't just sit back and hope this problem went away. We had to act."

"We had to do nothing. The situation was well in hand," I spit. "You have destroyed everything we've built, Mayor O'Brien. This town you've ruled like your own personal fiefdom for the last twenty years will now fall, and everything we have done in His name will be torn asunder. It is all for nothing now. Because of you."

"We can still salvage this. I can — "

I lash out, delivering a vicious backhand that rocks his head to the side. A thin rivulet of blood trickles from the corner of his mouth and he looks at me, his eyes wide with shock.

"How dare you lay hands on me," he mewls.

"How dare me? I told you to do nothing. I told you the situation was well in hand," I roar.

"Well in hand, was it? Then how is they got to Tony?" he argues. "It was only a matter of time before they connected Tony to the rest of us. Hell, he would have flipped on all of us to cut himself a better deal. You know that's true."

"We will never know now, because you have taken the choice out of our hands," I fire back. "You have made a decision for this entire group. And what makes your stupidity even worse is that you didn't even kill them. Both of those FBI agents are alive. Well, the other one may still die, but Blake Wilder wasn't even hit. You took this upon yourself, without our knowledge or consent, and you failed, Mayor. You failed and doomed us all in the process."

"I had to do something. We had to do something."

"You broke faith with us, Mayor O'Brien. You broke faith with our people."

He straightens up and looks at me. "Well, I'm sorry you're not going to get your old job back, Sheriff Montez."

I grit my teeth and clench my fists, feeling the rage surging through me. I want to lash out and beat this man to a pulp. All of my plans have been destroyed because he let his fear overcome him. I had perfectly set up Morris and his secret lover, Carville. Years of careful planning, setting up the perfect frame that would ruin them both, and allow me to step back into my old position atop the Sheriff's department, gone. Like a puff of smoke on the breeze, it's all gone.

And there is only one man to blame for it.

I look around at the circle. Even though their faces are hidden by masks, I would know my people anywhere. Members of the city council. Doctors. Lawyers. The people in this room are the ruling elite of Briar Glen. We made this city what it is today through our shared grief and pain. Through our sacrifice, determination, sheer will, and above all else, honoring our God and doing what He commands of us.

He showed the seven of us the way, that day He brought us all together in that dingy warehouse. St. Bernard's hosted a support group for survivors of violence. My own wife had just recently been murdered. She was so young and so beautiful. The love of my life. And she'd been snatched away from me in the prime of our lives.

But I was not alone. My story was echoed by the others in the group. Each one of them had lost somebody they loved to the animals that once roamed the streets of Briar Glen. But with God's vision and the determination and will he'd gifted to us, we took our city back. We got rid of the vermin in our town. Cut out the cancerous rot. We delivered God's true justice to the criminals and evildoers.

Oh, there were many shaky, fearful days early on. We always feared that we would be caught and that our dreams would be over. But the seven of us soldiered on, steadfast in the belief in our work. In our mission. In our faith in one another.

And today, Briar Glen is one of the safest, most beautiful cities in a country that's rotting from the inside out.

We had even bigger plans in mind. Things we wanted to do and changes we wanted to make. But that's all over now because of this man. Because of his fear and his lack of faith in us, and in our good works.

"A chain is only as strong as the weakest link," I say. "And tonight, you have proven that the weakest link is you, Mayor. You have condemned us all because they will come. Now they will come."

"I did what I had to do to protect this town, and protect this group," he says haughtily.

"You failed. And your failure has cost us everything," I say. "You did not keep your faith. And now, it is time to deliver God's justice upon you."

O'Brien's eyes widen comically large and his mouth falls open. Before he can utter a word though, I pull the gun out from beneath my robes, press it to his forehead, and squeeze the trigger. The recoil vibrates my arm, all the way up into my shoulder, and I watch as a spray of red mist bursts from the back of O'Brien's head. His eyes remain wide open but become unfocused.

He stands there wobbling on his feet for a moment, his mouth opening and closing like a fish on dry land. He takes a staggering step toward me but falls to his knees. O'Brien's eyes are on me, but I'm not sure he's actually seeing me, as a low keening sound comes from his throat.

With a sound like "gah" bursting from his mouth, O'Brien slumps over, hitting the concrete floor with a meaty thud.

He says no more. He doesn't move. And is still. As he will be forevermore.

I turn to my people. I can smell the fear wafting off of them. The uncertainty. They don't know what comes next. But I do.

"They will come for us, Brothers and Sisters," I intone, my voice reverberating around the room. "It is only a matter of time now."

All of them are looking at me, beseeching me with their eyes to provide them with deliverance. With the way forward. But there is no way forward. There is only now. And now is when we make our stand.

"We have two choices. We can run. We can be cowards and break faith like this man at my feet," I call out. "Or we can stand and fight the forces of darkness. Perhaps we won't win. But we can make sure they know there will be others like us. Others who will take up our mantle and fight the darkness. We can make this world a better place for our kids, and their kids after them, by showing the world that the darkness can be fought and beaten."

As the echo of my voice fades away, the only sound is the crackling of our torches. I can sense a sadness that our dream of utopia is over. But I also sense a grim determination in all of them. Nobody has left and I can feel everybody gearing up for the coming fight.

"I love you all, my brothers and sisters," I call out, my voice ringing true and bright. "And it is my honor to meet the enemy with you. Now. Steady your nerves. Calm your heart. Put your faith in your brethren. And arm yourselves. Nos servo fidem."

"Nos servo fidem!"

The eruption of applause and cheers of joy, of salvation, ring out through the night. It is a balm to my soul. If this is to be our end, it will be an end unlike anything the world has ever seen before.

I pull out my cellphone and make the call.

THIRTY-SEVEN

Pacific General Hospital; Briar Glen, WA

I SIT PERCHED on the edge of the chair in the waiting room, my hands clasped in front of me, rocking back and forth. The surreal nature of it all washes over me yet again. I can't believe I'm sitting here waiting to hear whether my best friend is going to live or not. I never in a million years thought I would be here, in this position right now. I mean, I know we work for the Bureau, and there are always the chances something like this could happen. I just never thought it actually would.

"How are you holdin' up?"

Sheriff Morris sits down in the chair next to me, his face etched with concern. I bite my thumbnail, which is a nasty habit I've had since childhood. But it's one that only rears its ugly head in times of great stress. And I'd say this qualifies. It beats smoking. Or drinking myself into oblivion.

"About how you'd expect," I tell him.

"They tell you anything yet?"

I shake my head. "They're not telling me anything other than she's in surgery."

"She's a tough one. I'd lay money on her pullin' through just fine," he says.

We sit in silence for a moment as my emotions churn inside of me. Morris' presence is comforting and I'm glad he's here. More than that, I'm glad that all of my questions and concerns about him were wrong. I look over at him and give him a shaky smile.

"I owe you an apology. Sofia too," I say. "Turns out you were right, and this was a frame job all along."

He nods, as if he expected the truth would win out. Eventually. But then he turns to me and gives me a gentle smile.

"I can't blame you for chargin' at me as hard as you did. If I had the evidence you had in hand, I'd have done the same thing," he admits.

"Well all the same, I jumped to conclusions," I tell him. "And I'm sorry."

"No apology needed. But I'll take it and thank you for it all the same."

"That leaves the question of who's behind all of this," I say. "Who would want to frame you and why?"

He shakes his head. "That I don't know. If I had to wager a guess though, I'd say it's the same person who came after you and Astra."

"Obviously, it's the head of this cult," I say. "But who is it?"

"That's something else I don't know."

"I wish I could go down into Highsmith's room and shake it out of him."

"That wouldn't be admissible in court."

I grin. "No, but it might make me feel a bit better."

"You're a good woman, Blake Wilder," he says. "You've got a good heart."

"You've got a pretty good heart yourself, Sheriff."

As we sit in silence, I ponder everything I've learned so far. Try to piece things together in a way that makes sense. It would be so much easier to drag it out of Tony, but I know that Morris is right. Nothing he says to me under duress will be admissible in court. And whoever's behind this would walk free. And after all we've been through, I'm not about to let that happen. This unsub is either going to prison, or into a hole in the ground. There is no other way this ends.

I run my hands through my hair, pulling on it hard in frustration. But then something occurs to me. I turn to the Sheriff.

"Tell me something," I say. "You ran for election against Montez, right?"

He nods, a small grin on his lips. "Beat him too. So bad he didn't even show for the second election."

"What if he's behind this? What if he's the cult leader? What if he's the one who's trying to frame you?"

"Now why would he do that?"

"How did the election go? How were relations between you during the race?"

He chuckles. "It was contentious all right," he said. "He didn't feel that one of his subordinates should be runnin' against him. Said it was disrespectful."

"Why did you run?"

"Well, Montez is a tyrant. Rules with an iron fist. It demoralized the entire department," he says. "I thought there was a better way. So I ran."

"He take it hard that he lost?"

"I've heard that, yeah. But then I heard he found religion and calmed — "

"Oh my God. It's him. It's Montez," I say. All the pieces suddenly fit. My mind is like wildfire. "He's been planning and plotting this for years. He and his cult were killing while he was the Sheriff. So he spends all these years after you deposed him plotting and planning, laying traps with the idea of destroying you and your reputation."

"To what end?"

"If you're forced to resign in disgrace, I assume the city council or mayor appoints a new interim Sheriff?" I ask.

He nods. "Yeah."

"Then that's it. That's what he was gunning for. Sending you down in flames so he could emerge victorious and regain his job," I say. "Which also tells me that he's got allies on the council. Maybe even the mayor himself."

He blows out a long breath. "Makes sense. But why wouldn't he just challenge me again two years ago?"

"Maybe his plan needed more time than that. He needed you not just to lose, but really fall from grace. That gave him time to plant all these murders – that's why in the last four years things have shot up so much."

He considers this with a nod, the information weighing heavy on him.

"You've also got to know he probably has members within the ranks of your deputies," I add.

"Nothin' I can do about that right now. Not until they reveal themselves. But I know I got some good ones too. Men and women I trust with my life."

"That's good. Keep them close."

All of these forces being arrayed against him are disturbing, to say the least. It makes for very dangerous times for the Sheriff. My cellphone rings in my pocket, so I slip it out and connect the call, already expecting Rosie and/or Potts to read me the riot act for Astra getting shot. But when the caller speaks, I don't recognize his voice.

"Is your friend dead yet?" he says.

"Who is this?"

"The man who put your friend where she is right now."

I feel the rage starting to build up inside. "Who is this?"

"I think you know who I am"

"Montez," I say.

"Give the girl a prize."

"I'm going to kill you," I hiss.

"Maybe. But I got a thousand bucks that says you don't ever get close enough."

"I guess we'll see about that."

"Why wait? Come on out to the old Montez factory," he says. "Meet me one on one and let's settle this."

"What's there to settle?"

There's a pause on the other end of the line, but then he speaks again. "It's because of you that all I've worked and sacrificed for is now gone. My dreams are in tatters, and it's your fault."

"I think you're mistaken. I haven't done anything. I didn't even know who you were until tonight."

"Well, now you know. Come meet me, Blake Wilder. Let's settle this as adults."

"What's there to settle? You lost this little war," I fire back.

'How about this... if you don't come, I'll make sure your little friend doesn't get out of Briar Glen alive. I mean, she might not make it anyway, but she does..."

The rage inside of me is white hot and I disconnect the call. Threatening me is one thing. But threatening my loved one is something else entirely.

"Don't do it," Morris says.

"Do what?"

"Whatever it is that has that 'I'm going to kill you' expression on your face," he replies. "You should stay here. Be with Astra when she wakes up."

"The doctors already said she'd be in surgery all night," I

tell him. "It was Montez on the phone. Said if I don't meet him, he'll make sure Astra dies in the hospital."

"I hate to sound like a callous jerk, but there's a chance she might anyway," he tells me. "Don't throw your life and your career away for this man. He's not worth it. Trust me, I know firsthand."

"He shot my best friend."

"And he's responsible for how many murders?" he fires back. "We know what he's capable of, Blake. Plus, he's got God knows how many people out there with him. You'd be walkin' into a buzzsaw."

"Good thing I never leave home unprepared."

"Blake — "

"I have to do this, Sheriff. I take monsters off the board. That's what I do," I say. "And Montez is a monster. So I have to go do my job."

He sighs. "Can't talk you out of it, huh?"

"Afraid not."

"Then count me in," he replies. "This is my town, I'm the Sheriff, and if you're gonna go in with both guns blazing, I'm going to be by your side."

I look at him for a long moment and see that there's no talking him out of it. He's a stubborn old goat. But I suppose the same could be said about me. Truth is, two against an army of religious fanatics sounds better than lonely old me against that army of religious fanatics.

"All right," I nod. "Let's go."

THIRTY-EIGHT

Industrial District; Briar Glen, WA

WE PULL to a stop about a quarter mile from the warehouse and get out of the car. I can see the building of the warehouse. It's set on a piece of land that juts out into the ocean a small way. It's run down but isn't falling down like some of the other buildings around this area of the city that's been left to rot.

"Lots of windows," I note.

"He's gonna see us comin' from a ways off."

"Maybe," I say as I look around. "But then, maybe not."

"Unless you can turn yourself invisible, there's that one spit of land the place is sittin' on. One way of approach."

I flash him a smile. "There's one other way."

I point to the narrow strip of sand that runs along a tall ocean wall. It's narrow and we're going to get our feet wet, but I don't think we can be seen. Morris looks at me and nods, impressed.

I pop open the trunk of my car and remove the false bottom. Underneath it is an array of weapons. I reach in and take the AR-15 and load it up, making sure to pack plenty of magazines into my belt. I then remove a 9mm Glock and tuck it into the back of my pants. Morris outfits himself the same way.

"This is a lot of guns," he says.

I shrug. "You should see what I've got at home."

"You obviously take your Second Amendment very seriously."

"Yes I do."

"All right then. Let's go," he says.

We cross to the ocean wall, using the trees and bushes for cover. We drop down from the top of the seawall down onto the sand, the water coming up to our ankles immediately, just as I thought it might. But wet socks aren't going to keep me from finishing this.

Crouching down, we move single file, me in front and Morris behind me. We cover the quarter mile in good time, reaching the end of the seawall, then use the pits and crags in the surface to quickly scale it. The moon is bright in the sky overhead, raining down a monochromatic silvery light over us. It would have been nice to have had some cloud cover tonight. But nothing is ever easy.

We make it to a row of windows. Or at least, the window frames. The actual glass was busted out long ago. I poke my head up and over but see nothing. I nod to Morris and we climb over the sill, quietly dropping down to the concrete floor. Weapons at the ready, we move room to room, looking for any sign of life. As of yet, there's nothing.

We're moving past a staircase, moving deeper into the ground floor when I hear a stifled sneeze. I look up in time to see a man wheeling around, an automatic rifle trained on us. I throw myself backward, crashing into Morris, knocking him to the floor, and we take cover underneath the side of the stairs. We quickly get ourselves untangled and back on our feet. The chatter of gunfire is impossibly loud in here. I clamp my hands over my ears.

The firing stops, so I swing into view and fire a burst up at the gunman. He grunts and falls away. Not taking any chances, I rush up the stairs, weapon leading the way.

"Blake, stop! Are you nuts?" Morris calls after me, though I hear his heavy footsteps pounding up the stairs not two feet behind me.

I reach the landing and find the man I'd hit. He's down in a spreading pool of crimson gore. I kick his weapon away and continue down the corridor, moving from room to room with Morris at my back.

At the end of the corridor, I push through a set of tall, oak doors to find who I'm looking for. There are a dozen people kneeling in front of Montez, who's standing on a podium behind them. All dozen people have their weapons trained on us, and Montez just laughs.

"Well, this wasn't very smart," Montez mutters. "But welcome all the same. Please, please come in."

"Yeah, I guess you're right about this too," I whisper to Morris.

"Maybe one of these days you'll listen to me."

"Yeah, maybe."

"Robert," Montez intones. "I didn't expect to see you here. What a pleasant surprise. And I have to say, getting to kill you along with her, well... that's just a special treat. Icing on the cake, as it were."

"You've lost your mind, Montez," Morris says.

"Quite the contrary. I found my way. We all found our way,' he calls back, his voice echoing across the cavernous room. "We found a God who loves us and a God who has empowered us to create this world as we see fit."

"By murdering innocent people?" I ask. "What God would ever condone the murder of innocent people?"

"Innocent? Is that supposed to be funny, Agent Wilder? These were animals who escaped justice," he says. "So we delivered God's true justice."

"We are Manus Domini Dei," the twelve kneeling on the ground chant in unison, which sends a chill down my spine. "Nos servo fidem."

When I spoke of this being a cult, I don't think I quite envisioned exactly what that would look like. Well, this is what a cult looks like. Twelve people in robes with the hoods pulled up, and creepy masks on their faces, chanting in unison like they're all linked to one hive mind. It's the most bizarre and disturbing thing I've ever seen. And I've seen some things in my time at the Bureau.

"Manus Domini Dei?" I call. "The Hand of God? A little pretentious and delusions of grandeur-esque, don't you think?"

Montez chuckles. "I would not expect a small mind like yours to comprehend what we are about," he says. "For somebody like you cannot grasp concepts like faith and fidelity. You cannot possibly know the bonds of fellowship like we do. Nor do you have the will it takes to do the things we've done."

"You're a chatty one, aren't you?" I fire back. "How about you and me settle this the old fashioned way. The two of us. Bare knuckle. Winner goes home, loser gets a ride to the morgue?"

His laughter is deep and bellowing. "Such violence. And you call me a monster," he says. "Please, step further into the room. I'd rather not have to shoot you."

My eyes flick around the room when I see the torchlight in the room glinting off small pieces of metal. When I realize what they are, my insides almost turn to liquid right then and there. This situation has gone from bad to worse. However, now I understand why this guy continues to blather on. He's trying to stall us. Keep us in the room. That tells me the bomb is on a timer, which is the only silver lining in this.

"The room is wired," I hiss to Morris, keeping my voice low so only he can hear me.

"Wonderful," he mutters. "Ideas?"

"Step further into the room please. The both of you," Montez calls, his tone growing impatient. "It is time for us to celebrate our ascension. Well, our ascension. Your oblivion."

I look at the kneelers and see that most of them are holding their weapons awkwardly and get the idea that this is probably the first time most of them have held a gun in their lives. Silver lining number two.

"When I say fire, squeeze that trigger and run like hell," I whisper.

Knowing most of these people don't know how to hold a gun, I'm assuming most of them don't know how to fire one accurately. Better than that, I'm rolling the dice on the idea that when they're being shot at, they'll scatter like leaves in the wind. I think it stands to reason that having never held a gun, they've never been fired at, and their primal instincts for survival will kick in.

God, I'm really hoping this isn't one of those things I'll have to apologize for later. But then, if I'm wrong, we'll be dead, so I can probably skip that part.

"I said, come closer," Montez roars. "Now!"

"You heard the man," I say. "Now!"

Morris and I both fire off several bursts as we scramble backwards. I hear several shots and feel a bright, hot pain lance through my leg. I tumble to the ground, gritting my teeth, and grunt. Morris stops and starts to come back for me.

"Go, you idiot. Get out of here!" I scream. "I'm fine. It's a scratch!"

I roll back over on my butt and fire into the room again. Without waiting, I get back up and run-hop along the corridor. The bullet just grazed my leg, but it still hurts like hell. Behind me, I hear screaming and the clatter of guns hitting the deck, as well as the shuffling of footsteps. And over it all, I hear Montez bellowing to his flock, demanding they come back. Ordering them to fight. It's chaos. It's perfect.

But then I hear a thunderous roar. The building around us shakes violently. Morris and I share a look and double our efforts. We make it to the staircase as the building heaves like a giant beast in its death throes. Plaster and concrete are falling down from above like a snowstorm from hell.

"Come on!" Morris calls.

I throw my arm over his shoulder, and together we scramble down the stairs as fast as we can. I hear concrete cracking and splitting, the loud, booming crash of chunks of it falling. The ground is trembling beneath us and the window still seems miles away. Behind us, I hear men and women screaming. They're on the staircase, but then I hear a violent rending sound, and a thunderous crack loud enough to rend the heavens. The panicked screaming behind us intensifies, but the roar of the building crashing down around them drowns out their cries.

I'm so caught up in the destruction behind me, that I'm not aware of what's happening in front of me. The next thing I know, I'm sailing out of the window. I feel weightless for a moment, and then I hit the hard packed dirt outside with a grunt as the breath is driven from my lungs.

But then Morris is there, dragging me to my feet, and helping haul me away from the building. We turn around in time to see the factory cave in on itself, the walls collapsing into a giant pile of rubble. Smoke billows up from the structure and tall orange flames lick at the sky overhead.

There is no screaming coming from inside anymore, and I see no movement on the pile of concrete and wood timber before us.

"Think anybody got out?" I ask.

"Doubt it," Morris says. "Montez started shooting those people trying to escape."

"So much for the bonds of fellowship."

"Having a building falling down on top of you definitely tells you who's with you to the end."

We stand in silence for several long moments. As we contemplate the scene before us, I feel the blood spilling down my leg and into my sock. The pain is intense. It's like the worst papercut I've ever had, magnified by a billion. Morris looks down at it, then up at me.

"I guess we need to get you back to the hospital after all," he says.

"It's just a scratch."

"Still needs attention. Stop being a mule."

I jerk my thumb at the burning pile of rubble. "What about that?"

"We'll call it in from the road."

"Fair enough," I reply. "Oh, and Sheriff?"

"Yeah?"

"Thanks for saving my butt back there."

He smiles. "Anytime."

THIRTY-NINE

UW Medical Center; Seattle, WA

"How's Sheriff Hottie doing?" Astra asks.

I roll my eyes. It's been a few weeks since the events in Briar Glen and Astra has not stopped talking about Sheriff Morris. She's got a bit of a crush. Word of the building collapse and the deaths of all the cultists got out and Grant, of course, seizing the opportunity to needle me with anything he can, has gifted me with a new nickname — Demolition Girl. Charming. Especially since it's caught on around the field office, which is really nice.

"Sheriff Morris is doing well. He said things are starting to get back to normal around there. Sort of," I say. "They've got to elect a whole new city council, and a mayor, since they were all killed in the building collapse, but he said it's a good time to start fresh... and make a few changes to the city charter. And I guess since he's temporarily the acting mayor, he can do that."

"And would one of those changes happen to be allowing him to date one Dr. Sofia Carville openly?"

"That would be a bullseye."

"It really is a shame," she says. "I mean, you were right. He absolutely fits perfectly with my daddy issues."

We share a laugh as I shift on the examination table, the paper crinkling under me. Astra and I are sitting side by side, waiting for our follow up exams. She's going to be out of action for a while. She's got rehab after she finishes healing. All in all, she was lucky. The bullet entered her upper right chest but ricocheted off a bone and exited through her shoulder, rather than turning inward on her. If that had happened, Astra would be dead right now.

It's a fact I'm cognizant of, and every time I think of what could have happened, it sends a lance of pain through my heart. I don't know what I'd do without her. Like Maisey and Aunt Annie, Astra is an integral part of my life. I'd be completely lost without her. It would be like losing a limb.

But, as she's reminded me a thousand times, it didn't happen that way. She's all right. She'll heal and will soon be back to her normal self. And by normal self, I assume she means out in the bars after work, trolling for man candy. She says often that somebody was looking out for her that night and made sure she was all right. I don't know what to believe in regard to that, but if it's true, I owe somebody one. A big one.

"Hey," I say and take her hand, giving it a firm squeeze. "I'm really glad you're all right. I was so worried. I'm just thankful you're fine, and I need to tell you that I love you. I never want you to not know."

"This is awesome. It's not often I get to see the soft and squishy side of Blake Wilder," she responds with a smile. "I wonder how long I can milk this?"

"Probably as long as you want," I smile. "Almost losing you, my best friend in the world, scared the crap out of me. It really did."

She gives me a soft smile and squeezes my hand tightly, not letting it go.

"How's your leg?" she asks.

"I'm fine. Like I've told everybody since it happened, it's nothing but a scratch," I say. "It was a graze, and not a very deep one at that."

"Yeah, but you know the Bureau, they will exercise an abundance of caution every single time," she replies. "Mostly so you have no grounds to sue them, but partly because they care."

I laugh ruefully. She's not wrong in that assessment. I've been on restricted light duty since we got back from Briar Glen. Meaning, I've had my butt parked at my desk for the last three weeks. It's been the single most annoying and humiliating experience of my life. To be chained to a desk for a scratch. I'd hate to see what they'd stick me with if they saw how badly I cut my legs shaving sometimes.

"You need to learn to relax, Wilder," she says. "Three weeks of nine to five days? Not having to do anything strenuous at the office? It sounds like heaven to me."

"That's bullcrap and you know it," I fire back with a laugh. "You're as anxious to be out on the streets catching bad guys as I am."

She looks pointedly at her arm in the sling. "I'm kind of rethinking that right about now."

"No you're not," I tell her. "You're a woman of action."

"That's definitely what the boys say."

I laugh. "What I mean is, you're not content behind a desk. You're definitely a kick in the door type of girl."

She nods. "That is true. You got me there."

We fall silent for a minute, simply enjoying the comfort of companionship between us. But then she turns to me.

"That was the first time I've really ever seen you get to be super FBI chick. You know that, right?" she asks.

"What? We've been on plenty of ops together."

She shakes her head. "We've been on plenty of other people's ops, as in backup, before," she tells me. "But this is the first time I got to see you running the show. And I have to say, I'm really impressed, Blake. You really know what you're doing, and you are one hell of a profiler."

"The same goes back to you. There's no way I would have made some of those connections that helped crack the case without you."

"We're both pretty fantastic and damn good at what we do."

I nod. "I'll drink to that."

"Believe me, when I'm off these meds and back to normal, I'll be drinking to everything," she says. "I'm gonna tie one on like you wouldn't believe."

"Oh, trust me, I believe it."

We're laughing together as the curtain is pulled back and a young doctor walks in, then pulls it closed behind him. He's tall and lean, and I can tell that beneath his lab coat, that he's very fit. He has sandy blonde hair that's neatly kept and styled, eyes a deep shade of green I've never seen before, and skin so smooth, it gives him a very baby-faced look. He's got high cheekbones, a chiseled face, and a square jaw. To use Astra's words, he's gorgeous.

"Oh, I get a two for one today, huh? And it's not even my birthday," he grins, delivering the joke in an exaggerated cheesy way. "How are you guys doing? I'm Dr Mark Walton."

"Nice to meet you Dr. Walton, I'm Astra, and this is my loyal sidekick, Blake."

"Nice to meet you both," he says, though his eyes linger on mine for a moment. "So, are you guys conjoined twins or something? Both of you have something wrong that I need to look at?

"Nah. She's just here for moral support. She got shot, but

she's fine," Astra says. "I got shot and I'm not okay. I might need mouth to mouth."

"Unless you're trying to get me to suck a bullet out of you, I think that might be unnecessary," he says with an easy laugh.

"I'm willing to give it a shot. For science."

"Science, huh?"

"What can I say? I'm a giver."

He looks at his chart and frowns, then turns to us. And when his eyes fall on me, I feel something physically shift inside of me. His gaze is intense. I feel like he can see down into the depths of my soul. I've never been around somebody who's ever made me feel that way before. I'm always very tightly guarded. Nobody ever gets in unless I allow it. And yet, he seems to get past my defenses without even trying. It's as disconcerting as it is exhilarating.

"So tell me, how is it you both came to be shot?" he asks.

"We both work for the Bureau," Astra says. "It's a natural hazard of the job."

"The Bureau," he replies. "As in, the FBI?"

She nods. "Seattle Field Office."

"Wow. That's impressive."

"Yeah, I think so too. Anyway, we got shot by some cultists we were investigating. No big deal, you know. Another day at work."

"That sounds like an incredibly dangerous line of work," he says.

"It has its moments," she replies.

Astra is working hard, trying to get this young, handsome doctor's attention. But ever since he walked into the bay, his eyes have been fixed on mine. My cheeks are burning with warmth beneath his scrutiny. I'm not used to getting any sort of attention from a man with Astra in the room, and I don't know what to do with myself.

Astra seems to pick up on it though, because she nudges me in the ribs with her elbow and makes a goofy face at me when the doctor's back is turned. She flicks her eyes to him and mouths the words, "go for it." I have to bite back the girlish squeal in my throat and take a deep breath, trying to remain calm.

"Remove your shirt please?" Doctor Mark asks.

"I thought you'd never ask," she purrs.

That finally cracks the façade, and he laughs along with her. His laugh really brightens up his face and makes him look like a boy. He just has this wholesome look about him that I find really appealing. Astra slips out of her shirt and Doctor Mark leans forward, gently peeling back the bandage, then studies the wound underneath. He's apparently pleased with what he sees because he gives her a smile.

"Looks like you're healing up just fine," he says. "You'll probably have a pretty cool scar to show off to the guys."

"I'm counting on it," she says.

He cleans out the wound again and packs it with antibiotic salve. With that done, he starts to dress the wound. And all the while, he keeps looking up at me and smiling. I'm absolutely not good with flirting. I don't know what to do. Do I smile? Do I try to make conversation? Do I just whip out my breasts like Astra does? What do I do?

Once he has a new bandage on her wound, Doctor Mark makes a few notations on the chart, and I can tell he's getting ready to go, which is unfortunate. I probably won't see him after he walks out of the bay and we go our separate ways.

"Hey, Doctor Mark," Astra says. "My good friend Blake here is totally single."

He laughs and I see spots of color bloom in his cheeks. "Is that so?"

"Totally so," she presses. "And she's actually not doing anything tonight."

"Astra!" I gasp.

She and Doctor Mark both share a laugh with each other at my expense. But then he turns to me and gives me a smile that sends a funny fluttering through my belly, then travels lower still.

"Coincidentally, I'm not doing anything tonight either," he says. "So how about we do nothing together?"

My jaw falls open, and I gape at him like an idiot. The idea that a man as gorgeous as Doctor Mark would ask me out when Astra is in the room is unreal to me. I subtly look around for the cameras, sure I'm being Punk'd. But there are no cameras. Just a gorgeous man looking at me, waiting for an answer. Astra nudges me in the ribs, prodding me along to make a decision.

"Umm... well..."

"She'd love to go," Astra finally says for me. "She'd really, really love to go."

"Great. Then I can pick you up around seven?"

"I... I mean, we..."

"Yes. She thinks seven would be fantastic," Astra says.

"It's amazing," he says to me. "I can't even see your lips moving."

I hang my head, my face turning some ungodly shade of red, which makes him laugh as Astra gives me a beaming smile.

"So, will you be bringing your translator with you?" he asks.

"I think I'll be fine by then," I finally manage to squeak out.

"Excellent," he says, and puts a card in my hand. "Just text me the details and I'll pick you up around seven tonight."

"Great," I say, feeling shellshocked. "I'm looking forward to it."

"Me too."

With a final smile to the both of us, he disappears through

the curtain and is gone again, leaving me alone with my humiliation, and a very excited Astra. She takes my hands.

"Girl, it's time to go shop. We need to doll you up so you can be sure of gettin' some tonight," she says.

"I may not want to get some tonight," I protest.

"Sure you do," she laughs. "But, whether you're getting some tonight or not, let's go get you a new outfit so you're lookin' your best when Doctor Hottie shows up. Let me work my magic on you, babe."

I turn to her and smile. "You really are the greatest friend ever."

"Yeah, I know."

EPILOGUE

Wilder Residence; The Emerald Pines Luxury Apartments,
Downtown Seattle

"HEY, COME IN," she says.

"Great, thanks."

I step through the door and see that she's not dressed. Which is fine. It looks like she got her hair done today, as it seems a bit softer and shinier than it did back at the hospital earlier. If I had to guess, her friend Astra hauled her out for a girl's day out. A little shopping, a few drinks, a little more shopping, a hair appointment, and judging by Blake's hands, a mani-pedi.

"Sorry," she says. "I'm running a little bit behind."

"That's fine. No problem at all," I tell her.

"Let me get dressed," she calls to me as she heads for the bedrooms in the back. "Help yourself to a drink. There's beer and wine in the fridge, harder stuff in the cabinet above the sink."

"I think I'll wait for you to have that drink," I call after her.

The door in the back closes, and knowing I have limited time, I get moving. Her laptop is sitting open on the dining room table, so I move over to it quickly and am pleased to find that it's still open and not on the lock screen.

"Thank you for making this part of it simple."

I quickly start searching her files, opening and dismissing them quickly when I see they have no relevance. I feel the precious seconds ticking by without finding what I'm looking for, or any trace of it. I scroll down to a file marked "Mom and Dad," and click on it.

The first thing I see are dozens of photographs of her parents and family back in Maryland. I click on one and feel a faint smile touch my lips as I look at a probably nine-year-old Blake Wilder. Who knew that such an awkward looking girl would grow up to be a genuinely stunning woman. Her friend Astra is beautiful, don't get me wrong. But she tries way too hard. Blake, I think, doesn't know how gorgeous she actually is. And she doesn't try. At all.

I've been watching her for some time now. At first, it was simply a job. This is what I'm being paid to do. I needed to learn everything about her that I could and find a way to ingratiate myself into her life. Mission accomplished. Having fake hospital credentials have come in handy more times than I can count.

But although it started off as just a job, and still is, there's something about Blake Wilder I find really appealing. There's something about her I genuinely like. Granted, I only know her from a distance. I don't know her, know her. But from what I've learned of her, even from a distance, she's... intoxicating. There's something about her that makes me feel things I'm not accustomed to.

I give myself a little shake and focus on the task at hand. Inside the Mom and Dad folder, I find a subfolder marked with a question mark. I click on it and I see dozens of reports from the NSA the DOJ, and of course, the FBI. A quick perusal shows that most of these seem to be related to the murder of her parents. I can see she's been trying to work it out for herself over the years.

But judging by the lack of activity on these files, most haven't been opened in several years. I'd say she hit a brick wall. Which is by design, of course. The murder of her parents is to remain a mystery that will never be solved. I personally don't know much about it, but I do know that my boss is insistent we keep tabs on Blake to ensure she's not looking into her family's case again. Especially now that her star is on the rise in the Bureau. My employer doesn't want or need the headache.

There's a one-page text document she wrote out, so I open it up and quickly read the several notes on the page. The one line that stands out to me is, *"FBI Dir. looking into same file/case as Mom? Why? What case. Do not have access. Must review Mom's cases."*

I look and see the note was written down a little more than a year ago. Suffice it to say, she never got the case file, and hasn't actively worked on the case for a while. Which is a very good thing. At least it is in my opinion, because if my employer got the idea that she was working on her parents' case again, he might decide it's time to move on her, and take Blake Wilder off the board. And I don't want that.

I close everything down and back out of her laptop, then pull out my cellphone and key in a quick message... *With target. Not actively looking into problem area. Has not for more than a year. But will remain close to target to ensure initial observations are correct.*

Finished with that, I send it away, then delete it from my phone. In my line of work, you can never be too paranoid. And you never, ever take chances. One wrong move and you're a dead man.

The door in the back opens, and I hear the click clack of her heels as she walks down the hallway and steps back into the living room. She's dressed in a form fitting blue dress that falls midway down her thigh, has a scoop neckline, and three-quarter sleeves. She's got on navy heels with black stockings underneath, and the dress itself compliments her figure exquisitely. It shows off the fullness of her breasts and the swell of her hips in the most tantalizing way.

"Wow. Blake. You look... amazing," I stammer. "Really amazing."

Her cheeks flush and she looks down. "Thank you," she says.

"So, shall we go?"

"Absolutely," she replies. "Let's go."

THE END

Thank you!

I hope you enjoyed *The 7 She Saw,* book one in the *Blake Wilder FBI* Series.

My intention is to give you a thrilling adventure and an entertaining escape with each and every book.

However, I need your help to continue writing.

Being a new indie writer is tough.

I don't have a large budget, huge following, or any of the cutting edge marketing techniques.

So, all I kindly ask is that if you enjoyed this book, please take a moment of your time and leave me a review

and maybe recommend the book to a fellow book lover or two.

This way I can continue to write all day and night and bring you more books in the Blake Wilder series.

I cannot wait to share with you the upcoming sequel!

Your writer friend,
Elle Gray

Made in the USA
Middletown, DE
04 June 2023

32054022R00155